"Oh, God!

The safe security of the cave dissolved into a suffocating closeness, and she could hardly breathe. She had no sense of direction, and suddenly felt completely disoriented.

The faint scent of cologne reached her. Someone was coming. She heard footsteps.

Frantically, KC searched the walls for a niche to hide in. It was useless.

Then two arms grabbed her from behind, and she flinched in terror. She twisted violently to see who held her, kicking out with her feet. It was a man.

KC opened her mouth to scream, but his hand clamped down over her face. "What the hell are you doing in here?" he hissed furiously into her ear.

"Mmmrrrggghhh!" She struggled, then kicked out again with her foot.

He loosened his grip, and in an instant, KC yanked furiously away, squinting in the darkness. Her backpack tumbled to the cave floor, but she was not going to get it. The only thing she wanted was to get away—far away. Footsteps clambered behind her, and she half stumbled, half ran toward the entrance where the brilliant stars beckoned through the hole in the cliff.

**Don't miss these books
in the exciting FRESHMAN DORM series:**

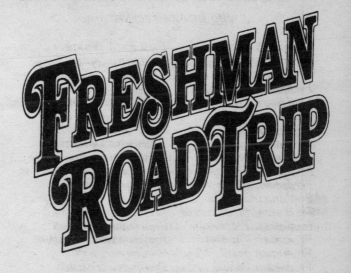

LINDA A. COONEY

HarperPaperbacks
A Division of HarperCollins*Publishers*

This book is dedicated to Laura Young—
who knows everything. . . .

HarperPaperbacks   A Division of HarperCollinsPublishers
10 East 53rd Street, New York, N.Y. 10022

Cover illustration by Tony Greco

First printing: April 1994

Printed in the United States of America

HarperPaperbacks and colophon are trademarks of
HarperCollinsPublishers

❖ 10 9 8 7 6 5 4 3 2 1

One

KC Angeletti leaned her head back on the scorching car seat as the hot sun washed over her cheeks. Her neck stuck to the vinyl surface, and when she moved, sweat trickled down her back. She was on a spring break southwestern road trip, and the temperature had soared to ninety-seven degrees. "Hottest spring on record," the gas station attendant had said at their last stop, a hundred miles ago.

Courtney Conner, her good friend and sorority sister from the Tri Beta sorority, was driving. In her floral scarf, sunglasses, and cool cotton shirt, Courtney looked as confident as ever. She even looked comfortable. The classic yellow 1957 Bel Air convertible sped toward a wrinkle of purple mountains on the horizon. KC licked her parched lips. She tilted her head slightly. It was no use. No matter which way she turned, her skin seemed to glue itself to the sizzling surfaces in the car.

"Winnie," she called to her friend Winnie Gottlieb who rode in the bathtub-size backseat. "Ice! I need ice! Could you get me some from the cooler?"

Winnie sat up. "Sorry, KC!" she called over the wind whipping across the windshield and into their faces. "It melted. Only thing left in this cooler is soggy lettuce, soggy cheese, and soggy bread all floating in lukewarm water."

"Then hand me that spray bottle, will you?"

Winnie reached down, grabbed something bright green, and slapped it into KC's hand.

"One spray bottle, doctor," Winnie joked.

KC pointed the nozzle toward her face, closed her eyes, squeezed the trigger-handle, and sighed as a cool spray of water hit her cheeks. It was dry in an instant, but it felt wonderful while it lasted.

She smiled as Courtney sang along with the country-western tune on the radio. There was a happy grin on Courtney's attractive face. KC envied her. Despite all the demands the sorority made on her, the daily meetings and social events—as well as her charity and hospice work—Courtney always seemed to have it together. KC, on the other hand, felt as if she'd fallen apart and all that was left were little pieces of herself.

"It sure is flat landscape out here," KC said, not really caring if anyone could hear her.

It was late afternoon and they'd been driving for two days straight, trying to make the trip from Springfield, Oregon, to the Southwest in record-breaking time. KC straightened her long legs. She felt as stiff as a railroad tie from sitting in the car for almost ten hours each day.

"Flat as a pancake," Winnie agreed. "No, make that a tortilla."

Courtney shot KC a quick glance. "That's part of why it's so . . . I don't know . . . attractive? The beauty is hidden. Subtle."

"Subtle. Right." Winnie was lying on the backseat, her pink-hightop-sneaker-clad feet resting over the side of the car. The rest of her outfit was just as flashy: a hot-pink cropped top and neon-green running shorts. "Hey, I mean, I love subtle. It's a great way to be."

KC nodded, spraying her face again and licking the cool water off her lips. "Oh, Winnie. You wouldn't know *subtle* if it landed on you."

"You're right," Winnie said. "But there is a certain mystery about it. You know, I've heard about desert spirits, cave spirits, rock spirits. And legends. Lots of legends. Hey, Courtney," she said, sitting up, "maybe you could track down some ancient sorority legends. And, KC, maybe you could find some ancient stock market legends."

"Oh, Winnie." KC sighed.

Courtney just shook her head.

KC stared at the fenceposts ahead. A huge hawk sat on one and gazed at them as they drove past. Maybe the landscape had subtle beauty, she thought. A certain mystery. It could be called attractive . . . in a way. But also desolate and bleak. The sun burned into her skin. They'd crossed four states, traveled over a thousand miles, and what had they discovered? A wilderness of rocks, dust, and sagebrush, and endless sky.

The glare off the road made KC squint. They were passing through a five-building settlement. The run-down houses by the side of the road all leaned crazily in the same direction. Faded and peeling paint hung off the weathered boards in curling strips. KC shook her head. The buildings out here seemed to blend into the desert like the rocks. Beyond, standing like statues in the blazing sunlight, stood a small herd of antelope. As the car sped past, the pronghorns bounded away, flashing their white backsides and flicking their black tails in annoyance at being disturbed. KC smiled. Something moving! For the last hundred miles she'd wondered if the whole world had emptied out, reflecting the way she felt inside.

Winnie's voice joined Courtney's in slightly off-key harmony: "'I'll find it at the end of the rooooaaaaddddddd!'"

Courtney glanced in the rearview mirror, and they all laughed.

"Winnie, how long has it been since you first heard that song?" Courtney asked.

KC shifted her body again, adjusting her sticky legs gingerly on the hot seat. She glanced over her shoulder and saw that Winnie was slathering more coconut-scented sunscreen on her arms. Winnie's spiky hair stood straight up in the wind, and she blew a huge bubble of bright purple gum. It splatted on her lips and nose. KC wrinkled her own nose as the smell of grape gum mixed with the cloyingly sweet smell of coconut.

"About fifteen years! No lullabies for baby Winnie," Winnie said over the wind. She pulled in her legs and bounced on the backseat. "My mom sang me Roger Miller and Loretta Lynn."

Courtney laughed again, checked her rearview mirror, and shook her head. "Would you look at those two? If they're not careful, they're going to end up in a cactus."

KC twisted around. A bright red Jeep, piled high with camping equipment, food, and rafting gear, followed the convertible. Its passengers were Faith Crowley and her boyfriend, Ted Markham. Ted had his arm clenched around Faith's shoulder, and she was leaning in to kiss his cheek as he drove.

Winnie crowed and waved like crazy. "Keep your hands on the steering wheel, Romeo!" she shrieked, the wind whipping her words away. Ted and Faith waved back wildly.

The two of them were doing well. It must be nice, KC thought, to have one person you could really trust, one person to rely on, depend on, to accept you for who you were. To share adventures with.

Ted and Faith were going to spend two days rafting the famous San Pico River that wound through the cliffs and sculpted rocks of the region. And so far, they'd spent every spare moment locked in each other's arms. KC inhaled a long, slow breath of the dry sagebrush-scented air. Well, Faith and Ted deserved a fun spring break. They'd survived some rough times. KC wondered if she'd ever figure out relationships, though. They seemed as mysterious as the desert landscape flashing past.

The air suddenly ruffled some papers at KC's feet. She quickly planted her shoe on an envelope that fluttered out of her open pack. The envelope and the letter inside it were the reason she was on this trip. KC reached down and clutched it firmly in her hand.

The scratchy handwriting in the upper left corner said "Maria Quintero, 341 Hermosa Street, Las Altas, New Mexico." KC's heart quickened as she looked at the return address and her throat tightened. It was the same sensation she'd had when she'd pulled the envelope from her mailbox at school two weeks before and discovered it was from her grandmother, a grandmother she'd never known she had.

Maria Quintero was her mother's mother. She was old, she'd said, nearing the end of her life. How had she put it? KC strained to remember. That's right, she called it "preparing for the next world." She wanted to contact her granddaughter, Beverly's girl, Kahia Cayenne Angeletti.

Earlier in the year, before her father's death, KC had found out she was adopted. She'd had an opportunity to meet her birth mother. That had been an emotional roller coaster, but she'd gotten through the ride in one piece. She'd even ended up understanding the pain her mother had suffered. Beverly Quintero had appeared during a terribly rough period in KC's year. And her mother had helped. She'd helped a lot.

Now, in the letter, Maria Quintero, her mother's mother, had asked KC to come to Las Altas. "It is time to speak," she'd written in the letter.

KC looked out at the expanse in front of her and saw that a huge thunderhead was forming in the distance. It billowed and rose, gigantic and white, towering over the scene, sending shadows sailing across the red ground below. A storm was coming. KC felt the envelope in her hand grow moist from the sweat on her fingers. Well, she'd gone through bad storms of her own right before spring break. A lot of people on campus had believed her responsible for the death of Brooks Baldwin. They'd pointed at her and stared and whispered until KC thought she'd go crazy. Even close friends had doubted her innocence. By the time it had finally been proven that Brooks's fall off the mountain near Springfield had been an accident, KC had lost her trust. It was the reason she now felt empty and alone.

Lightning flashed over the mountains as KC slid the letter back into her pack. A grandmother—her grandmother. Would she speak in unfamiliar words about other times? Times that had nothing to do with KC? Would she tell stories about people KC didn't know? Places KC had never been? Or *maybe* her grandmother would listen. *Maybe* she'd understand what KC was feeling. But KC doubted it. She doubted it very much.

Beside her, Courtney continued her duet with Winnie. KC had mentioned the letter to Courtney, and immediately Courtney had offered to drive KC to Las Altas in her vintage convertible. "After all," Courtney had said, "it's not every day that you get to meet a grandmother you didn't know you had." KC remembered the eager smile on Courtney's face. "And cruising through the Southwest in my car sounds like the perfect spring break to me."

KC noticed the wrinkles on the horizon were getting bigger. They were actually beginning to look like mountains. She wiped the fat beads of sweat off her forehead.

"So tell me, KC, do we ever get where we're going?" Winnie shouted over the wind. "There's been nothing for miles. And I mean zero. Good thing I went to the bathroom at the Last Chance Filling Station. They weren't kidding! Who would ever believe a sign that says 'No gas for the next 175 miles'!"

KC looked back at Winnie. "We're heading to Las Altas, a small university town at the base of those mountains," she said, pointing to the mountains growing bigger every minute. "About two hundred miles east."

Courtney nodded, then reaching over, flicked off the radio. "How much farther before we get to a place called Gold Hill?"

KC grabbed the map off the floor and unfolded it. She stuck her finger on a small blue dot. "About fifty, maybe sixty miles. Why the interest?"

"I thought we could use a rest," Courtney said, smiling. "I brought some brochures that the travel bureau gave me. And not only is there a place to stay at Gold Hill, but it has some fascinating attractions around it. All *very* educational."

Winnie leaned on the back of the front seat. "I hate to say this, Courtney, but education is *not* the reason I invited myself along. We just finished final exams. We need a break from education. That's why they call it spring break. I mean—my brain did a total short-circuit during that Western Civ. test. I mean, puhhllease! Dates of the Spanish Inquisition? That exam *was* the Spanish Inquisition!"

KC pulled her long dark hair off her neck. "You probably aced it anyway."

"Only time and Professor Hermann will tell," Winnie said cockily as she crossed her arms. "But it was *still* torture."

"Well, I think you should give Gold Hill a chance. Going to out-of-the-way places is part of the adventure."

"Okay, okay," Winnie said. "I'm starved, anyway.

So let's get to this mysterious Gold Hill fast and find someplace to eat." She turned back to face the Jeep and cupped her hands around her mouth. "Destination, Gold Hill!" she shouted to Faith and Ted.

"Lead the way!" Ted shouted back.

They drove on. The sun started to sink, sending bands of rose light spilling across the tumbleweeds beside the road. With every new color, KC imagined what Gold Hill would be like. A small southwestern town, with nice restaurants and flower boxes lining the wooden planked streets. Maybe there'd be a little general store, a quaint gas station.

For now, though, they cruised along, crossing the Hovantopi Indian reservation, where the only signs of life were a lonely windmill cranking in the distance and a small herd of sheep grazing not far from it. After that stretched total desolation for mile upon endless mile.

Finally, the car crested a small hill and KC gasped. Spread out before them was a wide valley splashed with red and gold light. The brilliant blue sky arched above, and gigantic clouds collected along the deep-purple mountains rippling the horizon. Courtney braked and KC craned her head to read a small wooden sign shaped like an arrow pointing down a dusty, pothole-covered road. In peeling red paint was written: GOLD HILL 25 MILES. Courtney waved and honked to alert Faith and Ted that they'd reached their turnoff.

After driving over a rutted road for close to an

hour, they finally reached the town. KC stared. Buildings lined one narrow street and seemed stuck amazingly on the side of the hill. A few dirt roads led off toward the cliffs. Tumbleweeds rolled along the planked sidewalk. Three cars were parked at the other end of the street in front of what looked like a general store. *This* was their exotic Southwest destination? KC felt disappointment land in her stomach. It looked like a ghost town.

"Whew!" Winnie breathed. "Move over, Wyatt Earp."

Dust blew up around the cars as they drove on. KC stared at the grit-covered windows of the buildings. She looked more closely. Gradually, she became aware of rustic, wood-carved signs and varnished window boxes. Some of the businesses had freshly painted storefronts. Slowly, KC realized that the buildings included a museum, an art gallery, a Mexican café, and something called the Antelope Trading Company. Maybe this wouldn't be so bad after all.

Courtney turned the car off the main street. At the crest of a hill, nestled at the base of the tall cliffs, loomed a neon sign. They had arrived at the Cactus Cottage Motel.

"All *right*, Courtney. I'll take a room *inside* a cactus as long as it's got a shower," Winnie chirped from the backseat.

As the car pulled up a rutted driveway, KC sucked in a tired breath. A central building stood before them, painted a faint shade of rose with windows trimmed in pale aqua. The main office was inside. To the right stretched a wing with about twenty rooms. To the left were five adobe cottages. Tucked against a hillside dotted with cliffs, trails, and cactus, the motel commanded a breathtaking view of the desert beyond Gold Hill. KC eyed Courtney skeptically and felt her frail optimism fizzle.

"What do you think? Great, huh?" Courtney said as she parked the convertible. She ran her long fingers through her hair, then pushed open her door and climbed out. "I'll check it out. No need to worry. Trust me. Everything's under control." She headed for the office.

Winnie propped her chin on the back of the front seat. "I'm beginning to wonder if everything in the Southwest is painted rose and aqua," she said.

KC sighed and got out of the car. Her legs felt like rubber and her shirt stuck to her back. She stretched her arms above her head and her spine cracked in protest.

It had been a long day. Her nerves and her sense of adventure had faded three hundred miles ago. She was hungry, tired, and worried. So far, the trip had consisted of eating quick meals in ancient drive-ins and sitting in the car for endless hours. She gazed at the Cactus Cottage Motel. And trust? KC wasn't sure she'd ever be able to trust anyone ever again.

Courtney returned from the office. "They have a cabin with three beds, including a little kitchen."

She pointed to the last cabin on the left. "The owner said it would be fine for Ted and Faith to pitch their tent in the back. I'll tell them when they get here. It's really a nice place."

KC wanted to believe nothing less. She inhaled the slightly cooler air as Courtney drove the car up to the cabin. Tall pine trees shaded the area and jays squawked overhead. KC got out of the car again and grabbed her suitcase from the trunk. She was the first to step onto the tiny front porch and pull open the screen door of their cabin. Inside were three single, wooden beds, each with a colorful Indian blanket as a bedspread. The headboards were carved to look like howling coyotes. The lamp on the bedside table was in the shape of a barrel cactus. And the ceiling lamp was made out of a wagon wheel suspended from a chain. A striped rug lay on the floor.

Winnie stumbled into the room behind KC. "Hey, check it out," she crowed, smiling. "Real authentic Southwest decor. Even the telephone is aqua."

Within a short time, everyone had showered and put on fresh clothes. Courtney sat on her bed combing her wet hair and studying a pile of travel brochures she'd retrieved from her suitcase. She'd changed into crisp chino slacks and a pink sweater. Winnie was in shorts and a cropped T-shirt, doing sit-ups on the floor. KC, meanwhile, was looking out the open window at the bright orange-streaked sky. The air drifting into the cabin was pungent and gloriously cool. It was amazing how fast the burning heat of the day had vanished.

"The café downtown serves real southwestern cuisine," Courtney read. "Blue tacos and red-hot chili. As well as tortillas, tamales, and something called Frito pie."

"Are you sure that's not red tacos and blue chili?" Winnie said, doing another sit-up. "It sounds like you need a cast-iron stomach."

"Well, I think you've got one from all those sit-ups," Courtney joked. "Now let's see." She flipped through another brochure. "Caves run in and out of the cliffs behind the motel," she continued to read. "A few old gold mines can be seen dotting the cliffs, reminding us of the glorious days of Gold Hill's past."

KC came away from the window and set out her perfume and makeup on top of the dresser. "Real caves and gold mines?" she asked, turning to look at Courtney. "How come people aren't crawling all over them, then?"

Courtney held up the brochure in her slim hands. "It says here that many of the caves are unexplored. And the gold ran out. Wow, KC, these caves and cliffs run all the way to Las Altas."

KC nodded. Las Altas. Her goal. She tried to imagine what meeting her grandmother would be like. But she couldn't. Her mind was a blank.

"The museum in town has special displays every week," Courtney went on. "And there's a bigger one about a hundred and forty miles east that's dedicated to the cliff dwellings. The Kanabi dwellings are the biggest in the whole region. We've *got* to see those. To the south is a 'painted desert' with petrified wood lying all over the place." Courtney's eyes shone as she turned over the brochure in her hand.

KC tried to call up some of Courtney's excitement, but inside she felt like flat soda pop. She wished she could feel the fizz of days before her troubles. Before her friends started suspecting her of killing Brooks.

"The river runs along the main highway but then veers off into the cliffs," Courtney explained in her tour-guide voice. She looked up. "I guess Ted and Faith will have a bit of a drive to the rafting place. It's behind a store called Flo's." She looked up at KC, her brown eyes sparkling, and smiled her sorority-president smile. "And after a week of fun and adventure, we'll head over to Las Altas and see KC's grandmother."

KC smiled back. "I really appreciate your driving me down here, Courtney. It was a good idea for all of us to get away for spring break." KC knew her thanks sounded inadequate. But it was the best she could do.

Courtney reached for her calendar organizer. "My pleasure, KC. Especially when I think about good old Springfield. Right now, the whole town is getting drenched with its annual spring rain." She shivered. "Now, let me write down an itinerary. Why don't we hit the local museum tomorrow? It's a good idea to get an historical overview, then—"

"Hold it there, Courtney," Winnie panted between sit-ups. "I'm not spending my spring break rummaging through some dusty museum looking at a bunch of old spoons and cups."

"The Indians didn't have cups."

"I don't care if they drank out of old moccasins. What I need is a whole different kind of adventure. We're here for a change of pace, right?" Winnie sat up and dove for the stack of brochures neatly arranged on Courtney's bed. Grabbing a handful, she bounced onto her own bed and, one after another, flicked the brochures onto the floor. Suddenly, one caught her eye. "Aha! This is more like it. 'Pinky's Dance Hall. Five miles past the Gold Hill turnoff on the road to Las Altas. Everyone Goes to Pinky's.'"

She looked up, her eager face shining with energy.

Courtney frowned. "Everyone is probably two cowboys and an antelope. And the road to Las Altas is twenty-five miles of bumpy road from here, remember?"

"Come on, Courtney! Live a little. New horizons," Winnie said, waving the brochure in the air.

"Pinky's Dance Hall is hardly what I would call a new horizon. It's probably dirty, dusty, and dull," Courtney said, brushing her hair vigorously. Disapproval was written in each stroke. "What do you think, KC?"

KC shrugged. "I don't know. Maybe it's worth checking out."

She sensed that Winnie was getting back to her old, risk-taking self. After a marriage, miscarriage, and separation, Winnie had plunged into a downward spiral of depression. Only recently had she been able to regain any of her humor and energy. KC saw Courtney study Winnie for a minute, and she could feel Courtney's diplomatic nature warring with her presidential side, the side that wanted people to do what she told them to. Then Courtney smiled and shrugged. "Oh, all right," she conceded. "But if it's totally boring, promise we'll leave?"

Winnie jumped off her bed and did a wild dance step around the room. "Promise! Pinky's, here we come!"

"After dinner," Courtney said, holding up her hand like a school crossing guard. "Then we can all go together if Ted and Faith want to come."

KC listened as Courtney and Winnie began discussing blue tacos, refried beans, and tamales. She turned toward the window and gazed outside, bending down slightly to view the sunset. Vibrant colors splashed across the deeply shadowed desert. As KC watched, the shadows shifted and moved, deepening the shades of violet and azure, blending the shapes and colors.

Suddenly, she didn't want to hear about Mexican food. She didn't want to hear about Indian artifacts or raft trips, petrified wood or caves. Grabbing a light sweater, she headed out the door and stood for a minute on the tiny front porch of the cabin.

Deep inside her something shifted like the shadows beyond the cliffs. What was she doing here? Why had she come to this empty place? To track down some unknown relative? To escape from school and routine and life? To escape from herself?

Courtney laughed inside the cabin. Winnie's loud voice spoke. "And what do *you* expect me to wear? Pearls and a black dress?"

Irritation bristled up KC's spine. She wasn't in the mood to mingle with a bunch of hicks at some local dance hall. Let Courtney and Winnie take charge of the adventure side of things. All she wanted was to be alone in the motel and watch the sunset. She'd never seen colors change so fast, vermilion to crimson to magenta. Indigo to sapphire. Something changed every second, and she didn't want to miss any of it. Maybe the landscape could teach her something. Maybe it could teach her how to live the rest of her life without trust, or hope, or purpose.

Two

F aith leaned back against Ted, whose arms were twined around her waist. They were looking at the stars twinkling across the vast deep blue of the night sky.

"Hmmm," Faith crooned as she let her head rest on Ted's shoulder. "Nice of the stars to give us a private show."

Ted pulled her closer. "I'll say. Between dinner and this gorgeous sky, I'm beginning to feel almost human again," he murmured. "And there's one other reason," he whispered, dropping a kiss along Faith's neck.

"Oh?" she teased. "What's that?"

"You," Ted whispered. He turned her around

slowly and let his lips find hers. Faith felt as if her blood had turned to warm honey. She kissed him back softly, then deeply.

"We'd better get that tent set up," Ted said when they pulled apart. He smiled. "Or we'll have to sleep under the stars."

His arms tightened around Faith's waist, and she breathed in the scent of his skin and the night and the pine trees. "That wouldn't be so bad," she whispered. Here she was, alone with the greatest guy in the world, a guy who'd given up chasing girls to be with her. And only her. It was a dream come true.

"Nope." He sighed. "Except I don't want to find a rattlesnake in my sleeping bag in the morning."

"Rattlesnakes?" Faith sounded alarmed. "Do rattlesnakes come out at night?"

"Search me," Ted said with a shrug. "But you know what they say about being safe or sorry." He took Faith's hand and led her to where their tent lay spread out across the grass. "Okay, let's get to work," he went on. "The directions say to insert the stakes into the ground before pulling the tent upright."

"Right," Faith said, reaching down and steadying the stakes as Ted pounded them with the mallet.

"They don't tell us what to do when the ground is like concrete, though," Ted said, wiping his brow. He hammered some more.

Faith handed him a collapsed corner, tripping over the stake they'd actually managed to drive into the ground. Ted reached out and caught her quickly, pulling her close. He gave her a quick kiss. She snuggled into his body, deepening the kiss.

Ted came up for air first. His eyes glowed in the dim light from the tiny back porch of the cabin. "We're not making much progress," he said, smiling.

"Not on the tent, anyway," Faith murmured.

From inside the cabin, the muffled voices of Courtney and Winnie reached them. They were still talking about clothes. Faith smiled. Courtney didn't know Winnie as well as Faith did. Maybe she should go in and warn her that Winnie wore what she wanted. She'd probably end up in biking shorts, a neon crop-top, and a bowling jacket no matter what Courtney said about "setting a good example."

Ted squeezed her hand quickly, and Faith turned her attention back to the tent. She grabbed a pole while Ted drove one stake into the little hole in the dusty earth. Puffs of dirt exploded around it, but Ted's determined blows with the hammer seemed to have an effect.

"You're doing it!" she cried.

"Yeah, but my arm feels like it's going to fall off. I can tell this rock has been here about sixty million years."

Ted finally jabbed all the tent stakes into the ground one by one. Making sure to pull evenly on both sides, they raised the roof. The poles snapped into place with a satisfying click. Faith examined their effort, her hands on her hips. In the dim light shining out the back window of the cabin, it looked like a cozy hideaway. "Well," she said, smiling with pleasure at the upright structure. "It leans a little, but it looks sturdy enough."

Ted slid his arm around her waist. "Yeah, I'd say we passed Tent 101. Now I can see why scouts are so proud of their badges." Faith stepped to the tent flap and crawled in on her knees. She was relieved to see that the floor was level, dry, and smooth. Going back out for their equipment, she arranged the lantern, her overnight bag, and Ted's duffel bag inside.

"There," she said, satisfied that everything was neat and orderly. All she needed was the cooler. She turned around to ask Ted where it was, when he dove in through the tent flap and grabbed her by the waist. "Hey!" she squealed, her feet flying up into the air.

He tackled her onto the soft pile of sleeping bags covering half the floor.

"What—what?" she gasped. Her questions were stilled as he kissed her.

"Hmmm," he murmured, his body stretching out alongside hers. "Just checking the condition of the floor. Seems to be fine," he said in a low voice as he ran his fingers along her waist.

Her thoughts drifted. This was what she needed. To get away from school, from the memories of Brooks's fatal climbing accident, from all the academic and social demands constantly pulling at her and Ted. Here, no one would interrupt them. They had all the time in the world. Time to share the outdoors, time to speak real words, time to just be. Faith sighed. This trip was going to be fantastic.

Heat coursed through her body as Ted drew his hand along her leg. She let herself move against him, feeling his strong hands, his chest, his legs.

"Now this is what I call a vacation," he murmured into her hair.

"Me, too."

"Even dinner was a blast," he whispered, his breath tickling her ear.

"Yeah, except Winnie was on overdrive," Faith said, thinking back over Winnie's excited chatter in the diner. "I guess it's nice to see her back to normal. But for Winnie, normal can be kind of abnormal. Like watching a Roadrunner cartoon on fast forward."

"There's definitely a wild look in her eyes," Ted teased.

"You think so?" Faith cuddled closer to him. "She's always revved up. Ready for anything."

"Well, better that than KC's blues or Courtney's camp-counselor organizing," Ted said. "Is KC going to mope through the whole trip?"

Faith punched him playfully in the shoulder. "Listen to you. Worried the others will spoil our fun? Nothing's going to ruin our time together," Faith said, her voice low.

Ted smiled at her in the darkness, and Faith could feel the heat in his gaze all the way to her toes. "What? Me worry?" he murmured. "The only camper I have eyes for is right in front of me. I just can't get over how I feel about you. I've never been able to manage a one-girl relationship before."

"Must be the girl you're with."

"It is. You're incredible, Faith." Ted's mouth found hers again, and Faith let herself float higher and higher.

Finally, she broke away. "If—if we're going to Pinky's we'd better start getting ready," she whispered. Ted made no response. He was busy kissing the palm of her hand. "And we have two whole days of rafting and camping to look forward to," she added. "Just you and me."

"About time, too," Ted said. "I thought I'd have to lasso and hog-tie you at school to get you away."

He moved close again, and Faith reached up and stroked his face, reveling in the warm, delicious sensation as his mouth touched hers. The sweet stillness swallowed them, and Faith drew him tighter into her arms.

Suddenly, right outside the tent, a coyote howled, and Faith jumped. "I thought coyotes stayed away from people," she said in a hushed voice.

"Yoo, hoo. The coyote alarm calling Ted and Faith!" It was Winnie.

Faith and Ted exchanged amused looks. "Shhhh," Faith said, putting her finger to her lips. "Maybe she'll go away."

They waited silently. Outside the tent, little thumps and rustles told Faith that Winnie was walking around the tent. Before Faith could take another breath, the tent flap went *zip* and there stood Winnie. Faith and Ted struggled up. Faith couldn't help but notice that Winnie's ruffled denim skirt, white tank top, and tight denim jacket showed off her fabulous figure. Her hair was freshly spiked. In one ear dangled a coyote earring; in the other bounced a miniature cactus.

"Wow," Ted gushed from beside Faith. "You look like you're ready for a hot time."

"Am I ever!" Winnie said, grinning. "Eat your heart out, Markham." She kicked out a little dance step as Faith and Ted stepped carefully out of the tent. But she didn't see the edge in the darkness and tripped on a tent stake. Swinging out with her arms, she tried to steady herself, but her skirt caught hold of one of the ropes. Suddenly, the tent shook with a violent motion. Then the whole thing collapsed with a *whoosshhh*.

"Winnie!" Faith shouted.

"Disaster!" Ted yelled.

Winnie was doubled over, laughing. "Sooorrrrrry!"

Faith started picking up the corners of the collapsed tent, but Ted went after Winnie. He put his hands around her waist and began tickling her. Winnie's laugh deepened. "Help! Faith! He's tickling me! Ted! Stop! Faith! Help! Call him off!" she shrieked, but Faith didn't move.

"You deserve it," Faith complained, irritation crackling in her voice. "You know how long it took us to set this thing up?" She gathered the gritty stakes in her hand and watched as Ted wiggled his fingers along Winnie's waist.

"Stop! Ted, please," Winnie gasped.

"Beg for mercy, Ms. Gottlieb, destroyer of tents. Say uncle!" Ted growled, holding on to Winnie's writhing body.

"Please, I beg. I give up! Ted! Uncle!" Winnie screeched, her laughter echoing around the cliffs.

But the more Winnie giggled, the more Ted tickled.

Finally, Faith stomped her foot. "STOP!" she yelled.

Ted and Winnie both straightened up and began dusting off their clothes, sliding glances at each other and laughing.

Faith shook her head. "C'mon, you two," she said, trying not to let their antics annoy her. "We'd better get going. We *are* going to Pinky's, aren't we?"

She gave Ted a searching look but did not wait for an answer. Instead, she spun on her heel and headed for the Jeep. Deep in the night, a hoot owl responded as Ted and Winnie quietly followed Faith.

Three

Courtney steered the car down the dark highway toward Pinky's. She hoped this wasn't a mistake. Above her, the sky was filled with stars, and the moon, almost full, hung over the ridge of mountains that had turned deep amethyst.

"It's amazing how cold it gets at night," Courtney said, trying to make conversation with Winnie, who bounced in the seat next to her.

Winnie nodded. "Sure is. That's why they've got to have a hot spot nearby." She laughed at her own joke, and Courtney smiled placidly.

Courtney hadn't spent much time with Winnie even though she knew a lot about her. She knew about Winnie's marriage, miscarriage, and separation. But hearing about Winnie's escapades and crises, and actually experiencing her energy, were two very different things. Courtney felt a little bit like she was sitting next to an overloaded electrical socket.

"Too bad KC didn't come," Courtney commented as she glanced again at the brilliant display of stars above them. "She would've enjoyed this."

"Guess she's in one of her moods. Says she wants to think," Winnie said. "Maybe we should have forced her to come. You know, tied her in the backseat." Winnie cracked her bubble gum.

"Forcing people doesn't usually work," Courtney said. "Being president of a sorority has taught me that much. I can't make people do things they don't want to. Otherwise, everybody's unhappy." She gave Winnie a quick glance. "I've learned to tell the difference between 'I'm-just-waiting-to-be-talked-into-this' and 'absolutely-not-no-matter-what.'"

Courtney was glad Winnie nodded. She wondered if common sense had any kind of an impact on Winnie. It was hard to tell. Winnie swayed back and forth to the beat of the song on the radio.

"And you think KC was in 'absolutely-not-no-matter-what' mode?" Winnie asked.

"I do."

Behind them, the Jeep's horn alerted Courtney that Pinky's was coming up. Faith and Ted had followed again, insisting that they take two vehicles in case someone wanted to leave early. Courtney had laughed when Ted had announced that he was going to "keep an eye on everyone." True, they didn't know much about the place, and it really could be a desert dive, filled with rough cowboys and ranchers. But Courtney had assured him that she could take care of herself. Fending off cowboys couldn't be any more difficult than discouraging fraternity guys from pawing her at a weekend frat bash.

Courtney slid her hands along the smooth surface of the steering wheel, then slowed suddenly as a kit fox shot across the road in front of her. Her main reason for suggesting this trip was to help KC pull herself together. Anybody could see she was in need of rest and relaxation. And if putting up with Winnie's carefree, frantic energy was part of the package, that was okay. After all, Winnie was one of KC's best friends. Courtney glanced over at Winnie, who was blowing a gigantic pink bubble. If their first adventure was to drive out to Pinky's just to prove the place was a dud, so be it.

She slowed some more as a bright red flashing light lit up the night from a large, log-cabin-like building off to the right. Cars jammed the parking lot. From inside the building came the sounds of a bass guitar thumping loudly.

"All right!" Winnie shouted. "Look at this place!"

Courtney pulled the car into the parking lot and cruised for a couple of minutes before she found a place to park. The gravel crunched under her tires. There were cars parked door handle to door handle on every inch of the lot. There were pickup trucks, sports cars, sedans, and minivans.

Winnie jumped out of the car and twisted like a Slinky through the tiny space between the neighboring vehicle. Her eyes gleamed in eager anticipation. "Come on, Courtney! Let's see how many coyotes this place really has!" She laughed loudly as Ted and Faith found a spot nearby and hurried up to them.

Courtney climbed out, smoothing her hands over her slightly flared skirt of deep burgundy and straightening her cream-colored sweater. At Winnie's insistence, she'd left the pearls behind, choosing instead her new delicate turquoise earrings and necklace that she'd bought at a trading post the day before. Even if everyone else was wearing denim and plaid, Courtney knew she looked good. She crossed around the back of her car to meet Ted and Faith. Ted wore an attractive dark-green shirt and new blue jeans, and Faith had on her denim split skirt and frilly white cotton blouse.

"Check it out," Ted said as he waved toward the sea of cars. "This looks like downtown Springfield on a Saturday night."

Faith's arm slid around Ted. She was smiling, and the flashing red light from the Pinky's sign pulsed across her face. "See you guys inside."

As Faith and Ted headed across the parking lot, Courtney smiled. It looked as if she might have been wrong about Pinky's. People stood clustered on the wide wooden porch, and flashing lights flickered in the big windows. Winnie jogged in place beside her. "Come on, Courtney. It's dance hall time." They followed Ted and Faith across the dusty lot, climbed the three wooden steps to the broad porch, and headed for the wide double doors.

Courtney hesitated on the threshold. The building was huge, the wooden walls polished to a deep, lustrous shine. Heat blasted into her face, and she gasped. Couples jammed the dance floor, and customers who weren't dancing lined up along a railing. Indian blankets hung above it along the wall, their red, blue, green, and yellow stripes adding splashes of color to the room. Interspersed between the blankets were neon signs in the shape of boots, guitars, coyotes, and cacti. The people, the walls, the floor, and the band were all lit by flashing red, green, and blue spotlights. Pinky's was a kaleidoscope come to life.

Most of the space was reserved for dancing. A long, wide wood floor sprinkled with sawdust ran from one end of the room to a raised platform at the other end where the band performed. Courtney felt the thumping base vibrate the floor under her feet. At the opposite end from the band, wooden stools were set up along a counter where customers could buy soft drinks and nachos.

Courtney smiled broadly at Winnie. "I guess it's like a waterhole in the middle of the desert," she shouted over the music.

Winnie nodded, then turned her eager eyes back to the dancing crowd. Gesturing for Courtney to follow, Winnie squeezed between two tall guys dressed in cotton cowboy shirts and a dark girl in a brightly colored flared skirt and red cotton blouse. Some people wore cowboy hats, and the flashing lights bounced off silver belts and bracelets. They made their way to the long railing. The music beat into a pulsing crescendo.

"Yes!" Winnie said. "Trust Winnie's instincts. I'm right again! Just look at that band!"

Courtney let her eyes follow Winnie's waving hand. The band, made up of six guys wearing blue jeans and colorful western shirts, finished up a country tune and launched into rock.

"They're good, aren't they?" Courtney shouted into Winnie's ear.

"Are you kidding? They're great! Catch you later." Winnie jumped into the mass of dancing bodies. She twisted, wiggled, and sang, smiling back at the people she bumped into.

Courtney shook her head in amazement. Across the floor, she spotted two guys staring at Winnie, obviously impressed with her sexy energy and contagious enthusiasm. A tall, dark-haired, muscular guy with short hair and blue eyes nodded appreciatively as Winnie gyrated with abandon, her arms upraised. He made his way toward her.

Winnie grinned as he clasped one hand around her waist and started dancing with her. Pretty soon, another guy approached her, and the two guys good-naturedly bantered back and forth, passing Winnie from one to the other. Not something Courtney would like, she reflected. Not in a million years. But she was happy that Winnie was having a good time. On the other side of the dance floor, Ted and Faith clasped each other in a sensual embrace, dancing to a beat of their own. The funky rhythm of the music was definitely contagious, but Courtney hung back, content to tap her feet to the music as she let the colorful scene swirl around her.

The trip had been a great idea. The minute she'd climbed behind the steering wheel of her car, she'd begun to feel the weight of classes and parties and charity work lift from her shoulders. She was beginning to feel free. And watching the couples dance, the flashing lights of red and blue and green across the smiling faces, she felt excited and happy, too.

The music cranked up a couple of notches, and Courtney felt the pulsing in her blood match the beat. She spotted an empty stool and slid over to it, climbing up quickly and leaning back against the railing.

The movement on the dance floor began to shake the building, and she smiled. Looking to her right, Courtney suddenly realized a guy had taken the stool beside her. His eyes were glued to the dance floor, so she studied him for a moment. He was handsome, with hair that shone with blue-black highlights, and he had an angular jaw and amazingly dark eyes. A small scar ran across one of his high cheekbones. She liked the way his mouth curled up even when he wasn't smiling. There was a sort of stillness about him, too. In contrast to the boisterous locals whooping it up on the dance floor, this guy seemed to be lost in thought.

Courtney found herself speculating. *I bet he writes poetry. Cowboy poetry. About the stars and the crisp, cool nights. Or maybe he's a graduate student. Intelligent eyes, serious. Writing a dissertation on local geology.* She looked at his hands. His long, thin fingers were deeply tanned and they rested on his knees. His pale-blue, tailored shirt fit loosely, and his jeans looked soft. Courtney found herself stealing glances at him. When she finally looked back at the dance floor, she could feel his eyes on her face.

"This is a nice place," Courtney said, turning to him. The guy nodded slowly. The music drowned out her voice, and she wondered if he'd even heard her. Maybe he was just acknowledging the fact that her mouth was moving.

"Do you come here much?" she shouted.

The guy nodded again, and gave her a quick smile. His straight white teeth contrasted with his deep tan. The scar wrinkled slightly. He took a deep breath. Courtney held hers, hoping he would ask her to dance.

But he didn't. Instead, he leaned back against the railing as the music changed to a slow, romantic tune.

Courtney frowned in thought. Was she here for adventure or not? What was the point of coming to a new place if you didn't try something new? What was the point of sitting beside this interesting guy and not doing anything about it? Maybe a little of Winnie's daring would be . . . educational.

She took a deep breath. "This is a great place," she said. The guy looked at her and smiled. "My name's Courtney Conner. I was wondering if you'd like to dance."

"How do you do, Ms. Conner." He held out his hand and took hers, shaking it slowly. His warm smooth skin sent tingles along her arm. "Why yes," he added, easing his long legs off the stool. "I'd be happy to dance."

Four

"I'm glad I stayed behind," KC said to the darkness surrounding her.

In the distance a coyote howled and another answered. She took a deep breath. Not long after everyone had left for Pinky's, KC decided to explore a trail in back of the cabin. It had almost seemed as if the path were calling her to follow.

She breathed in the sweet, desert air. The moonlight washed across the trail, lighting the path clearly. There was a steep incline, and KC panted a little as she clambered up. At the top, the trail evened out along a row of cliffs, and KC paused, turning to look out over the silvery expanse below her. Pools of deep shadows flowed out from rocks and ridges, making the flat land seem inhabited by large creatures. The brilliant reds and orange of the sunset had faded, transformed into muted silver, bronze, and slate.

KC was glad she hadn't gone to Pinky's. Being stuck inside a dance hall on a night like this seemed wrong. Being jostled and pushed was not what she was in the mood for. She knew Winnie had been annoyed at her decision. But now, KC was glad she'd stuck by her choice. This was where she was supposed to be. She knew it. She dragged her hands through her hair, pushing the thick strands away from her forehead, and walked on.

The smell of mesquite and sage added spice to the fresh air. Then something rustled nearby and KC flinched. Squinting into the darkness, she thought she saw something move, but the deep shadows by the trail concealed whatever was out there. It was probably just an animal. She was pretty sure she'd be safe as long as she stayed on the trail.

Climbing higher, KC marveled at the night sky. The stars appeared so low and brilliant that they seemed to touch the rocks above her. Suddenly, she sensed a rush of cold air and the damp, stale smell of moisture.

KC quickly flicked on her flashlight toward the cliff face and saw an opening gaping wide behind a tall, shaggy bush.

A cave.

What had Courtney said about caves and mines? They ran along the ridge all the way to Las Altas.

KC smiled. She'd always wondered what it would be like to go into a cave, to be tucked inside the earth.

Carefully, she readjusted her backpack, in which she carried a canteen as well her unknown grandmother's letter, stepped around the mesquite bush, yanking her sweater free of the clawing branches, and slid into the entrance. Her heart thudded in anticipation. The flashlight beam bounced off black walls that dripped with moisture. KC wrinkled her nose at the musty smell. Looking down, she saw that the floor was littered with chips of brown flaked stone, and as she walked deeper inside the cave, a weird sense of timelessness came over her. It was as if she'd stepped into an ancient world, and the world she lived in had suddenly fallen away. The quiet of the night seemed magnified. She released her breath in a slow hiss, and felt the cool air of the cave flutter back onto her face.

Following what seemed to be a path, KC stepped deeper and ducked as the ceiling became suddenly lower. The cave was about five feet in height, about ten feet wide. When she aimed her flashlight ahead, she saw the path curve sharply and disappear through a narrow slit in the rocks.

KC was glad for her flashlight and tightened her grip on the ridged handle. The beam sent an arc of white along the dark wall as she stepped slowly forward. Then the light flickered as she shone it up and down the base, where more chipped rocks and flakes ran along the floor.

The flashlight flickered again. KC shook it, rattling the batteries inside. It blinked. The cave had closed in behind her, and she felt the walls narrowing. Suddenly, the beam went out. She was plunged into blackness darker than anything she'd ever experienced. Total, utter blackness. The air felt tight around her ears. She closed her eyes. Her breath clogged in her chest, and a blind panic rose in her throat.

"Oh, God!" KC whispered. The safe security of the cave dissolved into a suffocating closeness, and she could hardly breathe. KC edged back, and gasped as she slammed into a hard surface. She had no sense of direction, and suddenly felt completely disoriented. Reaching out, she ran her fingers across a wall.

"Yuck!" She drew her hand away quickly and wiped it on her jeans. Her fingers were covered in slime.

The strange suffocating feeling intensified. Suddenly, she remembered being stuck in a closet when she and a childhood friend played hide-and-seek. KC flashed on the terror she'd felt. She'd started screaming, certain that the walls were going to close in and crush her.

She felt like that now.

KC edged back again, gasping for breath. Sweat trickled down her neck, and her hand slipped on the wall. Her heart felt ready to explode.

Suddenly, KC became aware of a dimness coming from behind her. There was a faint green glow. And it was moving closer.

The approaching light sent out a strange luminescent beam, and the minerals in the rocks started to glitter in eerie colors. She heard footsteps. Someone *was* coming.

Frantically, KC searched the walls for a niche to hide in. Her eyes focused on strange drawings along one side of the cave, where it appeared someone had sketched stick figures. Had someone come in here and etched these figures centuries ago? She stared at them, then turned toward the strange light as it grew slowly brighter. The faint scent of cologne reached her.

Before she could turn any further, two arms grabbed her from behind, and she flinched in terror. She twisted violently to see who held her, kicking out with her feet. It was a man. With a green face. His features were illuminated by the light in the hard hat perched on his head. In the dimness, she saw fierce light-colored eyes burning into hers, and a mouth set in a hard line.

KC opened her mouth to scream, but his hand clamped down over her face. His palm smelled of leather and mesquite.

"What the hell are you doing in here?" he hissed furiously into her ear.

"Mmmrrrggghhh!" She struggled, then kicked out again with her foot. He swore under his breath but held on tight. The stranger's muscular chest pressed against her back.

"What do you want?" he asked fiercely. He loosened his grip, and in an instant, KC yanked furiously away, squinting in the darkness. Her backpack tumbled to the cave floor, but she was not going to get it. The only thing she wanted was to get away—far away. Footsteps clambered behind her, and she half stumbled, half ran toward the entrance where the brilliant stars beckoned through the hole in the cliff.

Surging out of the opening, KC pulled away from the clawing branches of the shrub guarding the cave entrance. She tripped once, then scrambled forward and dashed down the trail, her feet pounding on the dry ground.

The cabins appeared below her, and she slid along the steep incline. Dirt ground into her jeans, but she didn't care. She wanted to get down as fast as possible. Only her hands steadied her somewhat as she clung desperately to the roots of trees for support. With a jump, she cleared the last cluster of boulders and landed with a heavy thud in back of their tiny cabin.

She was never so glad to see Faith and Ted's lopsided tent. Quickly, she dodged around it, charged onto the porch, and flung open the cabin door. Her fingers immediately searched for the lock, which she turned once she'd slammed the door shut. She didn't turn on the light, but instead collapsed on the bed in the darkness.

"Oh, please, Courtney! Ted! Come back. Soon!" she whispered, listening for footsteps over the rustling of the wind.

Five

....

Winnie couldn't believe how totally great Pinky's was.

Jake, the tall, dark-haired guy with the blue eyes, had grabbed her almost the minute she'd jumped on the dance floor. Now he clasped her hand tightly as he spun her around, his eyes sparkling. The guy who was with him was named Carson. He had red hair and a splash of freckles across his nose. He held her other hand. They were spinning her around and laughing, and she felt caught in a turnstile with no way out. Her fun meter was registering *Tilt!* The music was hot, the dance floor packed with bodies, and the night was young. This place would make her forget about ever being married. This place would blast any memory of matrimony right out of her heart.

"Hey, guys," Winnie called over the thumping of the music and the stomping of cowboy boots on the wooden floor. "Spin me the other way."

"All right, Winnie!" they yelled, turning her around and around.

Her feet clunked. She pulled her hands free and began swinging her arms.

Wild energy coursed through her veins and sweat dripped down her back. Nothing could ruin this! She spotted Ted and Faith, wrapped together like two snakes. They seemed to be having a great time, too. Faith had found love, at last. Part of Winnie was happy for her.

She pushed away thoughts of her ex, Josh Gaffey, of the times they'd gone dancing, or just hung out at home, studying, holding hands, laughing. She *wouldn't* think about it. Not now. She channeled her thoughts toward KC. KC was moping in their room. What a total drag *that* was. But Courtney was probably right. People did have to make their own decisions. Winnie grinned. Courtney could organize their field trips from now till doomsday. That didn't mean that Winnie had to go along. Winnie had made a decision of her own.

I'm going to dance until I drop, Winnie thought.

Her compact body wiggled as the two guys danced around her. Jake, in his straight-cut jeans and yellow and green plaid cotton shirt, reminded her of a rodeo rider, complete with cowboy boots and bucking-horse belt buckle. Carson wore a dark-red, tailored shirt and khaki trousers. He had a funny, high-pitched laugh that made giggles rise in Winnie's throat.

Winnie twisted out a funky dance step, laughing when Jake and Carson imitated her. As she spun, she caught sight of a tall, muscular blond guy, leaning back against the wooden railing. He watched her closely. Winnie smiled as his eyes swept down her body, then up. She liked the look of his broad shoulders and slim, powerful build. He reminded her of an Olympic swimmer. Girls swarmed around him, vying for his attention. He was obviously popular. And she could see why. His handsome face had a confident I-own-the-world look. Several guys clustered around him, too. When he spoke, they all bent toward him to listen.

And he kept watching Winnie.

Jake grabbed her by the waist and shimmied with her around Carson. The room was a blur. Suddenly, Winnie planted her feet, making him stumble off balance. He started laughing. Winnie twirled him around.

"Stop! You're making me seasick," Jake said as Winnie swayed and swished.

Beside her, Carson laughed his funny laugh. He saw his chance and grabbed Winnie, lunging away with her in a wild dance twirl.

"Yeeeee!" she squealed as Carson lifted her off the ground.

Carson leaned over and poked Jake in the ribs. "Give up, Jake. Go find your own partner."

Jake laughed, and continued to sway dizzily. He bumped into Winnie. "No way, Carson. I saw her first!"

Winnie ignored them. She was breathing hard from the dancing, and the heat made her throat dry. She twisted around to find the tall, powerful blond guy again. He was still watching her. Still leaning casually against the railing and ignoring the cluster of people around him. Bristling excitement crawled up and down her spine.

"Hold it, you guys," she panted. "I think one at a time would be better."

Jake and Carson started pushing each other out of the way. Winnie laughed and shook her head. A slow dance started. The excitement inside her built to an explosion. The blond guy had eased his elbows off the railing.

Then he caught her eye, his gaze burning into hers. He straightened, sliding forward gracefully, ignoring a slim brunette with pleading eyes who was asking him something. He didn't take his eyes from Winnie's face.

Winnie's heart hammered in her chest, and a tingle of electricity charged through her blood. He moved like a leopard.

Her two partners followed her gaze and moaned loudly. "So much for seeing her first," one of them muttered.

They peeled away, fading into the crowd without

saying another word. Before Winnie could form a coherent thought, the blond guy stood before her.

"Hi there," he said in a smooth voice.

"Hi there, yourself," Winnie said, grinning. This guy was even better close up. His tanned face was smooth, with a strong jaw and high cheekbones. He had a tiny turquoise earring in his left ear.

"Lance Putnam," he announced.

"Winnie Gottlieb." The pulsing energy between them was making her feel dizzier than ever, and when he swept her into his arms for the slow dance, she could feel her heart start to speed up.

His body screamed strength, and he moved like liquid gold. Winnie let herself fall into him as they covered the floor.

Wow! If I were mining for gold, I'd say I just hit the jackpot, she thought. She let her mind wander as she pressed her cheek against Lance's shoulder. He had a shirt on that smelled fresh and new. His hands slid down her sides, holding her to him tightly. Her body responded and they began to move as one, Winnie floating on a wave of sensation.

He kissed her neck, and she moved closer, pressing against him. This was a guy who could make her forget Josh. This was the guy to make her forget everything.

Across the room, Ted felt Faith's soft hair tickle his cheek.

"Hmmm," she mumbled. "You feel wonderful."

"Yeah," Ted said, pulling Faith a little closer. "So do you."

The slow rhythm of the dance echoed in his blood. He opened his eyes. Blue and red lights flickered across the bodies clutched together on the floor. The dance, the music, the lights, everything felt perfect. Almost. A tiny poke of restlessness jabbed at him. Just a twinge. He ignored it. It was just a passing sensation, nothing more. He'd given up flirting and wandering, hadn't he? He'd been loyal to Faith. Proved to himself he could be monogamous.

So why was he focusing on a couple coiled around each other so tightly that they looked like they needed to be pried apart with a crowbar?

Ted blinked. *Wait a minute*, he thought. *That's Winnie.* He let his eyes drift down her body, then turned firmly away. Burying his face into Faith's lemony scented hair, Ted took a long, slow breath.

No, he told himself firmly. He was with Faith. Period. He dropped both arms along Faith's back and she snuggled closer, sighing in pleasure. When Winnie had appeared at the front of the tent earlier in the evening, he'd been impressed by her sexy, funky outfit. She was so abandoned, so free.

He twisted his head a little again and spotted Winnie once more. She was still in the arms of a tall, muscular blonde with an earring. His hands were all over her. Ted stiffened as he watched the guy pull Winnie even closer and kiss her neck.

From somewhere he heard a voice. But he was

too busy staring at the guy touching Winnie to hear.

"Ted? Ted?"

"Huh?"

"Ted, what's wrong?" It was Faith. "You okay?" She was looking up at him dreamily.

"Oh, right." He realized he'd stopped dancing and was frozen in place, watching Winnie and her partner intently.

Faith followed his gaze.

"Do you think Winnie should let that guy put his hands all over her?" Ted asked.

"Winnie can take care of herself," Faith said, drawing him back into her arms.

"Maybe, but he seems kind of pushy," Ted complained.

The guy had moved his hands lower and Winnie wiggled happily, pressed against him as if they'd just been stuck together with glue.

"Forget them," Faith said. "They look happy to me."

"I don't know," Ted went on. "There's something about him. Something that bugs me."

Faith grabbed Ted's hand and drew it around her waist. He smiled at her, and she leaned her head on his shoulder. "Don't worry. She'll be fine. Winnie's smart. Smarter than all of us."

"I know. I just don't want to see her get hurt, that's all. I know she's been through some hard times."

Faith looked again at Winnie. "I want Winnie to be okay just as much as you do. Maybe even more. She's been one of my best friends forever.

But as I said, she looks perfectly happy."

Ted sighed quietly. He moved back into the dance with Faith, pushing thoughts of Winnie out of his mind. He was a fool to be fascinated by her. He had a great relationship with Faith. He loved her. She loved him.

So why did he keep wanting to watch Winnie? Why did he feel compelled to see what she was doing?

He swept Faith back into his arms, but guided her carefully, slowly so that he could keep his eyes on Winnie. The dance ended, and he stepped back, giving Faith a smile. Then he looked back toward the center of the floor where Winnie and the blonde had been.

They were gone.

He quickly searched the dance hall, and was annoyed to see them heading out the door toward the parking lot.

Six

The crescent moon hung lazily in the velvety night sky, its huge, white image smiling down at Winnie. A breeze ruffled the edges of her skirt as she leaned back against a cream-colored sports car. Lance Putnam stood in front of her, giving her a look that made her muscles weak.

"So this is the parking lot," Winnie said, gesturing toward the sea of cars. Beyond the bumpers and the windshields, she spotted Courtney's convertible gleaming in the pale lights that lined the area.

Lance nodded slowly. His eyes burned into her. "That's right. I just thought that Pinky's was getting a little too crowded. We can talk better out here." He paused and swept a warm look over her, heating her blood another twelve degrees. "You're not from around these parts, are you?" he asked smoothly.

Winnie shook her head. "No. My friends and I are down here for spring break. Road trip. Seeing the sights, you know. The cactus and the dust."

He grinned, his face shining in the dim lights. "That's what I thought," he said softly. "Maybe I could show you around. This is sort of, well . . . my town."

Winnie wrinkled her forehead. "What do you mean, *your* town?" she asked, taking a quick look around the parking lot. "What town? You mean Gold Hill?"

He shrugged. "Not just Gold Hill. We own a lot of land around here. My family, that is. I run the business. I didn't need college for that." He laughed deep in his throat.

Inside, Winnie felt a little flicker of satisfaction. He was trying to impress her. That was a good sign. He cared enough to try to make her think he was some kind of local big shot. "Really?" she asked, trying to sound intrigued. His family and how many acres of desert they owned obviously mattered to him. And if it mattered to him, it mattered to her.

"Yeah, really. I thought college was a waste of time. I mean, how many college guys have a car like this?" He pointed behind her to the car she was leaning against. Winnie edged forward. The convertible shone under the lights. The top was up, but through the side window she could see leather bucket seats and a wood-grained dashboard. The paint and chrome were spotless.

"Nice. Very nice. For a car." She gave him a smile.

"You bet it is." He reached forward and drew his hand along her wrist, under the cuff of her denim jacket. Little ripples of heat radiated through her.

Lance chuckled. His hand moved up to her face, and one fingertip slid along her jaw. The light in his eyes shifted a little. Winnie swallowed. The slow, fluid way he was touching her was making her insides turn all watery. "My dad and I run some successful gold mines around here," he continued. "Other stuff, too. Development. Construction. Everybody knows us."

Winnie smiled. She'd been right about striking it rich with Lance. "I didn't know there were any real gold mines in these parts."

Lance looked surprised, then he laughed again. "A lot of people think that, I guess. They assume the mines all played out in the 1880s." He shrugged, and his hands slid down her arms again. "The fools just don't know where to look. They let stupid superstitions stand in their way. Or they let some government agency tell them what to do."

Winnie liked the slow, smooth way Lance was touching her. She liked the way the music from the dance hall throbbed in the background, and the way the moon sent streaks of silver light across his hair. He moved closer, settling his hands on her waist.

"Uh, do you have any mines close to Gold Hill?" Winnie asked. "I mean, I've never seen a real gold mine." There was a persistent gleam in Lance's eyes as they traveled over her. He took another step forward until she could feel his legs pressing against her skirt.

"Our mines are way up in the cliffs beyond Las Altas, and they're off limits. We like to keep security tight. Everybody around here knows better than to mess with the Putnam family." He tried to smile, but Winnie noticed that a hard gleam had settled into his eyes. The soft, admiring look had vanished.

Winnie swallowed. "Oh."

"You're beautiful, you know that?" he whispered, pressing her against the car. His lips felt warm against the skin of her neck, and she tilted her head back a little.

He moved closer, tightening his grip on her waist. She tried to shift her position out from under the steady pressure of his hands, sliding a little along the slippery coat of the polished car. He pressed his lips on hers and at first she melted into him, enjoying the heat of his mouth. Then she drew back.

"Hey, Lance," she said in a soft voice. "Let's go inside." One kiss with this guy was plenty. There was something about the pressure on her waist that was beginning to bother her.

"I thought you wanted to come out here," he murmured, his mouth against her cheek.

"Well, I did." Winnie wriggled some more, but Lance wouldn't let go. "Hey, the music sounds great."

"Yeah, it does. From out here." Lance pressed his weight against her body, forcing her to lean back even farther against the car. "Come on, Winnie. Let's get to know each other better."

Suddenly, the warm pressure of his hands on her waist felt like steel. Winnie winced. "That's some grip you've got, Lance. What do you do, bend steel bars in your spare time? Let go, will you?"

He drew his hands forward, rubbing one hand down her leg and hiking her skirt up a little. She tried to push it back down, but he laughed low in his throat as he took her hand and pinned it at her side.

"Hmmm," he whispered, "I don't want to let go."

"Lance, back off. Please. I want to go inside now. You can stay out here if you want."

"Not by myself." He shoved her hard. This time alarm bells went off in Winnie's head. This guy was either too stupid or too persistent for his own good. Winnie flexed her muscles and pushed as hard as she could. He staggered back a step, long enough for Winnie to get past him. But he lunged after her and yanked her back in one fluid, powerful movement.

"Hey, Lance! Let me go!" she shouted, fear bubbling in her throat.

"Come on, Winnie. Don't stall on me now. Let's go for a ride. The desert roads are perfect for testing the limits of this baby." He patted the canvas top of his sports car.

"Take your baby for a ride without me," Winnie said. She shoved her hands against his shoulders again. It was like trying to move a mountain. He leaned forward, sandwiching her legs and back firmly against the sports car. She squirmed frantically in an effort to wiggle free.

It was no use. His mouth came down on hers, and he kissed her fiercely. Winnie knew she had to do something fast. She stopped fighting long enough for Lance to think she was giving in. Then, when his body relaxed, Winnie shoved up against his chest. He fell back, and Winnie grabbed her chance.

Pumping her legs, she made a dash for the back door of the dance hall.

Lance ran after her. "Come back here, Winnie," he shouted. "You and I have some unfinished business."

She ran faster, ignoring the sound of his approaching footsteps crunching across the gravel.

"Leave me alone, creep," she shouted over her shoulder.

With a burst of speed, she made it to the bottom steps of the porch of the building. She gasped for breath. The door opened. Jake and Carson stood on the wide-planked floorboards, big smiles on their faces. Relief flooded into her. Thank God! They'd be sure to help her.

"Hey, Carson, am I ever glad to see you," Winnie panted. Her lungs burned and her hands were shaking as she charged toward him. But Lance caught her from behind in his clawlike fingers and yanked her away from the steps. She lost her balance and stumbled.

Carson and Jake didn't move to help her. Winnie looked at them and was horrified to see that they were still smiling.

Then Jake let his eyes travel over Winnie's body.

"Hey, Lance. Need some help?" he asked.

Winnie was too stunned to react.

She watched as Jake *and* Carson stepped slowly toward her. "Yeah, Lance," Carson said. "Looks like you could use a little backup." He drew close to Winnie and flicked a finger under her chin. She punched his hand away.

"Hey," she said. "I need some help here." Her breath choked her as fear closed her throat.

Jake and Carson looked at each other, then nodded slowly. Carson stepped beside Winnie. "What do you think, Jake? Think we should give Winnie our help?" he said. "Or maybe . . ."

Winnie saw the two friends exchange smiles. Suddenly she realized they weren't going to help her. They were going to help Lance.

"Yeah, Carson," Lance grunted as he dragged Winnie off. "Grab her other arm."

Carson leaped to do Lance's bidding. The two of them started dragging Winnie back toward the sports car. They held her arms tightly, their fingers digging into her skin. She kicked madly at Carson, jabbing him fiercely in the shin. He winced. Winnie tried to kick Lance, but he dodged, and yanked her denim jacket harder.

"Come on, Winnie," Jake taunted as he looked on. "I think Lance wants your company a little longer . . . out in the desert."

They reached the car, and Winnie heard a door open. She tried to grab hold of the door frame, but

Carson peeled her fingers back and Winnie tumbled into the car. She screamed. The door slammed shut. She banged her fists on the window, but all three guys just leered and laughed.

Then Lance jumped into the driver's seat. He jangled a key, and Winnie heard the engine roar to life.

"Let me go!" Winnie screamed in raw terror. She was not going to let this happen. She clutched wildly at the door handle. "Let me out!" she screamed at Jake, who held the door shut. His face twisted into a gleeful smile. She heard his raucous laughter through the window. They were all laughing at her.

Then, suddenly, the back door was wrenched open. Someone grabbed her hand roughly and pulled her out of the car.

She stumbled forward. Whoever had grabbed her now let her go. The car engine died. When she looked back, she saw Lance catapulting out of the driver's seat. Winnie looked sharply around, terrified. Jake and Carson were backing toward the front hood of the car, stunned looks on their stupid faces. Suddenly, beside her, stood a tall, muscular figure, his familiar face contorted in fury.

Ted.

Winnie couldn't move or think or say a word. She stood frozen.

In one powerful motion, Ted leaped over the back of the car, drew back his arm, and aimed his fist smack at Lance's nose.

*　　　*　　　*

Right. Left. Right. Left. One of Courtney's hands rested on her partner's shoulder, the other in the warm clasp of his palm. The slow dance had eased into an old-fashioned foxtrot rhythm, and her partner moved slowly, gently to the music. At first, when she'd asked him to dance, Courtney had wondered if she'd made a mistake. Maybe he wasn't a deep-thinking cowboy artist or sculptor, after all. Maybe he was just incredibly shy. He danced with a sort of rigid formality that reminded Courtney of dance classes in junior high.

But then, he'd loosened up a little, and now his movements were sure and graceful. Even though he avoided her eyes, she could feel his interest. She was glad she'd asked him to dance.

Dancing had always been a way for her to get to know guys. Clumsy, eager ones tromped on her toes. Slimy, aggressive ones let their hands wander all over her. Dignified, stuffy ones held themselves rigid, as if they were afraid they'd break if they relaxed.

This guy was sort of in a new category. Gentle, but strong. A little tentative, but warm, too, with a kind of physical attractiveness that drew her like a magnet. It didn't matter that he held her at arm's length. Though part of her did wish he would hold her closer. She looked up, and her breath stuck in her throat. He was gazing down at her. A quiver of sensation swept across her skin. Maybe she didn't need to get any closer. The music stopped, and he stood, a second or two longer than he had to, his hand giving hers a little squeeze.

"Thanks," Courtney murmured. "I enjoyed that."

"Me, too." His dark eyes were still shining down at her.

She felt as if she were floating. As if the hot air inside the dance hall had buoyed her up next to the billions of stars outside.

Suddenly, the band cranked up the music, flooding the building with wailing guitar chords and a pulsating drumbeat. The dance floor exploded around them. Courtney and her partner struggled through the crowd and settled back onto their stools.

"What's your name?" Courtney asked.

"Joe Hillsey."

"Are you from around here—a local?"

"That's right. Of course, local means a radius of about two hundred miles. The county reaches all the way past Las Altas."

Courtney smiled, her interest intensifying. He had a rich, low voice, and sounded relaxed and thoughtful. Her smile deepened. That was almost three complete sentences, she thought happily. She was making progress.

"I'm traveling with my friends," she continued. "I know a little about the area, but we really want to get to see as much as possible. We're on spring break."

Joe raised his eyebrows slightly. "From the college in Las Altas?"

"No. University of Springfield in Oregon."

He whistled. "That's a good way from here." He gave her a quick smile again, and her heart flip-flopped in her chest. "There are lots of interesting things to see," he added. "The petroglyphs, for instance, beyond Little Canyon. Early cliff dwellers sometimes recorded ceremonial figures or important events on rocks or cave walls."

"Really?" Courtney felt a flood of satisfaction. She had been right about him. He was knowledgeable and confident. Between the two of them, they'd be able to figure out the best places to see. And talking about local sites seemed to touch a conversation chord in Joe. She'd lost track of the number of sentences he'd actually spoken.

He grinned again. "The Altaverdi of the late Pueblo period were pretty sophisticated."

"They were?"

"The cliff houses were almost like apartments," he said, his eyes softening warmly.

"You're kidding."

Joe gave her another rapid smile that looked a little apologetical. He folded his hands on one knee and leaned back, pulling his knee toward him. "Sometimes two hundred families could live in the cliff cities. The Altaverdi, you know, also used the caves for rituals." He grinned. "Uh—it's one of my hobbies," he said sheepishly.

"What?" Courtney asked.

"The artifacts, you know, the prehistory . . ."

Courtney smiled. "I would really like to see some artifacts, the real leftovers of the past. I mean, this whole area is dripping with history, isn't it?" she asked, leaning forward to touch his arm. She paused. He reached out slowly, dropped his knee, and let his soft fingers rest for a moment on her hand. His skin was warm and smooth. He held her gaze for a slow-as-molasses moment. The lights and the bouncing, hopping, whooping dancers faded from her view and all she saw was him.

He was about to say something. The words were half-formed and his face had registered some emotion she couldn't identify. He looked shy again. Then, in an instant, his face set, and he twisted his head away from hers and stared across the dance floor, a frown erasing the soft, almost eager look of a moment ago. He peered intently toward the door leading to the parking lot.

"I mean, I've seen pictures of cliff houses," Courtney continued. "But I've always wanted to . . ." Her voice trailed off. Joe wasn't listening to her. He sat completely motionless. She looked around quickly. The dancers had stopped, their expressions stilled, their smiles gone. Everyone looked worried, confused, and concerned. They buzzed like hornets around a mud puddle.

"Something's happened," Joe said simply. He edged forward, sliding smoothly off his stool, and headed toward the door.

Curious, Courtney pressed into the tightly packed crowd, wedging herself between the mass of bodies all rushing outside. Her pulse quickened. Something was wrong. Joe had burst out of the crowd and was running through the doorway and into the parking lot.

Pressed tightly beside two other customers, Courtney pushed herself onto the front porch. The cool night air hit her face, causing her to take a quick breath. Dust hung above the parking lot, and at first, all she could see was a dim yellowish light, and a small group of people clustered near some cars. Then she saw Joe, running fast.

He was headed toward two guys who were fighting. They rolled around on the ground, their fists flying. Courtney winced when a fist smashed into one guy's jaw. Before she realized it, she was halfway across the dusty gravel, grit sliding under her shoes. Ahead of her, Joe crossed the wide lot like a sprinter in a hundred-yard dash. Then, unbelievably, her quiet, reserved, mild-mannered dancing partner leaped into the middle of the fight. His hands clamped onto one guy's shoulder and he pulled him up. The movement yanked Joe's shirt out of his pants, and Courtney saw an odd shape tucked into a wide leather belt. Was it a gun? Did Joe have a gun in a holster? Courtney choked on the astonishment and sudden, intense fear.

Before she could react, the two fighters staggered away from each other. Courtney stumbled to a stop. She felt as if her blood had solidified into cement. The guy getting up from the ground was Ted. His nose was bleeding, and one of his eyes was starting to swell shut. Looking around, Courtney became aware of Faith and Winnie huddled close together.

Tears were running down Winnie's face, and

Faith had her arm around her. "Stop them," Winnie sobbed as the blond guy lunged at Ted. "Somebody stop them!"

"I said cool it, Putnam," Joe yelled, in a rough voice. The blonde staggered back, but when he glanced over at Ted, he surged forward again. Joe slammed him against a car.

"It's over, Lance. Now, back off!" Joe shouted again.

Ted wiped the blood off his face with his cuff. Faith left Winnie beside the car and ran to Ted. "Are you okay?"

"What's going on?" Courtney asked. No one paid any attention to her.

"Get your crummy hands off me," Lance was saying to Joe. "Stop pushing me around, you jerk."

Joe stood poised, ready to spring, but when he saw Courtney, he put his arms down. The tension hung in the air. For a minute, Courtney thought that Lance was going to start punching Joe.

"This bastard threw the first punch," Lance said, wiping the blood from his mouth and staggering a little as he took a step forward. He shoved Joe away from him.

"You bet I did," Ted snarled. "What the hell were you doing to Winnie?"

"Winnie?" Courtney repeated. "What do you mean, Ted?"

Ted poked a finger into Lance's chest. "He locked her in his car."

"What?" Courtney looked at Joe. He was standing beside Lance, looking embarrassed. Then Courtney turned to Winnie, who was still crying. "Is that true, Winnie?"

Winnie nodded. Courtney could tell she was on the verge of hysteria. Her hands were trembling and her face was white.

Courtney sent a fierce look at Lance. "Someone should call the police."

For some reason, that made Lance laugh. "Right. She was draped all over me. And she made the first move. Tell *that* to the cops," he sneered, raking Joe with a disgusted glance as he shoved past. Joe stepped out of his way.

"She threw herself at me. And I caught her," Lance went on, turning to Ted, who took a threatening step toward him. "Then this *turkey* punched me for no reason."

Courtney stepped closer to Joe. "Call the police!" she insisted. "This is an assault. Attempted rape. Aren't you going to *do* anything about it? Isn't anyone?"

She looked around at the crowd. There was a lot of murmuring, but one by one, the dancers headed back into Pinky's. Courtney was stunned. No one seemed to question Lance's statement.

"See?" Lance sneered. "Everyone believes I'm telling the truth." He gave his two buddies a smirk, and they all laughed.

"That's right," the redheaded guy who'd been dancing with Winnie spoke up. "She was plastered all over Lance. I'll testify to it."

Courtney's blood boiled. She spun back toward Joe. "Aren't you going to do anything?" she shouted again.

"I think we should just forget about it," Joe replied quietly. He was slowly tucking his shirt back into his belt. His face looked defeated and blank.

"Forget about it? Are you crazy? Winnie's almost been raped, and we're supposed to stand around and pretend it didn't happen?"

Lance laughed again. He flicked his head toward Pinky's, and the two guys fell in step beside him. Lance turned once and blew a mocking kiss at Winnie, then wheeled around and strode into the building.

Joe, Courtney, Faith, Ted, and Winnie were left alone.

"I can't believe this! Winnie, are you okay?" Courtney asked, rushing to her side.

Winnie nodded meekly. Her chin wobbled. "He wouldn't let me go. He kept pushing me against his car, and—and then he told me . . . he was going to take me out to the desert. . . ." Tears spilled out of her eyes and she broke down, her shoulders heaving.

Courtney spun back to Joe. "That guy should be reported. Ted's testimony will stand up. He was protecting Winnie!"

"Don't bother," Joe replied. "It's just his word against yours. Besides, your friend here admitted starting the fight. Now I suggest that you all go back to where you're staying. It's not a good idea for you to hang around here." He crossed his arms and held Courtney's gaze.

Courtney was dumbfounded. How could she have thought this guy was sensitive and strong? It was like he was two different people. He'd changed shape right before her eyes. "This is unbelievable! *You* are totally unbelievable," she spit out. "I suppose that gun at your belt makes you feel tough." She stepped toward Joe. "Well, it obviously doesn't do the job! You're not tough. You can't even stand up to some local big shot when there are witnesses to back you up."

Joe's face crumpled miserably. His eyes looked sad. "Listen—"

"I will not!" Courtney snapped.

They stared at each other for a long, painful moment, then Joe turned and headed back toward the dance hall. Courtney stared after him. How could she have been such a bad judge of character?

"God! What a jerk!" she fumed.

Faith patted Ted's face with a cloth. "It looks to me like Lance Putnam does what he likes," she said sadly.

Ted winced as she wiped blood from his nose. "And gets away with it. Ouch, that hurts!"

Faith tugged at Ted's arm. "Come on, we've got to put some ice on your face. Winnie, are you sure you're all right? Courtney will bring you back to the motel. Okay?"

Winnie nodded. "Sure. Thanks, Ted. I don't know what I would have done if—"

"Forget it, Winnie. I'm just glad you're all right. See you back at the cabin." Ted and Faith headed to the Jeep, and within minutes they pulled out onto the highway, followed by a trail of dust.

Courtney gently took Winnie's arm and guided her toward her convertible. Winnie began sobbing again as they reached the car. "Oh, Courtney," she gulped. "I was so scared! And I'm so sooooorrryyy!" She wailed as Courtney patted her arm.

"It's okay," Courtney said soothingly. "The important thing is that you're not hurt. And Ted's all right. I'm just glad he was here."

"Me, too! That guy was so awful! He wouldn't take no for an answer. I tried to get away, but he wouldn't let me."

Courtney frowned. She kept picturing poor Winnie being forced into the guy's car. "I know I was stupid, but that doesn't give that guy the right to force me!" Winnie went on.

"Of course it doesn't, Winnie. I can't believe that Joe didn't want to report him, either. I mean, he acted like it was okay that you were attacked." Courtney could still feel the swirling mix of fury and shock at Lance's attack on Winnie and Joe's total uselessness. She crossed to the driver's side, and her hands shook as she opened the car door.

Winnie sobbed. "Yeah. As if it was all my fault." She hiccoughed and gulped, trying to control herself. There was a long moment of uncomfortable silence. "I feel guilty," she said, her voice thick with tears. "I was stupid. I made a mistake. The guy is a total, undiluted creep. But it wasn't *all* my fault. I mean, that guy got to walk away with his stupid friends as if nothing happened." An angry edge crept into her voice.

Courtney nodded. It was obvious that Winnie felt lousy about the incident. Courtney recalled the numerous lectures she'd given younger sorority girls over the years about the dangers of encouraging guys they didn't know. It looked as if Winnie had just learned the same lesson. But the outcome still didn't seem right. Why should Winnie be made to feel guilty because some stupid bully abused her? Courtney despised injustice. And cowardice.

"Everyone was so intimidated by that creep," Winnie was saying as if thinking the same thoughts. "And now we're supposed to pretend that nothing happened. Give me a break!"

Suddenly, Winnie yanked open the passenger door of Courtney's convertible. She pulled out a box, flipped open the top, and snatched a Swiss Army knife that was lying on top of the screwdrivers and flares. "Emergency supplies," Winnie said. "And this is an emergency."

"Winnie? What are you doing? Put that knife down."

But Winnie didn't listen. She sprinted across the parking lot.

"Winnie!" Courtney screamed. "Stop!" She was certain Winnie was going to do bodily harm to someone. So she was relieved when Winnie stopped by Lance's car.

Winnie looked back, her eyes gleaming like dark coals. "Watch this!"

"No!" Courtney shrieked.

But Winnie plunged the knife into the smooth, canvas top of Lance Putnam's sleek convertible. And in one swift motion she pulled back quickly, making a sickening slice in the expensive roof of the car.

Courtney sucked in a horrified breath. A charge of energy jolted through her, and she jumped behind the steering wheel of her car and turned the key. The engine roared to life. "Winnie!" she screamed. Suddenly, from behind Courtney came a shout, and she twisted to see one of Lance Putnam's goons dashing down the wooden steps of Pinky's.

Courtney threw the gears into reverse, and a cloud of pebbles and dirt rose into the air. "Winnie! Get in! Quick!" she screamed.

Winnie froze for an instant, then looked over her shoulder. Her eyes widened as she spotted the figure running toward her through the dust. Instantly, she bolted away from Lance's car and made a dive for the passenger side of Courtney's convertible.

"Get in!" Courtney screamed again. Winnie plunged into the seat and slammed the door shut behind her.

Behind them, two more guys had dashed onto the front porch.

"My car! She wrecked my car! I'll get you for this!" Lance shrieked.

Courtney slammed her foot on the accelerator, and Lance and his buddies choked and coughed as dust shot into their faces.

"You'll pay for this," Lance sputtered.

"In your dreams, mega-jerk!" Winnie screamed as she looked in the rearview mirror and smiled.

Three guys, covered in dust, shook their fists at them. But they got smaller and smaller as Courtney sped down the empty highway, Winnie laughing beside her.

Seven

"*T*ell me again, Winnie," Ted said, laughter filling his voice. "Tell me what the top of that sports car felt like when you sliced it with the knife." Ted was sitting beside Faith on Courtney's bed, holding an ice pack on his forehead with one hand. Faith gave him a quick glance. His eyes were gleaming. He looked as if he were listening to the firsthand account of something really exciting, instead of the details of Winnie's stupid prank. Faith felt annoyance nettle her, crawling under her skin like a bunch of caterpillars. She'd had enough of Winnie's melodrama.

"It slid into that expensive top like a hot knife through . . . whipped cream!" Winnie said, laughing.

"But what you did is against the law," KC said, appalled.

Winnie made a face. "Yeah. And so is rape, KC. I mean, am I supposed to just sit around and feel victimized by that jerk? He deserved it."

"But what if he comes after you?" Courtney asked. "I wouldn't put too much faith in the locals around here standing up for justice. I mean, look at the way Joe reacted."

"Courtney's right," Faith said, leaning back against the cabin wall. "This is a really small town, Winnie. For all we know, your dance partner is out there right now, searching for you. Pinky's is only twenty-five miles from here, and in these parts twenty-five miles is like a short jaunt to the corner for ice cream. And maybe Joe knows something we don't about this Lance Putnam character."

Courtney sighed. "I have to disagree with you there, Faith," she said, her voice edged with irritation. "Joe was just a total coward. I thought he was being polite when he held me a foot away from him when we danced. But he just didn't want me to know he was carrying a gun."

Faith frowned. "I guess it's a good thing he's a wimp, then. I mean, he might have started shooting."

Courtney shook her head furiously, her blond hair flipping back and forth. "No way. He was inept. He would never have used the gun."

"Well, if Lance Putnam was as angry as you say he was, Courtney," Faith went on, turning toward

Winnie, "we'd better leave in the morning. We could head to the Little Canyon area that surrounds the river. Then Ted and I could get our raft trip in. I really don't think we should stay here a second longer than necessary."

"Excitement at last," Winnie said, bouncing on the bed. "Just like the Hole-in-the-Wall Gang. Head into the mountains where no one can follow us. Winnie Cassidy and the Sundance Gang."

Faith heard Ted chuckle beside her. The nettled feeling spread through her.

Courtney smiled at Winnie. "I guess you're right, Faith. I want to check out the Del Oro Spa. It's about seventy-five miles east of here. And if you guys head to the river, maybe no one will be able to find us. What do you think, KC? Want to luxuriate in a mud spa for a couple of hours?"

KC shrugged and started twirling a lock of hair around her finger. "I guess so," she said, her voice flat.

Faith thought KC looked worried. Maybe KC was imagining the sort of place where you had to slide into warm mud and take showers in freezing cold bathrooms with cracked tiles. Or maybe she was worried that Lance Putnam would come barging in after them. Faith could understand her concern. And KC had been pretty shocked by the whole story. When Faith and Ted had come stumbling into the cabin, Ted holding a cloth over his bloody nose, she'd screamed like a terrified rabbit caught in a trap.

Now she kept wrinkling her forehead and biting

her lip. Faith grabbed her braid and flicked the end back and forth against the palm of her hand. The whole evening had turned out to be a disaster. Her own nerves felt shredded.

"I never thought I'd end up an outlaw," Winnie chattered. "Did you know that the Hole-in-the-Wall Gang went out and had their pictures taken at the local photography studio after their first train robbery?"

"Yeah," Faith said. "And then the sheriff plastered the picture all over their wanted posters."

"Spoilsport," Ted accused, poking her gently in the ribs. Ted's eye looked better, less swollen and red. Faith gave him a worried smile. He stood up, crossed the room in two strides, and tossed his cold rag into the kitchen sink. "Don't worry, Faith. We'll be floating down the San Pico River before Lance Putnam scrapes together enough brain cells to figure out that we've gone."

"Yeah," Winnie muttered. "We'll stay out of Lance Putnam's way. He can't catch us."

"I hope you're right," Faith said. She took a deep breath, trying to calm her jittery nerves. Between KC's nervous glances at the door and Winnie's wild escapade, Faith felt on edge. The trip was suddenly feeling strange, as if there were currents of meaning running under the surface that she didn't understand. She was glad Ted had rescued Winnie. But couldn't he have simply told the guy to back off? Why did he have to start a fight?

"I think relaxing at the spa is just what we need," Courtney was saying to KC.

Faith turned to listen to Courtney when she heard something outside. "Shhh," she said quickly. "I think—"

Then she heard it again, more clearly. Footsteps. Rustling. More footsteps. Right outside the cabin. Gravel scraped. Another step sounded, closer this time. Faith felt her heart bang in her chest. She looked toward the open window. Then a heavy tread went clunk onto the front porch of the cabin.

"What's that?" Winnie hissed.

Faith pressed her back against the adobe wall. The surface was bumpy and rough. Everyone in the small room fell silent. The footsteps got louder, then they stopped right outside the door. Through the open window, Faith saw someone silhouetted by the faint porch lightbulb. She craned her head to see. Someone was there—a tall, dark figure right outside the door.

Faith looked over at Courtney, Winnie, and KC. They had all gone ghostly white, their faces stiff with fear.

"They're coming to get me," Winnie said, totally panicked.

"Shhh! Can you see who it is, Faith?" Courtney whispered.

Faith peeked out the window. All she could see was a tall figure. Deep shadows covered his face. She craned forward a little more, trying to catch the sounds. Whoever it was whispered to himself.

"I can't see his face," she whispered to the others.

Ted shook his head. "I bet it's the manager," he said softly. "The tent probably blew down and ended up stuck to his window." He tried to make his voice light, but Faith could see he was worried, his face rigid with anxiety.

"Faith," Winnie hissed from across the room. "You're closest to the phone. Call the police."

Faith saw that Winnie's eyes were huge with fear. But for some reason, Faith couldn't budge. What if the prowler had a weapon? What if he was just waiting for someone to make a move? Waiting until someone moved against the light. The light. She hadn't turned off the light.

Slowly, Faith reached for the fat cactus lamp on the bedside table when a loud knock sounded on the screen door of the cabin.

"It's Lance Putnam," Winnie shrieked. "I just know it is." She moved quickly, jumping right into Ted's arms.

Faith froze. She didn't turn off the light. Suddenly the menacing presence outside didn't seem half as upsetting as the sight in front of her. She couldn't believe what she was seeing. It wiped everything from her mind.

Ted was standing in the middle of the room, his eyes glued to the door, his strong left arm clasped firmly around Winnie's shoulders. He was holding on to her, tightly, securely. And Winnie, her eyes clamped shut, was hugging him, her arms wrapped around him as if she would never let go.

"Winnie!" Faith said sharply.

Another knock banged on the door, and everyone flinched. Then, slowly, the screen door creaked, the sound of its rusty hinges filling the room.

Faith couldn't think. She tried to catch Ted's eye, but he wasn't looking at her. She followed his gaze.

He was looking at the inner door as the figure on the porch pushed it open.

Eight

"Hello?" a rough male voice called from the door he held ajar.

There was a pause. KC could hear everyone's breath, raspy and harsh in the silent room. Then the voice spoke again. "Is there a KC Angeletti inside?"

KC flinched. She had thought for a moment it was one of the guys at Pinky's, too. But why would they want her? She hadn't even been at the dance hall. She hadn't damaged Lance Putnam's car. She'd been here and in the cave. The cave? Wait a minute. Maybe . . . KC rose and stepped toward the door.

Courtney reached out to stop her, shaking her head fiercely. "KC, don't."

"It's okay." KC crossed the small cabin quickly and pulled the door open a little wider.

Her breath caught. It *was* the guy from the cave.

"KC Angeletti?" he asked softly. His face looked guarded, wary. Now that KC could get a better look at him, she saw that he was about her age, with auburn hair a little lighter in color than his beard. He was wearing dirty, khaki trousers with bulging side pockets and a wrinkled cotton shirt. On his feet were thick-soled hiking boots, the kind climbers wore on rough terrain. They were scuffed and battered.

"Hi there. Uh . . . KC?" He caught her eye curiously. His voice sounded shaky. "Here. I brought this back. You dropped it." He held up KC's backpack.

KC reached out and took her pack from him. "Uh, thanks," she murmured.

"Who are you?" Courtney asked from the other side of the room. "How did you get KC's stuff?" The question just hung in the air. The guy didn't answer, and neither did KC, who felt everyone's eyes boring into her back as she clasped the doorknob and stared at the stranger.

Then, before anyone could say anything, the guy from the cave spun around, banged the door shut behind him, and disappeared.

"What a minute!" KC called. She dropped her pack and went after him.

She wanted to know who he was. She wanted to know why he'd jumped her back in the cave. She wanted to know why now, past midnight, he'd come to find her at the motel, then bolted away like a terrified animal. And, more than anything, she wanted an apology. After all, he'd scared her half to death in the cave.

She saw him sitting in an ancient-looking pickup truck, trying desperately to get the engine started.

"Hey! Wait a minute!" she called, stretching her long legs forward and crossing the ground in three easy strides. "I'd like to talk to you!"

She reached the door of the truck and rattled the handle.

The guy jumped as if she'd pulled a gun on him. His face froze in a look of sudden fright.

KC stared at him through the window that was streaked with dirt. She made a motion for him to roll down the glass, but he shook his head. "It's broken," she heard him say.

"Oh, no you don't!" she muttered, clasping her fingers on the door and finally managing to wrench it open. The guy looked at her nervously. KC showed no mercy. "You could at least say you're sorry," she said. "I mean, I just startled you, and *I'm* sorry. You seem a little jumpy. Someone after you or something?"

"Pothunters can be dangerous."

"Pothunters?" KC asked, confused.

"You know, thieves who steal stuff out of ruins. You never know around here. You can't be too careful." He waited, tightening his knuckles on the steering wheel. It had one of those old leather covers on it. "My truck is filled with valuable equipment," he muttered. He let his eyes linger on her face. "And . . . and

I am sorry," he finally said. He turned back to the steering wheel. He fumbled with the key, then pressed his lips together in an exasperated expression. The engine just moaned, then fell silent.

"Thank you. That's all I wanted to hear." She glanced over to the passenger seat, which was littered with a clipboard stuffed with papers, drawing pencils, and a trowel. What looked like a pile of black plastic sat on the floor, and on top of it was a rusty, metal toolbox. Suddenly, she wanted to hear more.

"So," she went on. "What's so valuable?"

He followed her gaze, and smiled slowly. "Well, this stuff is more valuable than it looks." The smile lit his eyes. She decided there was a sort of adventurer look about him. In his dusty boots and his khaki trousers with side pockets, he was the perfect advertisement for one of those outdoors-clothes catalogs.

"So you jumped me because you thought I was after your antique clipboard? Your flashlight? Or maybe that ancient pile of black plastic?" KC asked.

His smile broadened, but he didn't answer. He stared ahead, out into the huge, empty black space that stretched out around them. The silence lengthened. KC wondered if he was going to bother to answer her question.

"Well?" she asked again, feeling the urge to know the truth. She knew how hard the truth was to discover. Sometimes, it was nearly impossible to get people to believe it, too.

"Not exactly," he finally said. "You—you caught

me off guard, that's all. I wasn't expecting anyone."
He turned toward her again. "Listen, I'm sorry. I
didn't mean to scare you. I found the Cactus Cottage
postcard in your bag and tracked you down. I wanted
to let you know . . . well . . . I'm sorry. I didn't mean
to scare you or your friends back there, either."

He looked worried and frightened again. His
forehead wrinkled into a maze of dusty crevices. He
had brought back her pack when he could easily
have left it to molder away in the damp cave. "Well,
okay," she said. "Thanks for rescuing my pack. It
has some important stuff in it."

KC stood staring at him for a minute, then
turned to leave. She was pretty sure there was more
to his presence in that cave than he was telling her.
But she knew she couldn't force the story out of
him. Who was she to demand the truth? She'd been
telling the truth back in Springfield when everyone
thought she'd pushed Brooks off the mountain.
That didn't mean anyone believed her, did it? The
dark, heavy emptiness fell into her again as she
stepped away from the truck. What was the use? She
started to head back to the cabin.

"Wait a minute . . . KC?" the guy called from behind her.

She stopped and turned. "What?" she asked
wearily.

"You're right. I do owe you an explanation." He
looked at her almost pleadingly. She waited.

"I've been exploring those caves for over a

week," he went on. "I've been completely alone. I guess I'm . . . well, sort of out of touch." He slid his hands off the steering wheel and climbed out slowly. "I would like to talk about my work. That is, I need to talk. And you—"

Inside her head, KC heard an echo of the letter that lay in her pack. *It is time to speak.* The words of her grandmother. His words triggered a chord of response.

She stepped forward, pulled by the need he had to talk. She ached to unburden herself, too. Only, she didn't know whom to turn to. And the feeling of loneliness was starting to overwhelm her. Now she was face-to-face with someone equally lonely. Equally isolated. Maybe by choice, and maybe not. Maybe he'd been betrayed by his friends, too. Suspected and blamed by people he cared about. Maybe he'd run away to escape the pain of not being able to trust anyone.

Without speaking, she stepped past him and climbed up on the hood of the truck, its flat surface cold from the night air. Leaning back against the windshield, she stared out beyond the ragged little group of trees growing near the road that led to Gold Hill.

In an instant, he was beside her, settling against the windshield, too. The moon hung above them, casting its silver gleam across the desert. Out there, somewhere, was her grandmother, she thought suddenly. Waiting. Just as KC was waiting now.

She turned to him, and was startled to see that he was watching her closely. His face had settled into a serious expression, but there was excitement in his eyes.

"Are you heading toward Las Altas?" he asked suddenly.

KC nodded. "How did you know that?" she asked, wondering if he could read her mind.

"It's the only town of any size around here," he replied. "You're visiting, right?"

"Right."

"I go to school there," he added. He drew his knees up, twining his hands around them tightly. "At the university."

"Are you heading there, too?" KC asked, confused. She couldn't figure out what he was getting at, but he seemed to have something on his mind. Something important.

He shrugged, once again avoiding the question. A shooting star fell across the valley and a long silence ensued between them. KC could feel the windshield wipers against her lower back as she relaxed a little more.

"My equipment's on loan from the university," he said finally. "But I can't go back. Not just yet."

"Why not?"

He turned toward her again, and KC felt suspended by his gaze. He studied her face for a long time, searching it. It was almost as if he were asking her the same question that filled her brain, day after day, hour after hour. Can I trust you? he seemed to say. Can I trust you?

"I have more work to do," he murmured. He smiled again, a slow, gentle smile that made KC feel strangely at ease. "My name's Grady, by the way. Grady Kiesling."

KC returned his smile. "That's an interesting name. Are you from around here—originally, I mean?"

"No, my family's from Arizona," he said, turning his head once again toward the huge space below the truck. The air moved across KC's face, filled with the sweetly scented desert sage and pine. "Generations of Kieslings have been staking out land and ranching since the first movements up from Mexico. Our roots go deep into this crusty earth. I guess that's where I get my habit."

KC wrinkled her forehead. "What habit?"

"Anthropology."

"Oh," KC said, suddenly understanding the equipment in the truck. No wonder he looked like an explorer. "You dig up stuff, then?"

"Sort of. There's a lot more to it than that. Anthropologists study the remains and the artifacts. But we're mostly interested in the people." He stretched out his long legs and put his hands behind his head. "We try to discover the way people used the objects that archaeologists dig up. My dad was one of the foremost anthropology profs at the U. He discovered the Little Canyon cliff city."

"Was?" KC asked, her voice soft.

Grady stared up at the stars. KC saw a muscle working in his cheek, under his beard. A flash of deep sadness pierced his eyes. "He died in an accident when I was fifteen. They were setting up an important university dig, and a backhoe fell, trapping him underneath."

KC gasped. She didn't know what to say.

"I like to think I'm carrying on in his footsteps," Grady went on.

KC sympathized, opening a little gap in her defenses. "I lost my dad recently, too," she said quietly. "He wasn't my biological father. I was adopted. But he was my father in every other way. He cared for me, loved me, supported me. Even when I told him how to run his restaurant business. He listened to me." Tears pricked her eyes. She hadn't said this to anyone. Part of her didn't know why she was saying this to Grady. "It's been hard losing him. I want to tell him things, and then I realize he's not here anymore."

The silence that followed was a gentle one, one of understanding, of sympathy. They'd both lost someone they cared deeply about. KC let the night air flow into her. She watched him, watched the way his eyes registered every emotion, every flicker of interest or grief. They were shining with unshed tears.

Should she tell him about Maria? Nothing was as it had been. Nothing was as it seemed. KC opened her mouth to speak, but at that instant, Grady moved closer. He leaned against her, gently. The hint of the cologne she'd smelled in the cave drifted toward her. Then, without warning, Grady put his head on her shoulder.

KC flinched. His head felt heavy, strange. She pulled back, suddenly uncomfortable. No matter how sympathetic Grady was, KC felt that old flicker of alarm and distrust clamp down inside her. This guy might be understanding and kind. It seemed as if he'd had his share of tragedy, too. But how could she let her guard down? After all, look what happened with Brooks, someone she'd known since high school, someone she thought she understood. That empty feeling returned inside her.

If you can't trust your friends, she thought, her brain clicking back into its routine, how can you trust a stranger?

Grady pulled away. "I know. I feel it. It's so lonely, not being able to trust anyone."

KC's throat closed tight and tears welled up behind her eyes. Grady's arm came around her quickly, and he pulled her to him, sheltering her against him. His body felt warm in the cool night air.

"I know," he whispered. "I know how it feels. And I feel what you feel, your hurt. And . . ."

KC could hear his heart pounding in his chest. There was something soothing about it.

"I feel really close to you," he added so softly that KC could hardly hear him. But she had heard, and a flutter of hope moved in her heart.

"I—I know," she replied against his flannel shirt. "I feel it, too."

He shifted, and slowly, Grady touched his fingertips to KC's chin. He touched her lips with his. It was a light kiss. Sweet and full of tenderness and understanding. KC's heart vibrated with feeling, with hope. His lips were soft, and KC moved slightly against him. She felt there'd been a concrete mold around her feelings, and that Grady was breaking it open.

But the moment was shattered by the sound of squealing tires on the road leading to Gold Hill. Headlights flashed along the sagebrush and scrubby bushes that dotted the low, rolling hills. Grady flinched, pulling his arm off KC's shoulder and peering into the darkness. His face was rigid.

KC didn't quite understand his alarm. She watched as the stream of two bright beams turned off onto a side dirt road and bumped away across the desert. Probably some rancher going back to his spread tucked off in the distance.

Grady rolled off the side of the truck. He smiled at KC. "I've got to head out," he said suddenly.

KC shook her head slightly as if to clear the fog from her brain. She eased herself off the hood, brushed off the seat of her jeans, and skirted the front of the truck to stand beside Grady. "Where to?"

His eyes looked guarded. "To work. Can we meet again? I'd like to talk some more."

KC's brain clicked into gear. "Come tomorrow morning. We'll have breakfast. My friends and I are going to head over to the Del Oro Spa. It's east of here."

"I can't," Grady said. "Not tomorrow. Not here."

KC frowned. "Aren't you finished yet—with the caves?" she asked softly.

"The caves here are pretty well cleaned out. Those pothunters I was talking about are thorough." He chewed his lower lip. "The Del Oro Spa?" he asked, a thoughtful light growing in his eyes.

"Um-hm," KC replied. "I'm pretty sure that's the name."

Grady's eyes softened again. He placed his hands gently on her arms and pulled her to him. "I know that place," he said excitedly. "It's set along the cliffs above the San Pico River. There's a small settlement of cliff dwellings about ten miles beyond it. Toward Las Altas. The Casa Linda cliff dwellings. There's a parking lot and a small historical marker. Could you meet me there? At midnight tomorrow? I really would like to talk some more." His voice had a knifelike intensity. "I may need your help," he added.

KC thought quickly. She could borrow Courtney's car. Or the Jeep. She would probably have some time. But should she?

"If we lose touch with each other," he went on, "check at Flo's. It's a tackle shop combination convenience store on the highway. Let's see," he said, pausing. He squinted, obviously thinking. "It's about sixty miles east of here. Look for my truck, but *don't* ask inside for me."

KC stared at him. "Why not?"

"Everything, and I mean *everything*, you tell Flo will be all over the county in ten minutes." His mouth curled up in a quick, nervous smile. "She's information central around here. She finds out where everyone is going, and with whom. Then she relays the information to everyone else."

His voice sounded frightened. He looked around quickly. The night had remained quiet, and KC felt a chill run up her spine.

She wondered what he was hiding. He was obviously keeping a low profile in the area. What could he be doing? Why would mentioning his name at the place called Flo's matter? Her heart started pounding, partly in response to his sudden urgent energy, and partly in confusion. He needed help. That much was clear. But could she help him? Should she?

Before she could think of a way to ask him the questions tumbling inside her head, he pulled her in his arms. His mouth found hers. Passion, urgency, and need seared through his kiss. The warmth flooded through KC, making her knees weak. In an instant, he let her go, and she stumbled back. The truck door creaked open, and he jumped into the driver's seat, cranking the key ferociously. The engine turned over.

With one last smile at her through the gritty window, he was gone.

KC stood in the empty parking lot, with the dust hanging in the air. She wanted to trust him. The Casa Linda cliff dwellings. Midnight.

The voice inside her head that warned her over and over to stop trusting anyone grew fainter. She touched her fingers to her lips. But how could she trust him? He had danger written all over him.

Nine

A t seven o'clock the next morning, the sun streaked across the tops of the cliffs, sending warm rays of light and heat across Ted's back. He was standing beside the Jeep, folding the collapsed tent. Dressed in khaki shorts and a T-shirt, he felt goose bumps rise along his legs as a chilly breeze whistled through the juniper trees.

"There," Ted said. "That's done." He smiled as he checked his notebook filled with lists of supplies. Faith stood on the other side of the Jeep. She wasn't looking at him. "The clothes go in that dry bag," he went on. "Check." He grabbed a pen from the front seat and marked the list with an exaggerated flourish. "Safety gear, repair kit, cooking gear, gear gear." He grinned at Faith, who was surveying the food in a smaller dry bag behind the front seat. She didn't say anything.

As a matter of fact, she looked unhappy.

"I think we'll need more granola bars," Ted commented, leaning toward her. "And maybe some apples. I'll add those to the shopping list."

Faith made some sort of noncommittal noise and zipped up the dry bag, stuffing it into a space beside the cooler. Ted wrote a note in his book: "Buy energy bars and apples. Keep smiling."

If he could just figure out what Faith's problem was he'd feel ready to hit the San Pico River.

"So where are Courtney, KC, and Winnie going today?" he asked.

Faith finally looked up. Her expression matched the temperature of the cooler. "The Del Oro Spa. It's some ritzy layout tucked in the hills beyond Gold Hill," she replied. "I just hope it's well hidden."

"Why?"

Faith tilted her head to one side, causing her braid to slap against her shoulder. "So Lance Putnam won't be able to find them, that's why."

"Oh, come on, Faith. That guy has probably forgotten all about us."

"I don't think he's forgotten the ripped top of his car. He may not have caught up with Winnie last night, but that doesn't mean he's not close by, looking for her. I'm just glad we'll be on the river."

Ted came around the Jeep to stand close to Faith.

"Hmm," he said, letting his fingers run along her neck. "Me, too." She smelled like lemon. He wanted to hold her. But he could also feel the vibes. Worry. Anxiety. Tension. He stepped back to the front of the Jeep and reached for the map lying on the dusty dashboard. "Courtney said she'd drive her car and meet us at the pickup point. So let's see," Ted added, opening the map with a snap. "If we put the raft in the river at the place called Flo's, that means we'll float downriver about thirty miles."

Faith nodded. "At least Courtney will be sure to pick us up," she added. A jay cawed from the juniper tree above their heads, and Faith jumped.

Ted folded up the map and tucked it onto the dashboard again. "Well, why wouldn't she?" he asked, leaning over the passenger seat and tucking in a stray corner of the tent.

"Well, I mean, KC seems sort of—well—out of it. She let that guy Grady talk to her so long last night. I mean, she knows absolutely nothing about him. He could be a murderer. And she promised to meet him at the cliff dwellings near the spa. At some historical marker. She must be out of her mind." Faith shook her head again.

Ted tightened the ropes on the back of the Jeep that were holding the raft in place. He wished he could think of some way to get Faith's mind off the crises of yesterday and start enjoying the trip. He felt the stab of irritation slice into him, and pushed it aside. No, he wouldn't. He promised himself he'd be different with Faith. Every relationship had its ups and downs, its times of ordinary complaints and ordinary sensations. And even though he had a history of flirting, of never sticking with a relationship for more than a month or two, Faith had been worth giving all that up for.

He glanced over at her. She stood beside the front seat and was staring at the map. Sunlight splashed across her hair, highlighting the little golden flecks in the strands.

It's okay, he told himself. *I'm lucky to have Faith. She's honest, loyal, and sweet. She's the best thing that ever happened to me.*

Then why did he feel like he was a tire slowly being deflated? The relationship was safe. It was secure. But how much fun was it? For a crazy moment, he missed those wild days of seeing a new girl every couple of months. He missed flirting and laughing with whoever caught his eye. No. No. No. He wouldn't.

"It'll be okay, Faith," Ted said softly. He stepped back around to her side and slipped an arm around her shoulders. Her braid tickled his hand.

She sent him a quick glance that was hard to read. "I'm just worried about Lance and Grady, I guess."

"I know," he said softly, gently pulling her to him. He was relieved when she put down the map and threaded her arms around his waist. He felt the simmer of warmth, her soft skin, the smell of her hair. . . .

"Yooooohooooo!" a voice called from the side of

the cabin. Faith made an annoyed sound in her throat as Winnie bounced from the deep morning shadows.

Always the outrageous dresser, Winnie was wearing bright pink shorts and a yellow crop-top. A bright red baseball cap sat on her head and she was wearing roadrunner earrings. She had on pink high-tops that matched her shorts, and Ted thought she looked incredible.

"I don't know if you noticed, but the sun's up," she called. "It's time to make our escape. The posse's hot on our trail."

Faith stepped away from Ted and climbed into the front seat of the Jeep. She watched Winnie with a sort of blank expression on her face. Winnie jogged across the flat patch of grass toward them. "Courtney and KC are sort of ignoring me. Nothing major. Just one-word answers to deep philosophical questions. So I came out here to see if you guys were ready yet. I think *they* are. Ready, that is. To leave." Winnie crossed the flat patch of grass in a couple of steps. "You know, you'll take the high road—"

"And I'll cut 'em off at the pass," Ted said, laughing.

"No! You'll take the low road!" Winnie grinned, making an exaggerated face at Ted. "Winnie the Kid and her gang elude capture once again." She shimmied in the sunlight, and Ted suddenly felt charged up by her energy and good spirits.

"So, you're not freaked out about last night?" Ted asked, crossing his arms and leaning against the

Jeep. Behind him he could feel Faith stiffen.

"Me? Freaked out? No way! I'm ready for the chase scene through the canyons." Her eyes got suddenly brighter. "Hey! We could sell the story to the newspapers. 'I Escaped Power-Mad Sports Car Driver,' by Kid Winnie. You're a marketing major, Ted. You could run with this."

Ted laughed and shook his head. "Right, Winnie." He pretended to hold a microphone under her nose. "To what do you attribute your escape, Kid?"

Winnie crossed her arms. "Well, Mr. Markham, I guess it was just dumb luck."

"Would you say the vigilante driver's luck was dumber than your dumb luck?"

"Yes, that's right, Mr. Markham." Winnie's voice was getting lower and funnier by the minute, and Ted felt laughter building up inside of him. Strange that Faith wasn't amused. Maybe she had just gotten used to Winnie's sense of humor over the years.

Ted stumbled around to the driver's seat and climbed in. He was careful to avoid Faith's icy glance.

"Well, Winnie," he called as he started the engine. "See you at Flo's. Maybe you should buy a face mask and some sunglasses."

She waved as he eased the Jeep past her. "Good idea! If you get there first, save the rubber noses for me," Winnie said.

"You got it," Ted said, waving. Then he clasped the steering wheel tightly as he guided the Jeep around the cabin. A pothole bounced the vehicle back and forth, and he turned to apologize to Faith for the rough ride. But he stopped himself. Faith had turned her back to him and was facing out toward the valley filling up with morning light. She was ignoring him completely. *Okay,* he thought. *I won't notice. It'll be all right. She just needs to get on the river and float in the hot sun. She'll get over whatever is bugging her.*

He pulled out onto the road leading to Gold Hill. Heat rose in waves from the pavement. He tried to imagine the San Pico River, tried to picture the cold, rushing water and the sheer cliffs waiting for him. But all he could see was Winnie's body and sunny smile. The image cheered him up fast.

"When you said a road trip," Winnie called from the backseat of Courtney's convertible, "I didn't think you meant quite so much *road.*"

They were driving toward Flo's, speeding along a flat stretch of highway that looked exactly like the flat stretch of highway they'd driven the day before. Winnie draped her legs out over the car again. "Wow, it's incredible how hot it gets. Even my ears are steaming!" She blew a bright orange bubble, then sucked it back into her mouth.

Courtney and KC ignored her. They had continued their one-word-answer routine since leaving Gold Hill, and Winnie was beginning to get the picture.

"I'm sorry again for last night! I feel like you guys are sort of mad at me," she shouted.

"I'm not mad, Winnie," KC said without even

looking back. Her voice was flat and expressionless.

Winnie grimaced to herself. "Right, KC," she muttered. "And I'm not hyper."

"I'm not mad, either," Courtney said. She sent Winnie a little smile in the rearview mirror. Winnie winced. Ouch. This was going to be a long day.

"Okay, I used bad judgment. I made a mistake. I was stupid. I apologize! What do you want me to do, write it a thousand times in the dust by the side of the road?"

Winnie sighed. She'd come on this trip to have fun, to see the road, to see the Southwest. She gazed up at the blazing blue of the immense sky that stretched from horizon to horizon. She hated to admit it, but the most excitement she'd had so far was slicing Lance Putnam's car. She wasn't a violent person. Not really. Reckless, maybe. Wacky, occasionally. Bonkers, semicrazed, energized. But not violent.

She pulled at her spiky hair and looked again at the backs of Courtney's and KC's heads. How could KC criticize *her* when she'd agreed to meet some caveman at a historical marker near the spa? And at midnight, no less. *I mean, get real.*

Winnie watched the long ridge of cliffs flash past. According to Courtney's travel brochures, the cliffs led to the San Pico River, dipped along a plateau to the east of the Del Oro Spa, then rose again near Las Altas. They shone sort of flat, iron-brown in the sun.

She was really glad they were putting some distance between themselves and Gold Hill. There was no way she was going to admit it to the two sorority statues in the front seat, but she didn't want to face Lance Putnam either.

"You know that Lance was a real monster." Silence. "He could have raped me!" More silence. The wind whipped into her face and the sweat dried off her forehead. "But the only person who seems to understand is Ted!" Winnie shouted. Blank. Winnie shrugged. She might as well give up. They weren't going to crack. Conversation would be better with the rocks along the road.

Then KC turned her head a little and gave Winnie a mechanical smile.

Ted and Faith were ahead of them in the Jeep. Winnie could see Faith's braid frizzing in the hot wind as she stared out at the desert. It looked as if she was searching for treasure on the horizon. Winnie shook her head and fell back down onto the backseat. She grabbed a tube of sunscreen from her duffel bag and began spreading it on her nose.

About five minutes later, the car slowed. They'd reached a large log cabin, with huge windows all the way across the front and a big wooden porch all the way around it. To the left was a tall grove of trees, and out front, a huge parking lot. A wide sign on the roof read: FLO'S.

As Courtney pulled the convertible up to the store, Winnie stretched and took a deep breath. The air smelled fresh and clean, different from the parched, dry air on the road. She climbed over the backseat and stood in the gravelly dust, listening. A muffled whooshing sound was coming from the side of the building where Ted had taken the Jeep. Winnie jogged over and saw that across a field of brown weeds lay the river. Ted and Faith were unloading the rafting gear.

Winnie walked back to the store, realizing that Courtney and KC had already gone inside. The heat was becoming stiffling, but as Winnie entered Flo's a blast of air-conditioning hit her face.

The interior was cool and sunny, and smelled of new plastic, old wood, and blankets. It was a grocery store, plus tackle shop. At the back ran a long glass counter filled with fishing supplies. Long fishing rods marched across the back wall like some elaborate wall decoration.

Winnie bobbed her head. She walked past aisles of camping equipment, including cups, pots, coffeepots, and silver packs of freeze-dried meals. There were postcards, film, and booklets about the area. And there were about six aisles of groceries. She headed for the candy bars.

"Hey, Courtney," Winnie called. "What about a couple of days' supply of chocolate?"

Courtney glanced at Winnie and shook her head. "I'm dieting." Winnie looked her up and down. The slim Courtney was wearing dark-blue tailored shorts and a pink cotton blouse. Her blond hair was pulled into a ponytail. She was perfect. Of course she was dieting. Perfect people were always on diets.

"Okay," Winnie puffed out. She grabbed three candy bars and headed toward the chips. "KC, they have the tortilla chips you like so much. Want a couple of bags?"

A voice rose from somewhere at the back of the store. "No, thanks, Winnie."

Jeez, she thought. This was like traveling with zombies! Driving with the living dead.

Winnie heard the front door open and glanced up from the Cheez Whiz. Faith walked in. Winnie followed her to the natural-foods section. She was studying a selection of energy bars, granola bars, and raisins.

"Hard to decide, huh?" Winnie asked. "I'd go with the supercharged-survive-five-days-in-the-wilderness-on-just-one-bite bars. There." She stuffed four foil-wrapped snacks into Faith's hand.

"These are too expensive, Winnie." Faith chucked them back into the silver bin and selected some granola bars wrapped in dull-looking brown foil. She dodged away from Winnie.

Winnie headed for the fruit section right behind her. "Do you want some peaches?" she offered, picking up two perfect peaches. "These look good."

"They spoil too fast," Faith said as she walked quickly toward the bottled water.

Winnie felt frustration boiling inside her. *Have we got a major avoidance syndrome going or what?* she thought. She felt like a magnet with the wrong end sticking out, when everything bounces the opposite direction. Or maybe she'd become invisible.

For the first time since she entered the store, Winnie caught sight of a woman sitting behind the big block of wood that served as the front checkout stand. The space was covered with display racks. There were key chains and postcards. Tea towels and tomahawks.

Winnie dodged around a rack of decorated coffee mugs and headed for the counter. The woman had curly dark hair, sprinkled with gray. Her baggy dress was splashed with orange flowers and purple macaws, and when Winnie looked at her, she grinned a toothy grin.

"You want those candy bars, sweetie?" the woman asked in a cheerful voice.

"Yeah. I'm drowning my sorrows."

The woman cackled and nodded, her salt-and-pepper hair bobbing. "I know what you mean. Nothing works like chocolate."

Winnie paid for her candy, plopped one elbow on the polished wood counter, and leaned forward. "This is a nice store," she said. At least this woman was talking to her. Maybe Winnie wasn't invisible after all.

"Yep. Been here twenty years. Only place for about a hundred miles to get supplies. You visiting?"

Winnie nodded. "Yes. Spring break." She grabbed a map from a display rack beside the big, old-fashioned cash register and spread it open. "I'm Winnie. And that's KC. Courtney. And Faith," she said, pointing to each girl behind her.

The woman nodded again. "Well, it's nice to meet you, Winnie. You at the Cactus Cottage?"

"We were. But now we're headed up here." She pointed to the blue spot on the map that read "Del Oro Spa."

"Ooooh. Classy. Not many locals can afford that place," the woman said, smiling again. Winnie noticed about a thousand wrinkles spreading from her eyes. She smiled a lot. Winnie smiled back.

"My friend Courtney is treating. Then, after that . . ." Winnie studied the map for a minute. "Ah. Here it is. The Kanabi cliff dwellings. The ones that are up *this* road." She stuck her finger on a curving blue line that wound through some green blobby shapes on the map. "We're heading there, too. Then on to Las Altas."

"Well, you'll get in some of the nice sights. That Kanabi settlement is real pretty. Lots of rocks and stuff. Tricky road, though. Gotta be careful. I'm Flo, by the way." The woman stuck out her hand.

Winnie reached out to take it. A footstep clicked behind her on the tiles of the floor. Then, suddenly, Winnie felt her shoulder grabbed in a tight grip. She spun to see KC staring at her, her eyes huge. "Winnie! What are you doing?" KC snapped. Her face was white.

"Hey, KC. This is Flo. I was just— Ouch. Let go!" Winnie winced as KC's fingers dug into her shoulder. KC shoved her forward past the counter, then toward the front doors. "KC! Have you lost your mind?"

KC kept pushing her hard. Winnie stumbled out the doors, then tramped across the broad wooden porch. KC grabbed her wrist, then pulled her the rest of the way off the porch, into the broiling sun. Winnie yanked her wrist away from KC's viselike grip.

"Excuse me, KC? Do you mind?" Winnie yelled.

"What are you doing?" KC repeated. Her face was no longer deathly white. It was red, with two dark splotches of color high on her cheekbones. "That was Flo!"

"So *what*?"

"She's the local gossip. You *told* her what we were doing! Now she knows our plans. Why can't you ever just shut up?" KC spit out.

A hot flush washed over Winnie's face. "Oh, and I'm supposed to know that? At least she was willing to talk to me. And what difference does it make if she knows where we're going?"

"Just think for a change, Winnie. What if that guy from Pinky's comes in here?" KC snapped. "What if he asks about us? What if he asks where we've gone?" KC jammed her arms across her chest and gave Winnie a furious look.

Winnie felt the sweat puddling down her spine. The intense heat made her face burn. "Come on, KC. That guy isn't going to follow us. He probably lives a hundred miles from here."

"Right. Didn't the guy Courtney met say Lance is a local big shot?" KC said. "Didn't you say that, too?"

Winnie swallowed. That was true. Lance Putnam said his father owned mines along the cliffs toward Las Altas. But she wasn't about to admit that KC was right. Not in a million years.

"How can you be so irresponsible?" KC went on. "Why can't you learn any self-control?"

"Give me a break. Why are you dumping on me?

I made one measly mistake. I went out to the parking lot with some creep I didn't know. But you made a date with some caveman. And that's supposed to be okay?" Winnie felt a satisfying rush of anger pour through her.

KC just stared at her. Then abruptly she turned away and stalked around the side of the store toward the sound of the rushing river.

"I'm right, aren't I, KC?" she shouted. "You just can't admit it!" Winnie followed KC's furious footsteps across the dusty grass that covered the patch of ground running from Flo's to the river. The breeze from the water fanned her cheeks, drying the sweat that had started to drip into her eyes.

Across the small field, Winnie could see the bright yellow raft sitting in the water, tied carefully to a tree trunk. Faith was stashing food in it. Ted stood on the other side, tugging on ropes that lashed down the middle part of the raft.

"KC! What is your problem?" Winnie blurted. Then she stopped. Ted was dressed in a tight sleeveless T-shirt and running shorts. His arms and legs were brown from the sun. He was smiling broadly at Faith. The breeze from the river raised goose bumps along Winnie's skin, and she sucked in a slow breath.

KC spun back to her, startling Winnie from her thoughts. "I just can't believe you! You act like you're the only one on this trip. What if that guy comes after us?"

Winnie was aware that Ted and Faith had

stopped what they were doing and were staring at them. She wasn't about to let KC treat her this way.

"Lay off me, KC," she shouted. "It wasn't the crime of the century to talk to Flo. You're just so paranoid, you can't think straight." She pivoted her feet toward the river. Ted's eyes lit up when she got closer. Now that was more like it, Winnie thought happily. Someone who actually acted as if her presence was a pleasure.

But she could hear KC's footsteps behind her.

"But now everyone in the county will know where we're going!" KC shouted.

Winnie felt something snap inside her. The absolute last thing she wanted to do was go somewhere with KC and Courtney. Winnie could just picture it. Two days of being ignored, patronized, lectured, whined at, criticized, questioned.

"All right!" Winnie snapped. "If you're so afraid of that guy, I won't go with you. I didn't tell Flo the Foghorn about the raft trip." She turned her head to catch Ted's quick look. A smile flashed through his eyes. "I'll just go with Ted and Faith."

Faith gasped loudly, and KC stared at Winnie. There was a long moment when no one said anything. The river bounced and whooshed, the birds sang, even a few crickets chirped.

Then Winnie jumped into the raft and settled herself between the cooler and the dry bags. She grabbed a puffy orange life jacket and shrugged into it quickly.

"Now, see, KC, I am getting out of here before Putnam the Punisher finds me," she said. She smiled at Ted. "I'm ready if you are. Let's hit those rapids."

Ted stepped to the back of the raft, muscled it forward a little farther into the river, then waved Faith into it. She frowned, then stepped in, balancing carefully before settling herself on the left side and picking up a paddle.

"All right," Ted said in a cheerful voice. "One getaway raft, coming up. Hang on tight, Winnie. I've heard this is a wild river."

He pushed off, and the raft buoyed into the river with a bounce and a splash. Winnie settled back and smiled. A wild river would fit her mood exactly.

Ten

KC felt a rush of excitement flood through her as she looked around. She switched her overnight bag from one hand to the other, wiping her sticky palm on her dusty jeans. The wide, cool stone steps climbed through cascading ferns. Water trickled into a clear pool to one side, and on the other rose crimson cliffs. The Del Oro Spa, the landscaped retreat built against the red rocks of the cliffs, was absolutely, breathtakingly, unbelievably gorgeous.

"Courtney?" KC asked nervously. The air was hushed, the only sound the muffled roar of the San Pico River far below in the canyon. "Are you sure we should be here?"

Courtney gave KC a jubilant smile. "Of course. They're expecting us."

"They are?"

Together they made their way up a gently sloping flagstone path lined with lavender, geraniums, and daisies. Suddenly, the path opened to a wide, sun-filled patio. The heat seared her back as KC approached a tall arched, wooden door carved in an ornate Spanish design. To her right ran a stone wall about shoulder height. KC stood on tiptoe to peek over, and her eyes widened. On the other side, on a patio deeply shaded with acacia trees, was a cluster of glass tables all set with colorful burgundy place settings. Each table had a bowl of roses and lavender flowers in its center. Beyond the tables, a long stretch of turquoise water shimmered in the sunlight. A swimming pool.

Courtney took KC's hand, stepped to the wide doors, and shoved them open, leading her through the entrance into a vast, carpeted lobby. KC breathed in the heady scent of flowers and the unmistakable tang of sage. The interior had the clean, smooth lines of adobe architecture, with tall wooden posts supporting the arched ceiling. It gave KC the sensation of being in a designer chapel. The only color was provided by a huge handwoven blanket hanging on the wall. Across the back of the long room, glass windows opened onto the sheer rock cliffs across the river.

Courtney stopped at the registration desk to the right of the lobby. "Hello. I'm Courtney Conner," she said to a petite woman with short black hair and smiling, light-brown eyes.

KC was impressed. No matter how often she saw Courtney in surroundings like this, she always noted the ease with which Courtney slipped into the elegant "I belong here" manner. It still amazed her that someone so rich, so sophisticated, and so poised could be *her* friend. After all, KC had grown up in Jacksonville, Oregon, hanging out at her parents' health-food restaurant and eating tofu burgers and bean sprouts.

"How do you do, Ms. Conner? Welcome to Del Oro." The woman checked the large red leather book in front of her. "You and your guest have been assigned bungalow twelve. I think you'll enjoy it."

KC gave Courtney a quizzical glance. "You made reservations?"

Courtney beamed her a wide smile. "Surprise! My mother told me about this place when I let her know we were headed this way. It's one of the most exclusive spas in the country. I wanted you to enjoy a real holiday." Courtney gave KC's hand a squeeze.

"But—" KC glanced around at the muted tones of the furniture, the deep-pile carpet, and she swallowed uncomfortably. She pulled Courtney's hand and gently, but firmly, guided her to a pillar. "This place must cost a fortune!"

"My treat, KC," Courtney purred. KC shook her head violently, but Courtney held up her hand. "I mean it. It's the least I can do."

KC felt a sudden flash of unreality. They began their trip by driving twelve hundred miles. Then

Faith, Ted, Winnie, and Courtney got embroiled with a hotheaded bully at Pinky's. Then she was attacked in a cave and met Grady. Then Winnie disappeared on Ted and Faith's raft trip. She gazed around happily. And she ended up in paradise.

KC grinned at Courtney's shining face. The confused sadness she'd been feeling faded a little, and she took a long, slow breath. Leave it to Courtney to plan something spectacular. KC felt as if she'd just been handed the winning ticket in an all-expenses-paid sweepstakes to heaven.

"Well, if you're sure," KC said, her doubt slipping away. "You talked me into it."

A smile beamed across Courtney's face. "This is one of the reasons I was so eager to come. We could both use some real rest after last term at U of S."

The receptionist waved her hand toward a slim young woman wearing a white sundress. She had blond hair swept up into an elegant twist, big brown eyes, and a slightly crooked smile. "This is Sara. She will escort you to your bungalow. Feel free to ask questions."

Sara smiled at them. "This way, please. This stone walkway leads from the lobby to bungalows nine through twelve. We make sure there are only four cottages per section so that you can be assured of privacy. And quiet."

They stepped out the side door. "The spa facilities lead off from the other side of the lobby," Sara explained as they walked along a flagstone path curving between huge granite boulders. KC felt as if she were following a secret path to a retreat. This is what she needed, though. Quiet. Calm. Water and sun and saunas and massages. Maybe with enough pampering she could forget the nagging heaviness pulling at her heart.

"When you're ready, just head over there and sign up for facials, massage treatments, manicures, masks, steam wraps, and herbal wraps."

They reached a pueblo-style cottage nestled among a cluster of tall pine trees. Sara opened the French doors and stepped ahead of them into the sunny bungalow. Birds chattered in the tall trees above their heads, and the ever-present rush of the river was like a lullaby. KC gasped when she stepped onto the thick white carpet. Along the top of the white walls, in muted blues, browns, and salmon shades, ran a painted border of stylized lizards and birds. Rose-colored comforters sat on the twin beds. Between the two beds was a small, carved bedside table with a beautiful crystal lamp.

KC knew her mouth was open. She didn't care. Out another door was their own small, private patio with a trickling fountain. Behind the patio rose a high wall blocking their little sanctuary from the cliffs beyond where red rocks tumbled into the canyon. KC grinned gratefully at Courtney.

"I could get used to this, Courtney," KC whispered.

Sara laughed softly. "Some of our customers ask about long-term rentals."

KC set her overnight bag on the bed closest to her. "Sign me up," she said. "I'll take a ten-year lease."

Sara laughed again. "Let me know if you need anything. Anything at all." She walked quickly out the French doors and was gone, her footsteps fading on the flagstone path.

Courtney and KC unpacked their overnight bags. Within a half hour, they'd showered and gotten into their bathing suits. KC slipped into a thick terry-cloth robe provided along with the gigantic stack of towels in the white tiled bathroom.

They headed for the spa building, which was connected to the lobby by a glass hallway. When they entered the quiet room, a tall woman dressed in a crisp white uniform greeted them. "May I help you?" she asked in a low voice.

KC looked at Courtney, wondering what exactly they were supposed to do next. "Give us the works!" Courtney said, laughing.

The woman smiled. "Right this way."

The attendant guided them down another hallway. The swimming pool lay on their right, and KC saw couples lounging on huge towels, lying in the sun, talking, or reading. KC took another relaxed breath. The air smelled like water and suntan lotion.

Quickening her footsteps, KC stepped down the glass hall to a series of rooms facing the back of the building. Each room had an arched doorway, and Courtney stood beneath the door at the very end. KC came around her shoulder and stopped. The view out the back was of the cliffs, blazing red and gold in the afternoon light. Above the cliffs sailed white clouds across a brilliant blue sky, and in the far distance, just visible over the top of the canyon walls, loomed dark-blue mountains.

"Wow," KC whispered.

Courtney's eyes shone with excitement. "Isn't this amazing?" she asked.

The attendant guided them to two low reclining chairs. "Be seated here," she said. "We'll start with the facial massage, then move on to masks and the mud baths."

Reclining in the soft leather chair, KC felt fluttering anticipation run along her spine all the way to her fingers. It felt strange to give herself over so completely to other people. She sent a nervous look at Courtney, who'd settled into her chair and promptly closed her eyes.

"Have you ever had a facial before?" KC asked softly.

"I'm not going to spoil it for you," Courtney said, smiling. "Just wait and see."

KC closed her eyes, too. She jumped when a cool pair of hands touched her face. "It's all right," a soft female voice whispered above her head. "Just relax." As the woman's strong, supple hands began rubbing KC's face, KC felt the tightness in her jaw disappear. "Courtney, this is the life," KC murmured.

"You can say that again," Courtney muttered. She was receiving a facial massage, too.

Once all the muscles in her face and neck were free of tension, a cool, gel-like mask was dripped on KC's skin, then rubbed in slowly. Every inch of her face tingled with delight. The trip, Grady, the cave, Winnie, school, papers, exams, everything started blurring into nothingness.

After the facials, Sara returned to guide them to the mud baths, which were set up in an open area facing a thick garden of shrubs and huge cactuslike plants with spiky limbs.

"What are those gigantic plants?" KC asked Sara.

"Yucca. Fabulous, aren't they? And mixed in with them are teddy-bear cholla. Those trunks with the yellow fuzzies on the ends. Don't touch them, though. You'll end up with stickers embedded in your fingers for days. Sometimes, you have to take the spikes out with pliers. Here we are," Sara said, pointing to two long, shallow tubs of dark-brown ooze.

KC looked at Courtney. "We're supposed to get in that stuff?" KC asked.

Sara chuckled. "The mineral contents make these baths some of the most beneficial in the country. The blend of trace minerals is particularly advantageous, especially for someone with your coloring," she said to KC.

KC wasn't sure, but she took off her bathrobe and dipped a toe in the ooze. It squelched around her foot in slimy clumps. She lowered herself slowly into it, and was surprised to feel that it was warm, gooey, and weirdly comforting. It reminded her for a minute of the sensations in the cave, before her flashlight went out, when she felt the warm, ancient presence of some other life or some other time reaching out for her.

"Slimy," Courtney said beside her. She'd lowered herself as well. They both sank up to their necks in greenish-brown sludge. She looked at KC. KC looked at her. They burst out laughing.

"It's like lying in day-old pudding," Courtney said, giggling.

Sara placed a little pillow under KC's head. And when she leaned back, KC could feel the warm mud oozing around her. KC once again felt the subtle release of knots in her back and legs. She closed her eyes and stuck her toes out the end of the tub.

"This is absolutely incredible," she muttered sleepily.

"Hmmm," Courtney responded, her voice getting drowsy, too.

KC let her mind wander. Images of the desert, the endless road, and the clear moonlight flashed by her. Then there was Grady. She remembered his tense face and urgent voice. He needed her help. And she was going to meet him this evening.

It didn't matter that their rendezvous was at midnight. In a place where no one would see them together. She wasn't frightened.

The mud engulfing her body made her feel strangely protected, strangely engulfed in a secure cocoon of luxury and beauty and elegance.

What could possibly go wrong?

Eleven

"Two strokes left!" Faith yelled over the roar of the river. She paddled hard, and the raft pulled around a huge granite boulder sitting in the middle of the San Pico River. Icy water splashed over her as the raft hit the back-wave, and she shivered violently. The raft bucked, then dropped into a flat stretch that came up fast.

"Wow!" Ted shouted from behind her. "Good reading, Faith." The bouncing yellow raft righted itself and headed downriver.

"I thought we were going to die," Winnie shrieked from where she was sitting on the right-hand side.

Faith laughed. "Did you see your life pass before your eyes, Winnie?" she asked, looking at a rapidly approaching bumpy section.

"Yeah, and it lasted about two seconds."

They had floated out from Flo's toward a quick drop in the river, and had immediately plunged into a fast, whitewater section. So Faith didn't have time to scream out her frustration at Winnie's unexpected presence.

And now, as they headed toward the bumpy waves glistening with sunlight, she felt her anger dissipate. It was hard to stay angry. The river was too beautiful. Faith looked quickly at Winnie, who was gripping the narrow rope called a tieline that ran all around the raft. Her excited grin practically stretched from ear to ear. She looked like a smiling blimp in her orange life jacket.

Faith turned back toward Ted. His life jacket hugged his broad shoulders. His muscular arms gleamed in the sun, and he was smiling. "Some ride, huh, Ted?" Faith called.

He nodded enthusiastically. The water drops shone on his skin, and he looked like some enchanted river god. Faith's heart pounded harder. "So far, so fabulous," he said.

Until now, they'd been able to read the water and paddle around the big rocks and boulders that churned the surface at regular intervals. She felt a sudden bump. They were coming up on that choppy section she'd spotted. "Looks fast, but easy. Read it, and run!" Ted called.

Sticking her paddle into the surface of the river, Faith felt the current yank at it.

The raft bucked, and Faith slid her feet into the footcups placed on the bottom of the raft. The rubber felt slimy on her feet. She sent a quick glance up the tall cliffs that rimmed this section. The water reflected off the red rocks, flickering onto their faces in waving strands of bright, white light.

They hit the fast section, and the raft slid forward, the front dropping about a foot. Winnie shrieked as a wave splashed her face. Faith chuckled. Not even Winnie could ruin this for her.

The raft bucked again, the front rising and falling as they passed over the choppy water. The river carried them right, and soon they were in a slow-moving float section. Faith took a deep breath of fresh, cool air. The heat intensified, baking the rubber of the raft under her leg. Suddenly, she was hot.

Winnie tilted her head back, resting it on the cooler. "Ahhhhh. I think I could do this forever."

"Yeah," Faith agreed. "This is fabulous." The slow section was a nice break, but moving slowly made the heat more unbearable. Faith began to feel roasted.

"Look out," Ted shouted. "The river's dropping here. The slope will end up in some waves, I bet." Sure enough, at the base of the downward slope stood a three-foot wave. "Pull, Faith. To the right two strokes," Ted called.

Faith responded quickly. She grabbed her paddle more firmly and jammed it into the water, stroking twice.

The raft dropped forward, then turned right, just

missing the tall standing wave. The edges of it cascaded over her head, showering her with freezing
water. Faith sucked in a quick breath. Suddenly, she
was in churning water. She yanked hard at her paddle,
sensing more than seeing the current. The raft
bobbed into it, and the eddy shot them forward.
Faith breathed again. Good thing she and Ted had
signed up for a week of guide school back in Springfield. The man at the sporting-equipment store rec-
ommended that if they were going to raft the San
Pico alone, they'd better know what they were doing.

"Hey, Faith," Ted called. "Boulder ahead. Paddle
left!"

Faith jabbed her paddle into the water and back-
paddled so Ted could guide the raft around the
boulder. They sped past the churning back-wave.

"Wow, Ted. You could get a job river rafting,"
Winnie said, leaning back. "You're really good at this."

Faith was about to say that she was just as capable when the raft hit a sudden fast section. Skill-
fully, Faith paddled like mad to keep them in the
middle of the river. The cliffs sped past in a blur.
Water gushed into her face. Icy drops tingled along
her arms as she pumped the oar, the river tugging
ferociously at her side of the raft.

"Left, Faith!" Ted yelled, as Faith heaved her oar
against a run of rapids that came up so suddenly she
didn't even see them. Suddenly, they dropped forward.
Water was everywhere. They'd entered a small gorge,
the sunlight streaking fiery red across cliffs above them.

"AAARRRGGGHHH!" Winnie screamed as a wave splashed right across the center of the raft, drenching her. "HHHeeelllppp!" she screamed. The wave knocked her flat onto the bottom. The self-bailing raft drained the water quickly, but Winnie was soaked and she couldn't get her balance.

"Stay there, Winnie!" Faith screamed as they hit a standing wave. "And hang on!"

Faith fought the bucking raft. The power of the water pushed it up under her feet, and she felt herself falling backward toward the water.

"Faith!" Ted screamed.

At the last second, she shoved herself forward, and landed on her knees amid the freezing water sloshing around in the bottom of the raft.

She clambered up quickly, stuck her feet into the rubber footcups, and braced herself for more. The river turned suddenly. The current pushed them toward some big whitewater, and she heaved with all her might to maneuver past. Ted shouted something, but she ignored him. She braced her legs, curled her toes, and pulled again. The wide, floppy raft bumped and dove through a wall of water.

Wwhhoooooooossshhh.

The water smashed against Faith, and she sputtered, flicking the water out of her eyes so she could see. A rock appeared directly in front of them. "Right! Ted. Now!" she screamed as the raft twisted miraculously past the sharp rock.

Then, suddenly, they were jetting past the back-wave that crashed upriver just beyond the boulder. Faith fell back. Her legs throbbed from being tightly jammed against the side. Adrenaline pumped through her blood, and her hands shook.

"Whew!" she gasped. She turned and smiled at Ted. His eyes flashed with excitement.

"All right, Faith! We did it!" Ted crowed.

Winnie staggered up from the bottom of the raft. "And we didn't die. But there's an awful lot of water in here."

Faith shoved her wet braid back over her shoulder. She stood up and inched forward to a warm, dry section of the raft tube. The frigid water was making her feet feel like blocks of ice. "It's a self-bailing raft, Win. Watch."

In a couple of seconds the water was gone.

Winnie grinned at Faith as she plopped herself onto the tube on the other side. She straddled the hot rubber and bounced a little, her brown eyes twinkling. "Modern technology. What will they think of next? A raft that serves iced tea and chips?"

Faith sighed and looked at the bank, taking a moment to let her heart steady. A deer stood in the warm sunlight of a grassy bank. It watched them pass, and Faith smiled at the way its fuzzy antlers were outlined by sunlight.

The current was still fast, but ahead for as far as Faith could see was flat, soft water. A hawk soared above them, and windblown trees clung to the sides of the canyons that edged into the cliffs.

"Break!" Ted called and dove across the cooler toward Faith. "You did a great job of paddling back there, Faith. That rock could've done us in—big time. Come back here with me." Ted took her hand and guided her across the metal frame that was holding the cooler and their dry bags full of clothes, equipment, and bedding in the center of the large raft. Faith moved eagerly, settling down beside him, nestled in the corner with his arm around her shoulders. He leaned in and kissed her quickly.

"I could get used to this," she said. The hot sun beat down on her head, and the lazy feel of the river seemed to soothe her spirit. Ted's arm felt warm and heavy on the shoulders of her quickly drying life jacket, and the tension of running the rapids, and of having Winnie with them, eased out of her, flowing away in little currents that matched the rippling of the water.

She closed her eyes. The movement of the raft, the gentle back-and-forth, up-and-down, was like a massage. Her legs were warm. Every part of her was turning liquid. The sound of the water trickling past was suddenly quiet, different from the booming rapids. Ted's arm shifted on her back, his fingers rubbing her neck slowly.

Suddenly, icy water splashed her in the face. "Water fight!" Winnie screamed. Faith felt the raft buck, and her eyes flew open. A cascade of water came shooting at her and she dodged out of the way. The water splashed down Ted's legs.

Faith felt as if she'd been dropped off a cliff. The

shock of the icy water wiped out her warmth. Ted jumped up, leaned over the side, and drew his flat hand along the river, cresting an arching wave over Winnie. Pretty soon, Ted and Winnie were bashing each other with sheets of water, and Faith was drenched again. The raft bounced and rolled as Winnie dipped her hand over the side to pelt Ted. Then Ted leaned back and scooped another huge wave directly into Winnie's face.

Faith's relaxed euphoria was shattered. She huffed into the front of the raft, over the dripping wet cooler and dry bags. The water fight was getting as much water in the boat as any of the rapids they'd seen yet. Hobbling to her spot at the front, Faith propped herself in position with her leg braced against the tube, grabbed her paddle, and began pumping her arms to make the raft go faster. She wasn't going to lie around while Ted and Winnie covered her with water. This water fight was definitely no fun. But, as she tried to ignore Ted's and Winnie's shrieks and whoops, she realized no one seemed to notice. Or care. The raft sped up.

"Sit still, Winnie," Faith shouted. "This raft isn't made of iron, you know."

Her paddling was guiding them quickly past the slow stretch, and ahead the water churned and spray flew, catching the sunlight like flying diamonds.

"If you've got so much energy, Winnie," Faith added, "why don't you paddle?" She tried to control her sudden burst of temper. The river had washed away her annoyance, but now Faith felt it reignite.

Winnie wrinkled her nose. "All right. I will." She reached across the raft and took the blue and silver paddle from Faith, who held it out to her. Then she stood up, wobbling to get her balance, and sat down again facing downriver. "What do I do?"

She stuck the paddle in the water, and they immediately began spinning. "Winnie!" Ted shouted. "One-legged swans go around in circles."

Winnie laughed. "What?"

"One paddle working will spin the raft. Here, let me show you."

Faith watched as Ted climbed forward and straddled the tube behind Winnie. He reached both arms around her and positioned her hands on the paddle. "First, you have to know how to hold the paddle."

Ted's muscular chest covered Winnie's back. Faith sensed the pounding anger and jealousy she'd been feeling flare into a raging fire. She wished Winnie would just disappear! She was ruining everything.

"Hold your left hand at the top. Hold your right hand here, at the base." He reached forward and placed Winnie's hand on the pole section of the paddle. "The flat part, called the blade, controls the speed and power of your turn," Ted instructed, still smiling.

He placed his hand over Winnie's. And together they stuck the paddle into the water.

"Wow!" Winnie shouted. "Feel that water!" She wiggled backward to get closer to Ted. Faith frowned. It looked to her as if Winnie was using Ted as a pillow.

"Pull back," Ted instructed. Winnie leaned into

his chest, laughing happily. "Use your body for leverage if you get into rough sections."

"Hey, this is great. Private instruction and everything." Winnie arched a sexy look up into Ted's face.

"Now, lift the paddle out and start over," Ted said, scooting closer to Winnie.

"Like this?" Winnie asked, smiling.

"No, like this," Ted repeated.

Faith fumed. She watched as Winnie and Ted practiced together until Winnie could do the routine smoothly. Pretty soon, she thought, I won't be able to tell where Winnie stops and Ted begins. She couldn't believe Winnie was acting as if she had the IQ of a burned-out lightbulb.

Winnie leaned forward a little when some ripples of cresting white water appeared. "Hey, let me at this river!" she yelled. The ripples intensified, and suddenly a cluster of low-hanging trees appeared. Faith ducked as a tree branch headed right for her.

"Winnie, watch out!" Faith shouted.

"Yeah, Winnie. Watch your stroke." Ted grabbed the paddle from her as she snuggled tightly against his chest.

Faith's mood wasn't improving. She wished Winnie would fall out of the raft and disappear into the water. Then the raft bucked and bumped, and Faith looked ahead. She heard what sounded like thunder, but the sky was clear above her head. Suddenly, she realized what it was. A roar was booming out of a canyon downriver.

"Ted," she called. He ignored her.

"Ted," she repeated. "Hear that?"

Ted looked up, and his smile was wiped from his face. "Oh, no. Winnie, give Faith the paddle. Quick! Get to the side!"

Faith grabbed the paddle from Winnie, then jammed it into the water, pulling with all her strength. The muscles in her arms tightened and ached. Together, she and Ted managed to get the raft to a small sandbar nestled in some aspen trees.

Winnie clambered out and pulled the raft out of the water. "You scared me, you guys. What's going on?" she asked in a shaking voice.

Ted climbed out, too, and stood beside her on the beach. "Can you hear that, Winnie?"

Beyond a bend in the river came a thundering crash. "Yeah, it's loud. What is it?" Winnie asked.

"Devil's Canyon. The biggest rapids on this section. It's what gives the river its reputation as one of the best runs in the country." Ted took Winnie's hand and led her along a little trail that wound through some rocks. Faith watched them, biting the inside of her lip. *Wouldn't it be nice,* Faith thought, *if someone thought about anchoring the raft?* It would serve Ted right if, after his little tour of the trees and rocks and river, he came back and found the raft floating down Devil's Canyon without him. Faith flung the bowline around a spindly aspen tree trunk. At least *she'd* paid attention at the guide school. All Ted could think about was Winnie.

After tying the raft, Faith dodged through the trees toward a tiny, dusty trail leading up a steep, rocky incline to a cliff overlooking the canyon. Her feet burned on the hot sand as she trudged up the rise, the heat creeping up to her knees and matching the hot flashes of anger that overwhelmed her. When she surged over the crest of the cliff, she saw that Ted and Winnie were standing close together, staring down into the gaping space at their feet.

"Class IV all right," Ted said as Faith stepped to his other side. Her heart thudded uncomfortably in her chest when she saw the canyon.

Described as "intense" by the guide who had taught the school, the rapids looked impossible to Faith. Whitewater churned like the inside of a washing machine gone wild. Steep walls of dark-brown rock plunged into the canyon, forcing the river to boil through the narrow space. Huge, black boulders dotted the river along the left. In the middle, there was a foaming hole that looked as if it was covering a submerged mountain.

"That hole looks kind of intense," Ted said. He took her hand, and Faith felt relief rush through her. At least he understood that if they were going to get through Devil's Canyon, she would be the one to help. Not Winnie.

"What is a hole?" Winnie asked. "I mean, it's obviously not something dug out of the river."

Ted pushed a little closer to Winnie.

"A hole is where the water smashes against a big

rock or obstacle," Faith said before Ted had a chance to launch into his I'm-the-expert act. "There . . ." Faith pointed. "See how the water is crashing backward, upriver off that gigantic rock? The force of the water falling off rocks and boulders creates holes. The power of the backwash can trap stuff. We have to stay away from it." Faith's voice was ragged and tight.

She realized that she'd been sort of abrupt with Winnie. But she was tired of Winnie edging next to Ted, asking him questions, getting instructions, smiling, laughing, playing. It was time to get serious if they were going to get through Devil's Canyon.

"There's a drop to the left that we need to avoid," she said, pointing to a rolling section that was all whitewater hydraulics. "How about heading right, then a fast maneuver left across that eddy to get past that hole?"

"Good idea." Ted stared down for another long moment. "Just past that boulder, on the left, is a smooth patch. See it?"

Faith nodded. A small, dark-green patch shimmered on the left-hand side of the river, past the dangerous hole.

"We'll head there if we get into trouble. I think helmets would be smart for this one."

Winnie hunched her shoulders. "Helmets? Really? You guys think you can do this? I mean, it looks wild."

Faith tried to offset her earlier show of temper by smiling at Winnie. "You just need to hold on—tight.

Lean into the big waves. And if we tilt, move against the high side of the raft."

Ted laughed. "Faith's right. Just hang on." He gave her a quick, one-armed hug. "We'll take care of you."

The trio headed back to the raft. As they took their places and strapped on their helmets, Faith found herself wondering if Ted would even notice if she fell in. He sure seemed more concerned with Winnie. Suddenly, she felt like the extra wheel on a trip that had been hers and Ted's. All happiness was being squeezed out of the day.

They hit the river, and within a minute they were poised above the rapids, their raft tilting forward crazily over the brink of the flat surface into the canyon.

Instantly, they were in a hole that was invisible from above, and Faith had to paddle fiercely to keep the raft going. The front of the raft submerged in water, and she slammed herself back to compensate for the pull down into the icy water. The raft bucked up, wobbling crazily, and Faith churned her paddle into the bubbling wave beside her. They headed for the bank where the water looked a little less wild. The raft got slammed by a back-wave, and they struggled to line up with the current.

Winnie screamed.

Ted laughed.

Faith just clenched her jaw and hung on, straining her legs to keep wedged against the thwart.

The raft rocketed for a wall of crashing water. "Now, Faith! Left! Left!" Ted shouted. "That's a roostertail!"

They veered left and just missed the submerged rock that jutted up out of the water. The spray above it signaled one of the most dangerous hazards on the river, a sharp, submerged rock that sent water high in the air. Faith felt her breath stop.

The raft tilted sideways around a slide and shot forward, its front flying up. "All right!" Ted shouted as water splashed over him and they missed the sharp rock.

Sheer, intense power charged through Faith. She screamed, too. This was what she'd come here for! For pounding thrills. For thundering water and exploding rapids. One second she was underwater; the next, she was blazing through a patch of sunlight toward another wall of river. The canyon walls echoed the booming of the rapids and the water flew past her face. She whooped and hollered.

Suddenly the raft tilted wildly. Faith glanced to the side. Winnie was pushing herself up from the floor. She'd been thrown there by that last rapid. Faith saw her hands reaching for the tieline. Then she saw Winnie's bright red helmet leaning crazily to the side. The raft bucked at that moment as it hit a rock, and tilted right.

Winnie was there one second.

Then she was gone.

Faith blinked the water out of her eyes. *Winnie?* Her mind froze. The raft careened around the rock, then plunged into foaming, bubbling water.

"Winnieee!" Faith screamed.

In a flash, Winnie's tiny body disappeared into the whitewater, and Faith screamed again. She dove for the side of the raft, making it rock.

"Faith, the paddle! Get the paddle!" Ted screamed.

She dove back to her side, grabbing the paddle just before it disappeared into a foaming wave. Then she lunged against the tube, and craned over the side searching through curtains of water. "There! There she is." She pointed ahead as a bit of bright red flashed above the surface of a wave. The red helmet bobbed, then vanished.

"Winniieeeeee!" Faith screamed over and over till her throat felt raw.

Faith winced as Winnie's body smashed against the rocks downstream. Then there was nothing. She was gone again.

"Stay in the boat, Faith!" Ted screamed.

"But, Winnie—" She choked as tears streamed down her face. "We've got to help Winnie." The anger toward Winnie vanished.

"She's wearing her helmet. If she's smart, she'll ride downstream. I hope she was listening when I told her about pointing her feet downriver if she fell out. If she cushions the rocks with her feet, she may be okay. We'll get downstream and wait for her. Don't panic!"

Faith felt a searing pang of guilt. She'd just been wishing Winnie would disappear. How could she have been so resentful about Winnie nuzzling next to Ted? What did she expect? Winnie had been hyper for as long as she'd known her. So she did crazy things, so what? That didn't make Faith love her any less. She bugged her. Big deal.

"I'm sorry, Winnie," Faith said to herself. "I'm sorry for being angry with you. Be okay, please be okay."

The raft buffeted off the side of a ledge and shot forward again. Faith slapped her paddle fiercely against the water, unable to feel her hands or her feet or her legs. Unable to feel anything but terror. She had to get past Devil's Canyon. Past the boiling whitewater and deadly rocks. She had to find out if Winnie was safe. Or if she'd been trapped under the river. Forever.

Twelve

"Oooohhh." Courtney sighed. The mud oozed deliciously between her toes as she lay submerged in the mud bath at the Del Oro Spa. Her muscles felt loose. Everything was perfect. She reached out and grabbed a frosty glass of fruit juice that had been set beside her tiled tub. She took a long, cool sip through a straw. The air was warm, the mud was warm, and Courtney felt glorious.

All of her university worries—the Tri Beta sorority, her studies, her volunteer work, everything—disappeared, fading into a hazy memory. She didn't know how, but the mud bath had successfully erased all her anxieties about the trip, about Winnie, even about the fiasco of the fistfight at Pinky's. All she knew was bliss.

Something crawled along her shoulder. Drying mud, she told herself. She eased farther down into the goop.

Something scratched her head. It was probably a bug. She flicked her head sideways slightly.

A finger tapped on her shoulder.

"Hmmmmm," she murmured. "What is it, KC?"

"Excuse me," an unfamiliar voice spoke in her ear.

Courtney's eyes flew open. It was Sara, their attendant and guide at the spa. "Oh. I'm sorry," Courtney said. "I was spacing out."

"No problem, Ms. Conner. It's just that there's someone to see you." Sara smiled and sort of poked her head toward the foot of the baths. "He wouldn't leave."

Courtney felt dazed. What? Who? Her eyes were open but the world felt as if it had been turned into one of those soft-focus photographs, all filmy and gray-edged. Then she became aware of a tall figure silhouetted against the garden. Focusing her eyes, she saw the clothes the man was wearing and her breath stuck in her chest in a huge lump of suffocating air. He was in a khaki uniform. There was a gun at his belt and a shiny badge on his shirt pocket.

He was a policeman. A policeman? Here? And he'd insisted on seeing her?

Sara stood up beside the tub and grabbed a terry-cloth robe. Courtney struggled up, too, feeling the mud sliding down her legs and off her arms and chest. Her bathing suit was coated with slime. Courtney shrugged into the robe, wincing as the mud began to dry on her shoulders. It felt stiff and heavy.

KC's eyes fluttered open, then widened when she saw the policeman. "Oh! What's this? What's happening?" Her voice was groggy from sleep.

"Sorry to disturb you, but there's been a complaint filed about an incident at Pinky's Dance Hall," the officer said, looking at KC then at Courtney from behind his aviator sunglasses.

Courtney took a moment to study the officer. He was young, tall, with dark, wavy hair and a chiseled jaw. For some weird reason, he looked familiar.

"Oh, Pinky's," KC said, tilting her head up to stare at the policeman. "I wasn't there."

"Ms. Conner was. Weren't you?" the officer asked, removing a notepad from his pocket. "The complaint mentions a license-plate registration belonging to a yellow Bel Air convertible. 1957."

"That's mine, all right," Courtney said, crossing her arms. Under her robe, she could feel the mud dropping off her skin in chunks. "Did Lance Putnam file this complaint?" she asked, her voice sharp.

"That's right."

Courtney's skin prickled with annoyance at the mere thought of Lance Putnam. How he attacked Winnie. How Joe hadn't done anything about it. How angry she'd felt. She was remembering it very clearly now.

"And did he say what he was complaining about?" she asked slowly.

The officer frowned as he looked down at his little book. "Vandalism to his sports car. Damage to roof. Estimated repair costs, twelve hundred dollars."

"Twelve hundred dollars! You've got to be kidding! Padding the estimate, I'd say. How about two or three hundred," Courtney barked.

She watched her reflection in the policeman's sunglasses, and thought for a minute that he was going to leave. He was staring at her. Or at least she thought he was. It was hard to tell behind those stupid reflecting lenses. She raised her chin, determined not to look away. Everybody else in this county may be afraid of Lance Putnam, but she certainly wasn't. And no policeman was going to intimidate her.

He looked away first, letting his eyes rest on KC, who was still lounging in her mud.

"Maybe Lance is padding," he said finally. "And maybe not." He reached up slowly with long, tanned fingers. Courtney felt a flutter of recognition again.

He pulled down his glasses and tucked them into his pocket. She saw the scar on his cheek. His dark, intense eyes. The guy she'd met at Pinky's—Joe— was a policeman? He wasn't a sculptor or an artist or a poet. He was a cop?

Her heart stopped for an instant, and a realization flashed into her brain. Wait a minute, she thought. If he was a cop, he should have *done* something about Lance Putnam.

Anger flooded through her. She took a deep breath. "Are you dressed for a costume party or is that outfit for real?" she asked sarcastically.

He flushed. "It's for real."

"Then why didn't you do anything last night? Winnie was almost raped and you just stood there? What kind of a cop are you?" she snapped. "And now you've tracked me down here to register *his* complaint?"

"This is an official complaint, filed with the department," he answered in a stiff, cold voice. "I have to follow it up." He stuck his notebook back in his shirt pocket and crossed his arms, giving her a steady look.

"Well, you've done your job—*this* time," she added. The mud on her legs was drying, making her skin feel pinched and stiff. "Maybe I'll have to file a complaint, too. Or at least Winnie can. She may have damaged Lance Putnam's car. But you know what he did to her. Or maybe you don't believe her. Is that it? You don't believe Winnie's story?" Courtney could feel the color rising in her face. She willed herself to stay calm. She'd pretend he was one of her pledges who'd been caught after curfew. If it was the last thing she did, she'd keep her cool.

Joe looked sheepish. "All right. All right. Lance has been known to go too far. And that car of his . . . well . . . he probably did pad the estimate." He let his gaze drift to the side of the bricked area where the huge yucca and teddy-bear cholla stood. He stared at them. "The Putnams own half the county. They have friends in city hall *and* in the sheriff's department."

"But you're a state policeman, aren't you?" KC spoke up.

Joe looked at KC and nodded. The sunlight glistened on his thick, dark hair. "Yeah. First year. All first-year cops are on probation. We get a chance to do what we've been trained to do. But if we make any mistakes, we're out. No warning. No reason. Just out. And Lance filed an official complaint. I'm just doing my job."

"So you're scared of them," Courtney barked. "That's it, isn't it? You're afraid of losing your job."

Joe stared at her again, his dark eyes locking on hers. The simmering intensity that attracted her to him the other night was back. And his strength tugged at her again. But the intensity seemed to be in conflict with his desire to play it safe. She wanted to strangle him!

Joe uncrossed his arms and stuck his hands in his trouser pockets.

"Well, I didn't touch his car," Courtney added. "I swear. But I did drive Winnie away. I aided and abetted the culprit."

Joe's eyes widened in surprise.

"Isn't that what you call it?" she asked. "I took Criminal Procedures 121 last term. I got an A, too." She crossed her arms tightly in front of her. The dry mud rubbed against the inside of her sleeves. "Are you going to arrest me? Are you going to tell your boss that you tracked down the villain? That poor little Lance Putnam can collect his three hundred dollars? Make sure you take your gun when you go see the powerful Putnams. You may need it to feel important." Courtney took a breath. "I don't know why you're wearing that badge if you can't protect people," she went on, the words tumbling out of her.

Injustice got her angrier faster than anything in the world. But she was also angry about being deceived by Joe. He was obviously playing along with a powerful family, a local dynasty that called the shots and made everybody jump. She thought he was better than that.

"You might as well get a paycheck from the Putnams," she told him. "It sounds to me like you're really working for them."

She stared at Joe, his face frozen in embarrassment and discomfort. The sun beat down on his head and beads of sweat stood out on his upper lip.

"All right," he snapped, his voice suddenly sharp. "What if I had used my gun? What did you want me to do? Shoot Lance?"

"All I'm saying is that if you're going to carry it, you need to use it to protect people. It isn't a prop, you know," Courtney spat. Joe blinked.

She'd called his bluff. She knew it. And he knew it. And she was willing to wait there all day if that's what it took for him to drop the complaint.

Joe slid his sunglasses back on. "Guess I'll be going," he muttered.

Courtney stepped back toward her mud bath. "That's probably a good idea, Joe," she said. "You'd better report back to Lance. Tell him you found the getaway car, but the culprit is still at large."

Joe spun on his heel and disappeared around the side of the brick wall. Courtney flung off her robe, then stuck one toe into the mud. No one was going to bully her. She was going to stand up for what was right. Too bad Joe hadn't learned the same lesson.

Thirteen

The San Pico River thundered beside Ted as he sat down next to Winnie. It was an hour after sunset. The canyon was dark and crickets sang at the base of the tall cottonwoods that lined the shore. Faith and he had found a sandbar downriver about two hundred yards from where the rapids flattened out. They'd yanked the raft hard and pulled it out. And then they'd waited.

Ted could still feel the churning panic in his stomach. It seemed like hours before Winnie cannonballed out of the raging river, though it had probably only been about ten minutes. He was still weak with relief.

"You sure you're okay?" Ted asked Winnie. She

was dressed in dry parachute pants, a long-sleeved T-shirt, and an extra jacket of Faith's—not to mention being huddled under two blankets, and she was still chilled to the bone. At least she was alive and safe.

Across the campsite, Faith was scrubbing the little pots they'd brought to cook in. After Winnie had climbed out of the river, they'd quickly cooked a meal over the fire, and now Faith was doing clean-up, repacking the food, and making a lot of noise. The clang of pans echoed above their heads off the black walls of the shadowed canyon.

Winnie shivered some more, and Ted readjusted the blanket around her shoulders.

"How about another cup of coffee? Or maybe another blanket?" he asked.

Winnie shook her head. "N-n-no thanks. I just wish I could get warm." She huddled tightly into the rough wool and crossed her legs. Winnie had popped out from under the backwash like a cork, and Ted had instantly thrown her a lifeline. She floundered around in the rapids until she finally got hold of the end and he pulled her onto shore. When she'd dragged herself out of the water, she was blue with cold, her muscles limp and rubbery.

Ted looked at Winnie again. There was a bruise on her chin, and a scrape along her arm where she had slammed into a rock. He felt responsible. If he'd been able to keep the raft under control, she wouldn't have fallen out. It was his job to spot that chute, and he'd missed it. And she'd paid the price.

The fire in front of them flamed brightly. He reached beside him and grabbed a piece of wood, tossing it on the crackling wood that Faith and he had collected around the camp. The sparks crackled and flew up toward the cliffs high above their heads. Bats swooped through the light, and up on the cliffs a coyote sang.

"I stayed under that hole forever," Winnie said in a shaky voice. "I kept bumping around under the water. I couldn't tell which way was up."

Ted scooted a little closer to her. She was still shivering, and he pulled the blanket up around her ears. "Yeah," Ted said nodding his head slowly. "That's the problem. The current traps you and keeps recycling you back against the hole."

Winnie nodded, her damp hair wiggling. "That's me. Recycled Winnie." She giggled weakly and let out a long sigh. "I mean, for a long time, the water kept pushing me down. It was black. And *so* cold. But, finally, the river spat me out. I must have swallowed half the river."

Ted nodded, feeling the need to reassure her, the need to let her talk about her terrible experience.

She looked straight ahead toward the boiling rapids roaring through the darkness. "Well, maybe not half the river. It looks like most of the water's still there."

"It sure is," Ted said quietly. He filled his lungs with cold air. "Listen, Winnie. I'm sorry," he whispered. "If I'd been a better scout, this wouldn't have happened."

"Hey, not to worry." Winnie reached out and patted his arm gently. Her brown eyes shone in the firelight. The flickering, golden flames made her face shine. "It's okay. It was my fault. I chose a bad moment to let go. A rock came up from under the raft and next thing I knew I was in the water. It happened so fast, there was nothing you could've done."

Ted smiled at her. "How's your head?"

She touched the bruise on her chin. "Sore. But it's okay. Colorful, I bet. Like your eye." She reached up and let her fingers brush the remains of the bruise left over from his brawl with Lance Putnam. They laughed.

A relaxed feeling spread through him. He pulled his knees to his chest and crossed his hands in front of them. The fire's heat baked his jeans, loosening the tightness in his legs. He watched as the firelight played across Winnie's smile. She could actually laugh after being plunged into the river. She could make *him* laugh. She was amazing.

"We make a good pair," Ted offered. "People will think we're boxing partners or something." He looked over at Faith. She was still putting away pots, banging them into a pile. Ted sighed. She was angry. There was no doubt about it. When Faith was angry, everybody knew it.

Winnie followed his gaze. "Umm." She cleared her throat. "Faith? Can I help you do something?" she called.

Silence.

Ted felt irritation poking into him. Faith was ignoring them both. And for what? What had he done? Made sure Winnie was okay. So what? What did Faith want? To leave Winnie alone by the campfire while the two of them went off and looked at the stars? To leave her half in shock? He thought Faith was Winnie's friend. And she'd been practically hysterical on the riverbank as they waited for Winnie to appear. But when he had started taking care of Winnie, getting her blankets, tending to her bruises and scrapes, Faith had stormed off as if he'd done something wrong.

True, the rafting trip was supposed to be his and Faith's, but Winnie needed him. She had been badly shaken by her experience, and it didn't feel right to go off and leave her. Faith should understand that.

Ted glanced again at Faith's back. Her shoulders were tight. She stuffed a pan into the dry bag and zipped it roughly.

He inched closer to Winnie, and he could feel her slide toward him. Her body was relaxing a little, and she'd stopped shivering. The fire was warm, and the crackling logs felt soothing and comfortable. He looked at Winnie. Her brown eyes were shining.

Suddenly, he felt a familiar sensation. It was like a charge of electricity, a bolt of lightning, shooting right through him. And it magnetized the air between them. He was drawing closer to her. Her skin was like velvet. Her eyes looked like melting chocolate. She was sexy, energetic, funny, fun. She was different from Faith.

"She seems angry," Winnie said softly.

"Yeah," Ted agreed. They both knew they were talking about Faith. "She does." The magnetic feeling intensified. *Wait a minute,* Ted told himself. Winnie was picking up vibes. No doubt about it. She was feeling the magnetism, too. It was his old self, his flirtatious, always-interested-in-somebody-else self coming back. He wouldn't give in to it. He promised himself. He promised Faith. He inched away from Winnie.

"I think I should head to my sleeping bag," Winnie said slowly.

Ted felt relief flood through him. She understood. He didn't have to tell her that he couldn't give in. That this magnetic attraction wasn't okay. He wouldn't let it be okay. And he'd have to talk to Faith soon. If he didn't, the rest of the trip downriver, the rest of the road trip, would be torture. He smiled slowly at Winnie, whose gaze made him feel warm all over. Yeah, if he didn't talk to Faith soon, she'd freeze him the rest of the trip. And Winnie? It looked as if she was perfectly willing to thaw him out.

"I'll head over behind that tree, out of sight," Winnie said. She gathered her blanket, then picked up another one from the stack that Faith had laid out, and walked stiffly toward the tall cottonwoods. Ted could hear her scratching away the rough leaves, and fussing with her blankets.

A stony silence enveloped the camp. The river rushed, and the crickets still sang. Ted turned toward Faith. He could see her fussing with the food in the cooler, rearranging the blocks of cheese. She snapped the lid shut. His jaw clenched.

"You okay?" he asked from where he sat beside the fire.

Faith turned slightly toward him. "Who, me?"

"You've been cleaning for about an hour." He tried to make his voice light, but it sounded harsh, even to him.

She gave him a steady look. "Listen, Ted. This trip isn't turning out exactly like I planned." Her eyes were like darts.

Ted stood up. His legs were warm from the fire, but as he stepped away from the blaze, the cold of the night air hit him. He shivered. Crossing the twenty yards to Faith, he could feel her coldness, too. It suddenly seemed as if everything about Faith was hard and cold. "What do you mean?"

Faith squinted a little in thought, struggling with her words. "I love Winnie," she said, her voice dropping. "I was scared when she fell in. But—but she just has a way of making everything revolve around her. You know, upstaging people. And I get a little tired of it, that's all."

The icy blast from Faith reached right through him, and anger, outrage, and irritation all merged together. "Well, Faith, what do you want? Maybe we should push her back in the water. Maybe we should let her freeze to death. Would that make you happy?"

"Listen, Ted. Winnie invited herself. She's caused plenty of trouble already on this trip. Then she falls in the river. For all I know, she did it on purpose to get you to pay more attention to her!"

"What? That's a great thing to say!" he thundered. "I can't believe you think that! She could have been killed!"

Faith reached out her arm, her face wrinkled in worry and concern. "I—I'm sorry. I didn't mean—"

"I don't care if you're sorry. You're the one who's been moping and criticizing. You're the one who turns a cold shoulder to me whenever something goes wrong. Maybe you're the one who's trying to get attention."

"I'm sorry. Ted, listen," Faith said desperately. "Ted, *wait*!" She tried to put her hand on his arm, but he suddenly didn't want to be near her. He didn't want to be around her moods and her complaining.

"I'm going down by the river. Don't wait up for me."

He hurried past the campfire, past the cottonwoods where Winnie had laid her blankets, and headed to the riverbank. He needed some time alone. He needed time to think.

At the Del Oro Spa everything was quiet. Guests were tucked into their luxurious bungalows, all sleeping soundly. All except KC. Outside the French doors of her little cottage, the moon drifted across a cloudless sky. The shadows were deep and dark. KC rose from the soft, comfortable chair where she'd been reading by a lamp. She glanced quickly at Courtney, who had not stirred in her bed across the room.

"Courtney? You awake?" KC whispered.

Silence greeted her, and she shrugged. Well, it was after eleven. And with all their mud treatments, massages, facials, and wraps, KC herself was feeling pretty sleepy.

But she'd promised Grady she'd be at the historical marker at midnight. And that's where she'd be. It was important. He would be counting on her, depending on her.

She slipped on her shoes and tiptoed out the door. KC followed the path they'd taken that morning through the large granite boulders surrounded by ferns and shrubs. In the moonlight, everything looked mysterious and strange. The rocks looked like crouching animals ready to spring. The ferns looked like reaching hands.

KC headed along the path through the dappled silver splashes of light. Suddenly, she was in the large pool of moonlight that marked the front patio. She turned past the carved, dark door of the main entrance and rushed down the long steps that led to the parking lot, her footsteps thudding on the flagstones. Her hair flew out behind her as she hurried toward the wide expanse of blacktop at the base of the hill. The Jeep sat between Courtney's convertible and a BMW. KC quickly climbed into the driver's seat and jabbed the key into the ignition. Before long, she was driving down the long, sloping drive, away from the spa and toward a historical marker ten miles east.

Around her, the night sounds were muffled and faint. The river tumbled between the cliffs below, and above, the full moon hung low in the sky. Within minutes, she reached the turnoff and the Casa Linda cliff dwellings. Pulling the Jeep into the small graveled lot, she felt a shiver of anxiety. There was nothing but black rocks, gnarled and twisted trees, and moonlight. Then the headlights streamed across a wide opening in the trees and shrubs and she saw the cliff houses across the river at the end of a narrow footbridge. Flicking off the headlights and the engine, she sat quietly in the Jeep, listening.

Skittering and rustling sounded from the ground in front of the Jeep. Under the trees, something moved and squeaked.

She reached for her thick, green sweater and pulled it over her head. An owl swooped above her, a blur of white feathers and yellow-gold eyes. She flinched. Shivers galloped up her spine. The air was cold, and she rubbed her hands together. Then she climbed out and crawled onto the warm hood of the Jeep. She leaned back against the windshield and examined the dwellings through the framed opening in the trees.

The structures rose above the end of the sturdy footbridge. Some of them soared as high as four stories up the side of the cliff. The rooms were stacked one on top of the other, hovering above the ground like dragonflies. The ghostly, deserted dwellings, with their dark, empty window spaces, stared at her.

She peered through the moonlight at the small,

wood-carved historical marker that sat at the entrance of the footbridge.

> *The Casa Linda cliff house is believed to have been built in the late Pueblo period. It was occupied through three or four generations and then abandoned in approximately 1270 A.D. No one knows why. The dwellers of this cliff village enjoyed the security of their isolated and self-contained village. About one hundred families lived on this site. Climbing is prohibited.*

One hundred families. A small town, clinging to the cliff, going about its daily life. The reflection of the river flashed across the face of the rooms. KC began to feel a strange attraction to the empty houses, as if they spoke to her, whispering of the long-forgotten people whose lives had filled each room. It made KC feel terribly lonely.

She shook her head to clear her imagination. The air was cold. She flicked her sleeve up from her watch. It was 12:15. Grady was late. Probably tied up with some anthropological detail. Measuring or scraping or digging or classifying something. Or . . .

KC felt the prickling of fear along her arms and neck. She heard the voice inside her head, warning her, cautioning her not to trust anyone. But another, softer voice whispered that Grady needed help.

Stretching her long legs, she felt the cold tighten her muscles. Relaxing at the spa had given her a chance to clear her mind of her dark empty feeling. She'd been floating, disconnected from life. But now she felt the familiar tightening of her neck and jaw. She felt the flicker of fear again in the muscles along her spine. The fear was not just of being alone amid the dark houses. It was the fear of living a life without trust. The fear that she'd always feel this empty.

The moon slid a little farther across the sky, and the shadows deepened. KC yawned. Time hung suspended from the cliffs. The Jeep engine had cooled, and all around her the rustling in the leaves and the trees had stilled.

KC checked her watch again. Grady was thirty minutes late. She began to wonder if she would have to wait all night. An owl screeched, and KC climbed off the hood. She stretched her arms above her head. She listened intently for the sound of a truck in the distance. But there was nothing. Only the whispering of the brittle leaves of the craggy trees and the rushing of the water far below her.

The empty night filled her. Grady wasn't coming. She'd been set up, again. She looked at her watch one more time. The second hand swept around and around. She wouldn't wait any longer. Climbing back into the Jeep, she sat for a minute staring at the flickering light running across the front of the cliff houses.

She started the engine, threw the Jeep in gear, and sped out of the parking lot. Within a half hour, she was back at the Del Oro Spa, climbing the stone stairs quickly and hurrying through the deepening shadows to her bungalow. Quietly, she slipped into the warm room, changed into her pajamas, and slid into her soft bed.

In the other bed, Courtney was still breathing deeply. KC stared up at the ceiling. The sheets smelled fresh and clean. The room was filled with slanting shadows and quiet. The whispering breeze rustled the shrubs outside the window. But her eyes stayed open. She watched the moon's shadow move across the wall. Inside her head, the chant started again, the flat, nagging voice that had followed her from Springfield. The voice that grew louder by the second. "You can't trust anyone, KC. I don't know why you try."

"Let's get away," the voice inside Faith's head was saying. "Let's raft the San Pico while we're in the Southwest. It'll be romantic. . . ." Isn't that what she'd said to Ted back in Springfield?

"Ha," Faith muttered out loud. She was tucked inside her sleeping bag. Her feet and arms and legs were warm. Then why did she feel like ice water had been poured into her veins? Faith stared at the leaf shadows on the side of the tent. Beyond her, the river rushed and roared, never ceasing its tumultuous plunge through the canyon. The sound should comfort her. But it didn't.

She'd been wrong to snap at Ted. After all, the fact that Winnie had taken over their trip wasn't *his* fault. She shouldn't have said that Winnie had fallen in on purpose. But she'd been angry, and hurt. This was her trip, too. And it was going all wrong. It wasn't romantic and fun. It wasn't turning out the way she'd planned. In her mind, Ted and she would camp out under the stars and watch the moon, wrapped in each other's arms. They'd drift down-river in the relaxing heat. They'd share adventures and new places. They'd make memories they could talk about later, and laugh about. But somehow, Winnie was taking center stage. Spotlighted. Solo. Upstaging Faith and her daydreams.

Faith sniffed. Tears pooled in her eyes. It was all so unfair. Here she was, lying in her sleeping bag, alone. Ted sat by the river, alone. This wasn't what she'd had in mind at all. Her ears pricked. Beyond the sound of the river and the wind, another sound reached her, a different sound, something that didn't fit in the murmuring hush of the trees or the tumbling crash of the river.

Footsteps.

She squeezed her eyes shut, deepened her breathing, and lay still. The footsteps were coming closer. Then the tent flap zipped quietly open. Faith commanded herself to relax, to loosen her clenched jaw. Ted must be standing there, watching her. She wanted to apologize, she wanted to talk to him, but something kept her poised, still, and silent.

"Faith?" Ted's soft voice called. "Are you awake?"

In her mind rose the image of the smiles between Winnie and Ted. Ted tickling Winnie. Ted teaching Winnie to row, his arms clamped tightly around her waist. She heard their jokes and laughter ringing in her ears. Her muscles froze and her voice clogged in her throat.

She had laid a blanket across Ted's sleeping bag beside her, and now she felt it shift, brushing her leg quickly. He must have picked it up. The movement stopped again, the muffled world inside the tent hanging quiet and still. Then she heard the quiet zip of the flap being closed, and he was gone.

Faith sat up. She wanted to go after him. She wanted to talk to him. After all, he'd just come to be with her, to talk to her. And all she could do was pretend to be asleep. What was *wrong* with her?

The night sounds returned, muffled chirps and creaks. The trees above the camp fluttered. Faith listened. Beyond the sounds of the night, she heard something else. More footsteps. And whispering.

Crawling out of her sleeping bag, Faith carefully lowered the zipper and inched through the tent flap. Then she paused. There it was again. Giggling. Down by the river.

Faith waited. From behind the trees crept a small, muscular figure, crouching in the darkness, heading toward the water. Faith heard laughter, then a "Shhhhh."

Winnie.

And Ted.

Faith saw them both plainly. Winnie's crouching figure flashed through a bright pool of moonlight. Then Faith saw Ted. He was looking at Winnie. He raised the blanket that had been draped around his shoulders. Faith's eyes widened. Winnie ducked to his side and sat down quickly, settling herself under the blanket. She giggled.

"Shhhh," Ted hissed.

They nestled together tightly, their shoulders touching. The blanket came up, merging the two shapes into one. Faith imagined how close they must be sitting. Their hips were probably pressing into each other, their legs . . .

Ted turned toward Winnie. Faith held her breath. *No!* she thought. *No! Ted, please don't.* She wanted to scream. She wanted to stop him. But she couldn't. Part of her was too horrified to speak, to move, to think. Her heart pounded in her chest so loudly, she was certain they could hear it. No, she knew she was a fool. Neither Ted nor Winnie could hear anything. They were too wrapped up in each other. They probably couldn't hear the thundering river right beside them. They were too busy.

Slowly, Ted leaned forward and Winnie tilted her head back. The moonlight lit their faces as their lips touched, gently, tentatively. Faith could see Winnie's hands twine up around Ted's neck in encouragement. A gigantic swell of wrath raged through Faith. She could see everything.

Fourteen

s KC trudged toward the main lobby of the Del Oro Spa the next afternoon, she berated herself for being a fool. Her flutterings of hope and curiosity had crumbled into disappointment and disgust. She'd waited for Grady, and he hadn't shown up. Then she'd lain awake staring at the shadows on the walls of her bungalow. Finally, just before dawn, she'd fallen into an exhausted slumber.

"Okay, KC," Courtney chirped as they passed bursting planters and dappled ferns. She was wearing new jeans and a crisp white, sleeveless shirt. Her designer overnight bag hung smoothly from her shoulder, and her blond hair was pulled back into a neat ponytail. "You'll check out the museum for us, right? It's twenty miles east, on the way to Las Altas. Get all the brochures and pamphlets you can. I'm really curious about these cliff dwellings."

KC nodded silently. Birds sang in the trees around them, the only place where the heat was diminished.

Courtney paused, allowing KC to catch up with her. She fell into step beside her as they entered the French doors leading to the carpeted lobby. "And while you're doing that, I'll drive to the raft pull-out place. Let's see. . . ." She hesitated, wrinkling her forehead in thought. "Thirty miles west of Flo's. We'll meet at Flo's at sundown." Courtney laughed merrily. "It sounds like one of those spy movies, you know. Synchronize our watches."

KC didn't answer. Courtney was in president-of-the-sorority mode, and KC knew there wasn't any point in complaining. Anyway, KC could barely put two complete sentences together. She was tired, and her brain felt as if it had chewing gum stuck inside. Good thing Courtney wanted to take over. KC followed Courtney to the registration desk.

A tall, dark-haired man with a pencil-thin mustache and narrow brown eyes greeted them. Courtney signed out and handed in their key. "Well, Ms. Conner," the man said in a rich, deep voice. "I trust the Del Oro Spa met with your approval?"

Courtney set down her bag, then laid her manicured hands on the marble counter. "Absolutely." She hesitated a little, a flicker of a shy look crossing her face. "I hope no more policemen showed up. I apologize about that."

The man gave her a thin smile. "If he hadn't insisted on seeing you, we would never have disturbed you. Our patrons' privacy is crucial. But officers of the law can get very insistent." The smile faded. A serious, almost severe, expression settled on his face. "And I have to admit that around here, we are often grateful for their efficiency."

Courtney tilted her head. "What do you mean?"

"This area seems to attract all sorts of questionable characters. Drifters. Scruffy undesirables. I warn you to be very careful in the desert, Ms. Conner. You must never trust anyone. Especially not strangers."

KC stared. The light in the lobby suddenly seemed very bright and blinding. Strangers? Like Grady? Her palms grew damp.

"Thank you. We'll remember that," Courtney commented, her voice steady.

They made their way to the parking lot and quickly stowed their belongings in the two cars. The heat radiated off the blacktop and crept up KC's legs even through the thick soles of her hiking shoes. She climbed into the driver's seat of the Jeep. The heat broiled her back.

"Do you think the manager was right?" Courtney spoke up. "I mean about strangers in the area? You waited for Grady a long time last night, right?"

KC nodded. She'd told Courtney about her futile wait in the dark. Courtney had been sympathetic, but wary.

"I'd be careful, KC," Courtney continued. "You really don't know anything about him."

"I know. But he seemed so sad, so—"

"Desperate?" Courtney finished, her smooth forehead crinkling in worry.

KC nodded. "A little."

"Well," Courtney went on, her voice gentle. "Maybe it's a good thing he didn't show up, then. Especially after what the manager said about drifters."

KC frowned. "I guess he could've made up that story about being an anthropology student," she said. "Who knows? I've decided to forget the whole thing. Forget Grady. Forget last night." She coiled her fingers around the steering wheel. "I'm going to stop worrying about him."

"Good." Courtney patted her arm. "Have fun at the museum. I'll see you at Flo's."

She hurried to the driver's side of her car, jumped in, and drove off with a quick backward wave to KC.

KC *was* determined to forget Grady. She pushed away the image of his face, his light-green eyes, and his intense voice. She pushed away the tentative flicker of hope that he'd stirred in her. She squeezed shut the tiny crack in her heart. And cemented it.

The road to the museum twisted along the cliffs. It was a sizzling gray ribbon curling eastward, and as KC drove, she felt a sort of numb, hypnotic peace settle over her. The glare off the road beat against the windshield, and KC squinted, feeling sweat trickle down her temples and along her neck. The distances here seemed to stretch time and space. Everywhere they went, they had to drive and drive to get there, crawling along the broiling roads in the sun. KC reached behind her and fumbled in her pack for her canteen. The liquid soothed her dry throat. She retightened the top and tossed it onto the seat beside her.

Glancing left, KC sped past the Casa Linda cliff dwellings where she'd waited the night before. In the afternoon sun, the cliff houses looked flat, dusty, completely ordinary, and completely deserted, the remains of a now-dead life. She'd been foolish to think the spirits of the residents still hovered over the stones. They were simply clever buildings stuck in the rocks.

"Seven hundred years ago, these villages were alive with laughter and conversation. Women gossiped around the fires, children played in the courtyards, dogs barked . . ."

KC listened as the guide led the small group of visitors through the exhibit of artifacts and maps. The woman, dressed in the khaki uniform of a park official, had been telling them about the history of the region, and about the mysterious disappearance of the inhabitants. Now she led them toward huge glass cases filled with pottery.

"These pots were found at the magnificent Kanabi cliff dwellings, located just forty miles east of here. The settlement contained more than two hundred rooms. Sophisticated planning allowed the people who lived in these villages a strong defense as well as comfortable quarters."

KC stared at the exhibit. Again, the strange awareness she'd felt for the people who had lived here washed through her, and she shivered. She felt the same tug of connection as she had the night before at the Casa Linda dwellings, and in the cave where she'd first encountered Grady. She remembered the reflection of the moonlight and river across the face of the cliffs. The dwellings had been the homes of real people, with real lives. Their history spoke to her from the bowls and pots. There were bracelets and necklaces, tiny incense burners, and figures of animals. There were grinding stones and knives, pipes and whistles. The objects of life.

KC felt tears sting her eyes. These were the objects and treasures Grady supposedly worked with. No wonder he was so intense. No wonder he wanted to carry on the work of his father. His father had taught him about the ancient people, about the value of discovering and reconstructing their lives. KC sucked in her sudden breath. It was almost as if Grady were in the room with her, speaking to her. *See?* his voice seemed to echo. *See? These are the lives of those who have gone before us.*

The guide's voice penetrated her thoughts, ringing through the large, sparsely decorated chamber. "But many of these dwellings have been destroyed.

Commercial mining wants to carve into the cliffs, particularly those closest to Las Altas, to extract the valuable minerals. Already three cliff-dwelling villages have been lost because of greed. These mining ventures blast away any remnants of the past."

KC wanted to scream. Her heart pounded as the guide went on to explain the threat of mining to the region and to its unique heritage. How could anyone destroy the precious voices speaking through these objects?

The guide led them toward the gift shop adjacent to the museum. There, she explained, local crafts were for sale, providing an income for the tribes that still lived in the area. "Even though the cliff dwellers have disappeared," she said, "we can still help their descendants." She paused, her clear blue eyes sparkling in enthusiasm. "Are there any questions?"

"Why did the residents leave?"

"Where did they go?"

"Were they chased away?"

The guide responded patiently and cheerfully to the barrage of questions. "No one knows for sure why the cliff dwellers abandoned their homes. Some say drought caused the mass exodus. Some say the tribes were absorbed by other groups. Perhaps by the ancestors of the Zuni, the Hopi, or the Navajo. But no one knows for sure."

After everyone in the group fell silent, the guide thanked them, then disappeared through the museum door. KC wandered through the shop, admiring the intricate jewelry, baskets, pots, and figures for sale. She picked up some booklets explaining the tradition of the pottery makers. Another booklet called "Cave Dwellers" caught her eye, and she took that. She made sure to get a stack of brochures on the Kanabi dwellings, the ones they were going to visit the next day.

"The museum will be closing in ten minutes," the girl behind the counter suddenly announced. KC realized with a jolt of surprise that it was past five o'clock. She'd been in the museum all afternoon.

KC paid for her books and returned to the Jeep. The sun was slipping down toward the horizon, casting crimson streaks across the flat desert in front of her. As she drove to Flo's, she could still feel the spirits of the cliff dwellers speaking to her.

But their voices were faint, and they spoke in words she didn't understand. "Shut up!" she screamed over the dry wind. "I won't listen!" She gripped the hot steering wheel harder and sped past the rising cliffs. Whatever message the ghosts of the ancestors were trying to communicate, she wasn't going to listen anymore.

By the time she reached Flo's, KC felt as if she'd been roasted alive. Her seat was sore, her legs were stiff, even the bottoms of her feet were numb. She glanced quickly around the dusty lot. There was one dilapidated Volkswagen van and that was all. She pulled the Jeep under the shade of the tall cottonwoods and climbed slowly out.

The large windows of Flo's, decorated with posters advertising sales on bait and tackle, glinted reddish orange. KC staggered up the wooden steps and hobbled into the air-conditioned store. The blast of cold air on her face offered immediate relief.

Flo was still behind the counter. She was wearing a bright turquoise dress that looked a little like a feed bag. She gave KC a toothy grin. "Can I help you, honey?" she asked in a loud voice.

"I'm just looking for my friends. We were all in here buying supplies yesterday."

Flo squinted at her. "You know how many people come into my store? It's the only place for miles." She cackled.

"One of my friends was wearing an orange Dayglo crop-top. She was talking to you about our plans to go to the spa," KC said. *And I could have killed her for it, too,* she added silently.

"Oh, yeah. Nice girl. With spiked hair and bubble gum?"

"That's right."

Flo shook her head. The tight, gray-streaked curls bobbed back and forth. "Haven't seen her. But someone was asking about her."

KC felt her heart stop. "Asking about her? Who would be asking about Winnie?"

"Lance Putnam. He came in trying to find a short, brown-haired girl, built like a runner. Said she had spiky hair and a sexy grin. That sound like your friend, sweetie?"

KC swallowed. "You're kidding! What did you say?"

"I didn't say anything," Flo said, her face flushed. "What do you think I am? A gossip?" She started straightening the boxes of matches on the counter.

"Did you tell him where we were going? I mean to the cliff dwellings?" If Grady had been right about Flo, that meant everyone knew their plans. Including Lance Putnam.

"Are you sure you didn't say anything?" KC asked again.

Flo's hands fidgeted, and her face pinched up into a nervous expression. She finished straightening the matches and moved on to the rack of plastic key chains. "I said no, didn't I?" she replied. "Now, you just relax, sweetie. There's nothing to worry about. Except maybe that road to the Kanabi cliff dwellings. Tricky. Gotta be careful."

KC fumed. Even if Flo had told Lance Putnam their plans, she wasn't going to admit it. And what could KC do about it now anyway? She'd have to warn everybody. That meant they'd probably have to change their plans. Again. Just because of Winnie.

KC charged out of the store. The sun on the horizon looked like a big, red beach ball, and the air was already getting chilly. The shadows lengthened across the parking lot, and KC crossed to the Jeep to get a sweater. She yanked it on over her head. Just as she was tugging her hair out, a truck spun into the lot, kicking up gravel and dust.

Tires squealing, the truck skidded toward her. KC leaped out of the way, ducking behind the Jeep.

"What do you think you're doing?" she screamed when the truck stopped.

The person who jumped out of the driver's seat had a black eye. His left cheek was swollen, and a jagged cut slashed across it. The cut was puffy and discolored. His shaggy auburn hair was ruffled and windblown, and his beard was dusty. His face under the cut was pale.

"Grady?" KC gasped. "Oh my God, what happened to your face? What happened to you? Where were you last night?"

He didn't answer, but instead grabbed her hand and pulled her to the side of the store. "KC! Thank God, you're here! I need your help."

KC reached for his face, but he flinched back. "That looks bad, Grady," she said. "That cut is deep. And where are your glasses?"

"They broke. It's okay. Listen, I've been driving back and forth in front of this store all afternoon hoping you'd come back. I—I really need you." He looked so frightened, KC felt the sudden tugging she'd felt the night they'd watched the stars in front of the Cactus Cottage Motel. The feeling that they shared something. But he'd abandoned her last night. And she was still furious with him. And angry at herself. *Don't be fooled again*, the warning voice cried in her head.

"Where were you last night?" she asked again. "I waited forever! What is going on?"

"I can't tell you," he said. "It's safer if you don't know." He took her other hand and held it firmly. "You have to trust me, KC."

His hand gripped her tightly, and in spite of herself KC stepped closer to him. She saw it again, deep in his eyes, the soft pleading light that shot straight into her heart. The spark of some indefinable emotion reaching for her. She groaned.

The sizzle of her anger sputtered slowly out of her.

"Are you still headed for Las Altas?" he asked. He glanced over his shoulder, then back.

She nodded once. "After we visit the Kanabi cliff dwellings. Why?"

"Could you do me a favor?" Before she could even respond, he'd let go of her hands, dashed back to his truck, grabbed something in the bed of the truck, and run back to her. In his hands he held a cardboard box. It was sealed tightly with layers of tape.

"Here. Could you deliver this for me? To Dr. Carlos Sanchez. University of Las Altas." His voice was edged with desperation.

"Why can't you deliver it yourself?"

"I just can't." He glanced again at the road. "It's *really* important, KC. Now, listen. Don't open the box. Whatever you do. Unless—unless you get into trouble or something."

KC cocked her head to one side. "What kind of trouble?"

"Just hand it to Dr. Sanchez as soon as you arrive. The university is pretty small. You won't have any trouble finding him. Anthropology Department. Field Division."

KC puffed out an exasperated breath. "Grady! What kind of trouble?"

"You won't regret this, KC. It's okay. Really. Trust me. You have to trust me!" He grabbed her shoulders. Somehow the box ended up in her hands.

Her anger was completely gone, dissolved by his intense plea. But she still felt doubt and confusion. His eyes held hers again. The light in them changed. Slowly, he leaned forward and kissed her. His lips were soft, warm, and as he deepened the kiss, KC could feel joy spinning through her. The kiss turned strong, fiery, demanding. And she felt herself losing track of her questions, of where she was. . . . Then, suddenly, he stepped back, leaving her weak and dazed.

"Thanks, KC. Thanks for everything," he murmured softly. In an instant, he was gone, and the only sign that he'd been there at all was the box in her hand and the pounding of her heart.

KC was still standing in the shadows when Courtney's convertible pulled into the parking lot. Winnie sat in the front with Courtney, and KC had to admit that Winnie looked great. Her eyes were shining, her skin tanned, her hair was freshly spiked, and she was blowing a huge, bright-green bubble. KC let her eyes travel to the backseat, and a flicker of surprise and alarm passed through her. Ted and Faith were sitting as far apart as they possibly could. Faith's cheeks were flushed, and even in the fading light, KC could see she was very angry.

"Well, the explorers made it down the river," Courtney called. "We spotted a motel farther down the road. It looked nice. I thought we could head there tonight."

KC nodded, casting a quick glance at Faith and Ted. Ted's eyes were avoiding everyone, especially Faith. Something was wrong. Courtney was doing her scout-leader routine, but KC could see the strain around her mouth and in her eyes.

The only person who looked normal was Winnie. She had a strange bruise on her chin, but besides that, her skin almost glowed. Her hand was beating out a drumbeat on the side of the car.

"What's that box?" Faith suddenly asked from the backseat.

"It's—it's something Grady wants me to take to Las Altas," KC said, a slow flush stealing up her cheeks. "To Dr. Sanchez at the university. I guess I'll put it in the trunk."

Courtney held up her keys, and KC took them, stowing the box quickly in the trunk to one side of the rafting equipment and the camping gear.

"What's *in* the box?" Faith demanded, her voice sharp.

The sun had dropped below the horizon and the air was cold. The cottonwood trees fluttered, and in the branches, birds were winding down their chatter.

KC handed Courtney the keys and stared back at Faith. "I don't know," KC said, trying to keep her voice steady. Faith was beginning to get on her nerves. "I just feel like I can trust Grady."

"Are you kidding me?" Faith exploded. "You're crazy!"

KC let her eyes meet Faith's. "Maybe it's time for me to start trusting people again. *I* think it's time. I don't know why. And taking this parcel doesn't seem like a big deal."

"You don't even know him! Of course it's a big deal! You must be out of your mind! That box could have drugs in it! Or explosives. Anything."

KC frowned. "But it's going to the university, Faith," she replied, annoyance making her voice tight. "What's wrong with you?"

"Dr. Sanchez could be a terrorist for all you know. Or a drug pusher. You're *totally* crazy!" Faith seethed, crossing her arms tightly and glaring at KC. "And as for trusting people again," she continued, "trust is useless. Completely pointless! A totally meaningless concept!"

Fifteen

Courtney felt the pull of the ruts and rocks on her car as they bumped and bounced up the steep, winding road that led to the Kanabi cliff dwellings. It was the following morning. They'd spent a quiet night in a small motel down the road from Flo's, and now they were going to explore the ancient ruins ten miles up the curving mountain road. Clinging to the side of the plateau, the road wound through stands of juniper and pine, and jays shattered the silence of the morning air with their sharp cries.

KC sat in the seat beside her, and Winnie was once again in the back. Behind them, following in the Jeep, were Faith and Ted. But this time, Courtney thought, no one had to worry about Ted not keeping his hands on the steering wheel. He stared ahead, his angry eyes burrowing into the back of Courtney's head, and Faith sat as far away from him as she could, squashed against the passenger side as if she were part of the door.

Courtney glanced down across KC's lap toward the sharp drop to the valley floor. She smiled. "That's an amazing view. I hope no one here is afraid of heights."

KC shook her head, her long curls dancing in the sweetly scented morning air. "No, not really. I'm not scared of heights, exactly. It's not having a guardrail that's making my heart skip every other beat."

Courtney laughed. "Well, it looks as if the road levels off and heads across that plateau area." She glanced again in the mirror at the Jeep. "Faith still looks pretty unhappy, doesn't she?" Courtney commented.

KC nodded, glancing back briefly, then looked at Winnie. "Any ideas why Faith's so upset?" KC asked.

Winnie blew a pink bubble and shook her head. "Nope. I don't even think she knows. And if she does, she's not telling me about it. She's not speaking to me. Or Ted. I mean, in my psych-major analysis, I'd say she's into communication meltdown."

Courtney glanced at Winnie in the rearview mirror. Something had happened on the raft trip. She was sure of it. But the question was how to ask Winnie in a tactful way. Then again, there was no need to be tactful around Winnie.

"I mean, how can you talk to someone who

won't communicate?" Winnie added. "It's like talking to one of those rocks out there. Or that tree. Or that canyon. Or that gully. Or one of those gigantic clouds. Big waste of energy."

Courtney shook her head and looked over at KC. The sun was beating down on her dark hair and she was smiling, leaning her head back on the seat as they climbed the last incline toward the scenic plateau that led to the cliffs. At least KC was beginning to lose that tight, nervous look around her eyes. Maybe that had something to do with this Grady person, but maybe not. Courtney had to admit that she wasn't thrilled at carrying a mysterious package in her trunk. But even though Courtney didn't know Grady, she knew KC, and she would do anything to make this trip work for her. Even if it meant going out on a limb and transporting something she shouldn't.

Gripping the steering wheel a little more tightly, Courtney negotiated a hairpin turn, then accelerated as the road leveled off a little. Her muscles felt warm and relaxed. And she felt as if she could accomplish anything. Especially after standing up to Joe. He'd misjudged her, that's for sure. He really thought she was going to agree to pay for Lance's convertible top. She felt a deep ripple of satisfaction at having taught him a lesson. She giggled a little, and KC gave her a curious look.

"I was just thinking about this marvelous drive, KC, and how much fun we're having."

Winnie snorted in the backseat.

"Well, *some* of us are having fun," Courtney added. "And this drive is worth the extra wear and tear on the tires. I mean, look at that!" Below them, as far as the eye could see, stretched a wide, flat valley, colored with reds and browns and dark blues in the morning light. Courtney studied the road ahead and noticed a turnoff to the right, where they could stop and admire the view. A little wooden sign read: "Scenic Lookout."

Courtney pulled the car to the right, settling it securely in a rutted gully about twenty feet from the edge of the plateau. Behind her bumped the Jeep. It parked right behind her convertible.

They all climbed out and stood looking over the amazing panorama. The valley stretched out like the bottom of some vast, dry sea. Along the horizon, thunderheads seemed to be gathering, casting pools of shadow.

"Major rain time, folks!" Winnie screamed suddenly as a thundercloud appeared directly over their heads.

Courtney jumped for the convertible top. "KC!" she yelled. "Grab the other end." They fumbled for the wide canvas top and wrestled it out of its cover and over the car. Thunder boomed, echoing all around them, and the wind swirled up big clouds of dust.

"Get the Jeep!" Ted yelled.

"It's raining!" Courtney screamed as fat cold drops started splatting on her face.

Courtney was barely aware of Faith and Ted struggling to fasten the Jeep roof.

Snap. Click. The canvas top snapped on. Stabs of lightning crackled, and volleys of thunder poured off the walls of the cliffs.

Suddenly, a sheet of rain pounded from the sky, and Courtney, Winnie, and KC dove for the doors of the convertible. Fat raindrops pelted the roof. Steam rose on the inside of the windows. The loud battering drops sounded like crazy drumbeats. From inside the drum. Walls of water flowed down the windows.

In twenty minutes it was over. Peering out the window past KC, Courtney smiled at the rain-washed land. The shrubs by the road were glistening with sparkling drops, and the trilling song of a canyon wren filled the air. "I hope we see a rainbow," Courtney said, pushing open the door. She gasped. Her foot sank in mud up to her ankles. "AAAHhhh-hhh!" she moaned. "Help!"

KC dove across the seat. "What is it?" Then she looked down at the ground. "Oh, no!"

"Stay in the car, KC," Courtney commanded. "I'll see if it's like this all on all sides."

When Courtney squelched her way around the back, she realized that she'd parked in a gully. Water rushed around the tires toward the cliffs and over the sides in its enthusiastic tumble toward the lowest point. There was mud everywhere. And they were parked right in the middle of it.

Ted leaned out of the Jeep. "Try to get the tires out of that gully, Courtney. We'll stay here in case you need a push."

Courtney climbed back in the driver's seat and started the engine. She pushed her mud-covered foot gently on the accelerator.

EEerrrrrrrrggghhhh. EEerrrrrrrrggghhhh.

The tires spun like tops.

She lifted her foot, then tried again.

EEerrrrrrrrggghhhh. The car dropped deeper.

"Stop! Courtney!" Ted shouted. "Stop!"

Courtney brought her foot up off the accelerator pedal. Ted stumbled toward her door. "The tires are down about a foot in this stuff. You stay there," he suggested. "We'll get everybody out and try to push."

"Okay," Courtney said in a brisk voice.

Winnie and KC climbed out the other side.

"Oooohhh," KC moaned as she stepped into the mud at her feet. "This feels like the mud baths. Only worse."

"Yuck!" Winnie complained. "This is really disgusting."

Courtney shook her head. She stayed behind the wheel, praying that they'd be able to budge the gigantic convertible. "Now, push!" she yelled. As she touched the accelerator, she could feel four pairs of hands trying to propel the heavy car forward. The seat bounced. The engine chugged.

"Stop! Stop!" yelled Faith. "I'm getting covered with mud!"

Courtney glanced behind her. "Try propping something under the tires!" she called. They stumbled through the mud to find old tree limbs. They wedged rocks. They were even prepared to wedge sleeping bags until Courtney stopped them. "Ted," she said, feeling desperate. "Try pushing with the Jeep."

He nodded, lines of worry creasing his face. "Okay, Courtney. But that car of yours outweighs mine by about a ton and a half."

"I know. But it's our last chance."

They tried. Courtney felt the bumper of the Jeep touch the back of her car. She felt the slight jump forward. Her heart jolted in hope. Then she heard the Jeep's wheels spinning. And spinning. And spinning. Ted gave up.

They were stuck. Miles from anyone, miles from anywhere. Her boat of a convertible was trapped.

"Don't do that, Courtney," Ted snapped. "You're making it worse!"

"But I have to keep putting on the gas!" Courtney called from the driver's seat.

"Wait till I say so," Ted ordered.

"Okay. Okay," Courtney replied.

It was an hour later. Faith watched Ted as he dug little holes around the tires of the car with his camp shovel. He was grimy with mud, and he looked angry, frustrated, muddy, and wet. Faith bit the inside of her cheek. For the first time in a long time, she didn't feel the fizz in her blood when she looked at him. She felt nothing.

All she could associate Ted with now was Winnie.

She saw their lips touching. The image replayed itself over and over in her mind. Her stomach churned violently and she looked away toward KC, who sat on a rock under a twisted juniper.

"But we have to get to Las Altas! I promised Grady," KC moaned.

"If you have any suggestions, KC," Ted said, standing up, "I'd really like to hear them."

KC blushed furiously. "Sorry, Ted."

Faith sat in the passenger side of the Jeep, her feet stuck against the dashboard, her knees against her chest. KC crossed and uncrossed her arms. She'd been moaning about getting to Las Altas by that afternoon. Faith shrugged. At this rate, they'd be lucky to get it there by Christmas.

Winnie had climbed over to the cliff and was sitting on a rock. Now and then, Faith could see her watching Ted, a sly smile on her face. Faith wanted to scream while she tore Winnie's spiked hair out by the roots.

The sun had come out again, blazing down on them perversely as if the rainstorm had never happened. The pungent scent of rainwashed pines scented the air. Courtney worried about water. They'd only brought one water bottle, and the day was getting hotter by the minute.

"Ted," Courtney called from the convertible. "Maybe you should take the Jeep for help. We're going to run out of water." The statement hung in the air. They all knew that the most dangerous peril in the desert wasn't rattlesnakes or scorpions or coyotes. It was lack of water.

Faith stuffed her hand into her pocket. Her set of Jeep keys jangled in her hand. "Hey, I'll go," Faith said. "If we stand around here staring at one another much longer, we really will run out of water." She shoved herself from the passenger side into the driver's seat and stuck the keys in the ignition. "I've been wanting to get away anyway," she added.

Faith flicked on the engine, and spun the tires as she turned savagely in the small space between the edge of the turnout and the convertible. The Jeep rocked violently, and mud flew everywhere.

"Faith!" Ted screamed.

Faith steered the Jeep in a circle.

Ted leaped in front of the bumper. "Hold it!" he yelled, slapping his hands on the hood. "I'm going, too."

Faith bit the inside of her lip. "Why?" she asked. "I can do it. And what if I don't want you to go?"

"It's my Jeep," he snarled. "And even with four-wheel drive, the trip will be tricky. Come on, Faith," he added in a calmer voice.

Before she could respond, another voice piped up. "I'm going, too!"

Winnie. Of course. Who else?

"There isn't enough water for all of us," Winnie sang out. "KC and Courtney can guard the ocean liner."

Before Faith could say anything, Ted and Winnie

had climbed in, Winnie cramming her tight little body into the back. They'd transferred all the camping gear and rafting equipment into the Jeep from Courtney's car, but Winnie just plopped herself on top and scrunched down into a corner.

Faith's anger mounted. But it wouldn't do any good to complain. Winnie did what she wanted. With whomever she wanted.

Not waiting to see if Winie was settled into the Jeep, Faith popped the clutch, gunned the engine, and flew out of the mud and down the road. She caught a final look in the rearview mirror at KC and Courtney as they waved good-bye.

She slowed around the hairpin turn. The mud slid under the tires, and she swallowed hard. "Look out!" Ted barked as the wheels slithered toward the edge. Behind her, Winnie gasped.

Faith slowed down. The road was steep; even with the deeply grooved tires of the Jeep, control was difficult.

"Listen, Faith," Winnie said from behind her. "I want to talk to you. I mean, the last couple of days have been weird, uh?"

Faith remained silent.

Ted took a quick breath beside Faith, but she kept her eyes glued to the road.

"And I'm sorry if I helped make the trip, uh, weirder," Winnie added.

Faith waited. Waited for some mention of Winnie's behavior in the camp. Of her kiss. Her flirting.

Her making trouble at Pinky's. But silence settled into the Jeep. The only sound was of a blue jay cawing in a pine tree and the slushing sound of the Jeep tires plowing through the mud.

This was really too much! Why couldn't Winnie just come out with the truth? That Faith's wonderful, romantic trip with Ted was ruined because of her!

In the distance, a car whizzed across a flat space below them. The highway. About a mile away. *Good*, Faith thought. *I won't have to listen to Winnie much longer.*

She pulled the Jeep around a wind-croded rock, and headed for the dirt road that joined the highway. In one direction lay Las Altas, the other Gold Hill. They could go either way for help.

Winnie leaned toward the front seat. "I'm sorry, Faith," she said again. "I guess I'm just a troublemaker. But—but you just make things worse by being so uptight."

Rage knifed into Faith. A wave of nausea swept over her. She spun around. "Uptight! I'm uptight?" she screamed. Ted tried to touch her, but she shoved him back hard against the passenger door. "Get away from me," she yelled. She lifted her foot off the clutch and the engine died. Turning back to Winnie, she glared pure hatred. "You're right, Win. This is some weird trip. *You* flirt with some maniac at Pinky's and everyone is supposed to feel sorry for you! KC is smuggling contraband for some crackpot who lives in a cave! And my *boyfriend* makes out with my best friend under the stars. Why shouldn't I be uptight?"

Winnie's face froze in a look of horror. Faith knew Winnie was realizing that Faith had seen them the night before. That made it worse. It made everything worse. Winnie was trying to make *Faith* feel responsible for her disgusting behavior.

And she wasn't going to do it!

Faith took one look at Winnie's stunned expression, then turned to glare at Ted. His face flushed bright red. She was not going to take this one more second!

"I'll show you who's uptight. I'll *show* you," Faith fumed.

She grabbed her backpack, then banged the door to the Jeep shut so hard that Ted's head bumped against the passenger-side window.

"Good!" she snapped. "I hope you end up with two black eyes." She thumped to the side of the road, the heat of the blacktop hitting her like a sauna. She headed across the highway to stand on the eastbound side—away from Gold Hill and Flo's and the river. She wanted to go toward Las Altas, as far away from Ted and Winnie and her miserable fantasy of a romantic vacation as she could get.

Planting her backpack on the dusty ground, she stuck out her thumb. Tears spilled down her cheeks. They were hot and sticky and made her face feel on fire.

But she didn't care. She didn't care about anything. All she could feel was the heat of the roadside, the dust sticking to her skin, and her piercing, intense anguish.

Suddenly, in front of her, a huge semi truck

braked, sending a wave of heat into her face. She could see a blue and silver cab, giant wheels, shining chrome. It squealed past her, then pulled slowly into a long, deserted lot that was in front of an abandoned gas station. A horn tooted.

Faith froze. Cars whizzed past. She looked across the road, right at Ted and Winnie, who stared at her. Winnie had climbed into the front seat beside Ted. Their faces were pale, horrified.

The truck's horn tooted again. Faith picked up her backpack and spun on her heels. *Why not?* she asked herself furiously. *Risking my life will show them! I'll show everybody!*

She ran along the gritty shoulder of the highway until she reached the side of the truck.

"Where ya headed?" a cheerful voice asked.

Faith didn't answer. Instead, she slapped her hand around a long silver pole that was positioned on the side, set her foot on a small ladder above the tire, and with a surge, pushed up into the cab. It was air-conditioned, and cool air swirled around her as she slumped into a soft, plush seat. Images flashed into her mind. Ted kissing Winnie in the moonlight. Ted and Winnie staring at her from the Jeep. The long stretch of gray, sizzling highway in front of her. She sniffed loudly, then swallowed past a huge lump of fear and rage and desperation that clogged her throat. Then, in one fierce motion, Faith grabbed the handle of the door and slammed it shut.

Sixteen

Dust. Rocks. Blinding sun. Towering heat. And thirst. KC tried to swallow, but her throat was so dry, the effort hurt.

"How long has it been now?" KC asked, her voice hoarse.

"About three hours all told," Courtney answered. "Since we first pulled in."

The convertible sat in the mud like a beached whale. KC stared at the horizon. She sat in the front seat, her legs swung sideways. Courtney sat in the backseat, facing outward, too. They were still waiting for Faith, Winnie, and Ted to return with help. Or without help. It didn't matter to KC. She just wanted them to come back.

"Do you think we should start walking down the road?" Courtney asked, a frightened quaver in her voice.

KC shook her head. "It's about ten miles. We're almost out of water."

Courtney leaned her head against the seat wearily. "I know."

The sun scorched the side of KC's face. She brushed the salty sweat out of her eyes with the back of her hand. Even though the sun was headed for the horizon, its rays were still parching her throat and drying her lips. The whole valley felt like one gigantic baked oven. KC took a deep breath, trying to calm the rising panic in her dusty throat.

"Do you want to sing some more?" Courtney asked, smiling.

"I think I've run out of camp songs," KC said. "And if I sing one more verse of 'A Hundred Bottles of Beer on the Wall,' I'll scream." KC glanced past Courtney toward the water bottle on the backseat. "Besides, it just makes me thirsty." KC's mouth felt as if it was part desert already.

Courtney had retrieved her travel brochures from her suitcase. She'd read aloud from them for a while, then stopped when she'd read that visitors in the desert needed a quart of water every hour in hot temperatures.

They hadn't even come close.

Courtney nodded. "Yeah, I know."

KC glanced at the water bottle. It was almost

empty. A half hour ago she'd taken a tiny sip. The water sloshed pathetically in the bottom.

As if reading her mind, Courtney reached over and picked up the bottle. "I've got to have another drink. Want some?" Courtney asked.

KC felt panic rise, closing her dry throat. "I'm so thirsty," she moaned.

"Me, too," Courtney whispered.

They looked at each other, KC's desperation mirrored in Courtney's eyes.

Wordlessly, Courtney handed the bottle to KC. She let the water brush her lips, and a small sip dripped out of the opening and down the back of her parched throat. KC was beginning to understand how people could have shoot-outs over waterholes. She handed the bottle to Courtney, who tilted her head back to lick the last drop.

"That's all there is," Courtney said.

KC sighed heavily and turned back to watch the sun edge its way toward the distant horizon. "What if they don't come back?" KC asked.

Courtney stepped out of the car and poised herself at the edge of the cliff. Beyond her lay the empty valley. "I—I don't know."

"What if the Jeep broke down?" KC went on, a wave of jittery panic coming over her again. "What if we're out here all night?"

"I guess we could sleep in the car. At least we'd be safe from coyotes and rattlesnakes," Courtney said.

KC swallowed and let her mind drift back to the

night she'd climbed to the cave behind the Cactus Cottage Motel. The night she'd wondered about animals prowling the area. None of them really knew much about the desert. And this was where it had landed her, stranded in the middle of nowhere with no food, no water, and no equipment.

Thinking back to the cave made her remember Grady and her promise to him. What would he do if she never delivered the package in the trunk to Dr. Sanchez in Las Altas? She'd never find out what he really wanted from her. Or if she could trust him. And he'd never know what happened to her. What if she died out here? From thirst. They'd find her parched bones baking on the hillside. She licked her dry lips.

Courtney hummed a little beside her, and when KC glanced at her, she could see that her friend was frightened, too. Her nervous gestures gave her away. She'd unhooked and refitted her ponytail five times in the last half hour. She kept wiping her sunglasses on her shirt.

KC rose from the front seat and crossed the muddy patch beside the car to rest her hand on Courtney's shoulder. "We'll be okay," she whispered. "It'll be a great story."

Courtney smiled. "If we live to tell it," she replied.

Suddenly, a flash of light made KC turn her head. "What was that?" she gasped.

"What?" Courtney asked.

"Down there." KC pointed to the distant road that curved around the base of the plateau. Something moved, something edged around the side of the mountain. The sun shone in her face, blinding her momentarily. The deep shadows growing against the mountain made the road dark. KC squinted.

"Headlights!" KC screamed. "Those are headlights!"

Courtney started jumping up and down. KC grabbed her arms and whirled her around in a circle.

"We're saved! We're saved!" KC screamed. She pulled Courtney into a tight hug, tears of joy stinging her eyes.

Together, they looked back down the mountain. The headlights crawled closer and closer up the winding road.

"Hey, look out, guy!" the driver called as a jackrabbit shot across the road in front of the truck. "Missed him. Good."

Faith sniffed. She'd been crying for about thirty miles. Her face burned and her eyes were swollen. She felt miserable. Since hitching a ride, Faith hadn't said a word. Instead, she just stared out the side window watching the scrubby bushes and telephone poles flash past.

The driver had finally thrown a tape in the tape deck. A soothing country-western ballad drifted through the cab.

"Nice evening," he said. His voice was soft, kind of low.

Faith let her eyes drift toward him. He was about

her age, she guessed, maybe a little older, with curly brown hair and clear gray eyes that shone brightly from his tanned face. His nose was a little crooked, and when he smiled, little wrinkles fanned out from his eyes. He wore a pale-blue T-shirt and jeans. So far, he'd kept his hands on the steering wheel and his eyes on the road. But now, as Faith watched, he lifted his right hand and laid it on a storage box on the floor of the cab.

She held her breath. *What am I doing?* she asked herself furiously. *This guy could be a pervert or something, and I'm trapped in this truck with him. I must be out of my mind!* Maybe Winnie was right. Maybe she *was* hysterical and crazy. Why else would she have climbed aboard this truck with a total stranger? Faith shook her head slowly. And she had told KC that *she* was asking for trouble!

Beside her, the trucker's hand drew something slowly out of the box. He kept his eyes on the road, Faith noticed. Fear slid along her body and she broke out in a cold sweat. He was lifting something. Faith's eyes widened. He handed it to her. It was a box of tissues.

"Thanks." She sniffed. She wiped her eyes and blew her nose, and felt a little better. If he was planning on attacking her, he must be waiting until they got someplace really desolate, off the heavily traveled two-lane road leading to Las Altas. They passed a sign. LAS ALTAS NINETY MILES.

She looked around the cab. It was large, with

about fifteen dials clustered around the dashboard. The tape deck was built into the dash to the right of the dial and a wide case of tapes sat below it. Faith surveyed the titles. Mostly country western, she realized, but some folk music, and two Mozart tapes. There were also a couple of books on tape. Some mysteries. And *Great Expectations* and *Moby Dick*.

Under the dash was a stack of notebooks. Faith took a deep steadying breath. There was nothing tacky or obnoxious in sight. No soda-pop cans, no candy wrappers, no decals. No strange magazines. Just a clean, sort of cozy cab, driven by a clean, sort of cozy driver.

They passed through a crossroads. There was a rose-colored adobe house and a filling station. Beyond it, a dirt track led off across the sagebrush. Several people standing at the gas pumps waved at the trucker as he sped past, and he tooted his horn.

"That was Arthur and Mort," he said. "They run the Circle K out past Gold Hill. Mostly cattle, a few horses. We had the cattle-roping trials out there last year. Nice spread," he added, nodding slowly. She liked the way his voice always seemed to have a laugh floating around in it somewhere.

"Yeah. Nice place," he said again to the windshield.

She glanced at him again. He was smiling. Even though he kept his eyes on the road ahead, Faith got the feeling he was smiling at her.

"Do I pass?" he asked with a little laugh.

Faith let herself look at him directly. "What—what do you mean?" she whispered. Her voice felt scratchy from crying. She hiccoughed a little.

"You just gave me the once-over, didn't you? It's okay. I did the same to you. I have to be pretty careful, you know. There are a lot of crazy people on the road." He risked a quick glance at her, and Faith found herself smiling back. His eyes sparkled as his mouth curled up into his cheeks. "You don't look crazy to me," he added.

"I'm not. Not too crazy, anyway," Faith said softly.

"I'm Jeff, by the way. Jeff Warshasky. Where ya headed?"

Faith clenched her jaw. Where was she going? All she knew was she wanted to get as far away from Ted and Winnie as possible. Away from the fiasco of her ruined romantic getaway.

"Gosh," she said. "I—I guess I don't know. I just want to get away. I guess that does sound a little crazy," she said uncomfortably. "My name's Faith Crowley. I go to school up in Oregon," she murmured, looking back out the window at the flashing shapes along the road. They passed a large, jutting outcrop, its slanting ribbons of rock glowing vermilion in the sunset.

She guessed she'd head back to Springfield. Might as well console herself at home. "I—I guess I'll head home," she said finally. "Is there a bus station around here somewhere?"

Jeff nodded. "There's one down at Santa Clara.

It's off the highway about twenty miles, but I'm deadheading home, so that's okay. I could take you there. I live at Verde Flats, you know. Down toward the Wapatki reservation."

"Deadheading?"

"Yeah. Carrying nothing but air." He chuckled. "My dad owns the company, so he lets me take the jobs I want. I just dropped some avocados in Chaco. What a relief that's over! I hate hauling produce. You never know when the refrigeration is going to go out and you're stuck with forty thousand pounds of rotten, smelly carrots. I sweated all the way that I'd be left with guacamole before I unloaded."

He laughed again, and this time Faith joined in. He bobbed his head enthusiastically. "Hey, that's nice. Hearing you laugh," he said happily.

He *had* made her laugh, Faith suddenly thought. She hadn't laughed in a long time. A thin thread of joy snaked into her.

They sped east, the center line flashing past. A car passed them, gunning its engine as it cut in sharply to avoid an oncoming pickup.

"Idiot," Jeff muttered.

Faith pressed her back into the deeply cushioned seat. "So you drive this truck for a living?" she asked, a little shy.

He grinned. "Nah. I do this to earn money so I can go on and do what I want."

"And what's that?" she asked.

He hesitated, glancing quickly at her, his eyes serious. "You won't laugh?"

Faith shook her head. "I promise."

"You're sure?" he asked. He was smiling, but Faith could tell that whatever he was talking about was important.

"I *promise*," she said.

He reached over and grabbed one of the notebooks stacked under the tape deck. He handed it to her. "Here. Take a look."

Opening the first page, Faith was startled by the photograph. It showed a low, curved coffee table, polished so it shone with a deep reddish-brown gleam.

"I want to design and build furniture . . . like that," Jeff said in a soft voice.

"Wow," she said as she studied the picture. "This is beautiful. You *made* this? I like the way it seems to move and flow. It almost looks alive."

He sent her a sudden, intensely grateful look. "Yeah. That's what it's supposed to do! I designed it after I made a trip to the ocean last year. I'd never seen the ocean before. I just couldn't get over how it was always moving. So, when I got home, I picked up a piece of wood and started working with it. I think it turned out pretty."

Faith laughed at his humility. "So do I. The ocean in wood." If Ted had created something like *this*, he'd never stop talking about it. Deep inside somewhere, Faith didn't feel comfortable comparing Jeff to Ted. It felt disloyal.

Anger flashed through her again. Well, why shouldn't she compare Jeff to Ted? Hadn't Ted been comparing her to Winnie? And by the way he'd been behaving, it looked as though Faith had lost that contest.

Faith glanced again at Jeff. For a split second, their eyes met, and Faith felt a tug of sympathy from him. And warmth. "So, you want to head to Santa Clara to the bus station?" he asked again. He sounded eager, and a little shy at the same time. "No problem. I'll just mark the detour in my logbook. That way Dad will know where I was with his rig," he said. A small, dusty town appeared at the side of the road, and Jeff grabbed the gearshift, changing its position with a rapid flick of his hand. The gears changed pitch, and Faith felt the truck heave into a lower gear.

"That's nice of you," Faith commented. She nestled further into the deep seat, aware of the comforting way it supported her body.

"That's a swivel seat," Jeff said to her, dragging his fingers quickly through his curly hair. "Flip that lever at the front and it'll swing this way."

Faith succeeded in readjusting her seat, and smiled as it clicked into position facing Jeff. "Hey, this is great," she said. To her left, she was aware of a brown leather flap hanging down like a curtain. "What's this?" she asked. When she tapped it, it flapped a little inward.

"Uh—this is a sleeper cab," Jeff said, a red blush

stealing up his face. "That's my bed." He flicked her an embarrassed glance. They passed quickly through the small town, and Jeff shifted again. The truck roared as it gained speed. "There's a closet to the side and storage underneath the bed. Some rigs have refrigerators—even televisions in them."

"Wow! I never knew you could sleep in trucks," Faith said, peeking behind the curtain. A neatly made bed lay in the dark space. "That must save you a lot of money."

"Yep. Sleeper cabs have really helped operators keep traveling costs down. Hang on. Here's where we turn for Santa Clara."

The truck engine roared again as Jeff maneuvered around a sharp bend. A road sign pointed south. SANTA CLARA TWENTY MILES. QUINTA JUNCTION ONE HUNDRED MILES.

The light turned orange as the sun sank below the horizon, and the shadows of the rocks lengthened. Faith felt a sense of ease crawl into her as Jeff drove her southward, off the main highway toward Santa Clara and the bus station. Everything suddenly felt safe and right and comfortable. She was out . . . away from Ted. Maybe this hadn't been such a stupid thing to do after all.

In twenty minutes, Faith saw the twinkling lights of a town shimmering in the clear evening air. The truck engine roared as they began the descent into Santa Clara. The outskirts appeared, and then Faith realized with a sudden jolt that they were on the other side of the town. The bus station was off to one side of the road, and Jeff maneuvered his long trailer into a wide, gravel space under a lone streetlight. He kept the engine running, looked at her, studying her face closely. "Sure you want to go out on the local run? It takes six hours to get to Las Altas from here." His voice was soft, with the lilting sound of a smile in it somewhere. But his eyes were steady and concerned. They held hers for a long, slow minute.

She turned around to the window to eye the bus station, and her sensation of happiness wavered. The bus station was located in a cinder-block building painted a dirty shade of beige. The front was lined with big, paned windows and, through them, Faith saw dingy linoleum tile on the floor and a bare light-bulb hanging from the ceiling. There were two red seats with the stuffing coming out of them.

"It does look kind of lonely," she said in a small voice.

"Yeah. Santa Clara has a population of about thirty-five. And that's in the tourist season." Jeff laughed softly. Faith knew he was watching her. But she didn't know what else to do. She had to get back to Springfield. Didn't she? But waiting in that desolate bus station didn't appeal to her at all.

"Any suggestions?" she asked, her voice flat.

"Well," he said slowly, "since I'm heading home, I could run you down to Las Altas to pick up the direct coach north. It'd save you time. I mean, the local won't even get here till ten o'clock. And then they stop at every one-horse town between here and Las Altas."

Faith bristled with excitement. She turned again to face him, to see if he was serious, or if he was just offering her a ride out of sympathy and pity. But his eyes were shining and there was a big, happy grin on his face. He looked excited and eager, as if he really did want her to go with him.

She knew she wanted to go with him. He brushed his hand through his hair again. She smiled. "Will that be okay with your dad?"

"I'll give him a call on the radio and let him know what I'm doing." Jeff nodded quickly. "Well, what do you say?"

"If you're sure it's okay—" Faith hesitated. She wanted to be completely sure. It would take them a few more hours to get to Las Altas. If he changed his mind . . .

"All *right*!" Jeff whooped, grabbing his CB microphone from over his right shoulder and flicking on the set. "It's more than all right! It's stupendous!"

The crackle and hiss of the CB filled the cab. Jeff got his dad on the radio and told him their plans. *"Okay, Woody,"* the voice crackled. *"But get the truck back by ten A.M. sharp. You've got computer desks to take to Tucson. Over and out, Woody."*

Faith wrinkled her eyebrows at Jeff. "Woody?"

"That's my handle—you know, my CB name. My dad thinks it's pretty funny that I want to hang out with wood all the time. He thinks I like it because wood can't talk back," Jeff said as he rehung the microphone on its cord.

Faith laughed, feeling light and giddy. She'd get to spend more time with Jeff, as well as a free, comfortable ride to Las Altas. "Well, I think you're an artist. And you make the wood talk—it says just what you want it to say."

Jeff opened his eyes wide, and a flush stole up his cheeks. "Why, thank you. That's a nice thing to say . . . especially to a woodworker."

"Breaker. Breaker," the CB squawked. *"Lance, respond, you turkey. What do ya want?"*

A jolt of surprise stabbed into Faith. Jeff was busy negotiating the light pole and wasn't paying attention. When he reached his hand back to turn off the radio, Faith stopped him. "Wait a minute," she said urgently.

The voice on the radio was obviously calling Lance Putnam, the guy from Pinky's. She was curious.

Jeff shot Faith a smile. "Listen all you want. When you're done, flip that switch." He spun the steering wheel and guided the long trailer across the gravel lot in front of the bus station. The rig swung gracefully out onto the road and they headed back toward Las Altas.

"Jake, we've found them. We're heading up the Kanabi road. Get here fast. It's party time."

Faith gasped. That sounded like Lance Putnam had found Ted and Winnie. But how could they have?

Unless Ted and Winnie had headed back up the Kanabi cliff dwelling road and gotten themselves stuck in the mud, too. Or maybe they never went to get help. A flash of deep, hot fear exploded through her.

Lance's voice crackled again on the radio. *"I can see the yellow convertible parked in the turnout."*

Faith felt a wash of panic. "Oh, no!" she gasped. "That's Lance Putnam!" she gasped.

Jeff gave her a serious look. "You know that guy? He's a total jerk. His dad owns most of the valley. Their mining company has done some terrible damage up in the hills. They actually blew up an ancient ruin last year just to get a slim vein of silver."

Faith felt the pulsing fear heating her blood. Her face flamed and her hands were warm. "My friends and I sort of ran into him. He's mad at us."

Jeff frowned. "Not good. He's *not* the kind of guy anybody wants to mess with."

The CB squawked again. *"Jake, get here now! They're alone! I mean alone! Stuck on this hillside like sitting ducks,"* Lance's voice crowed.

"They've found them. Oh, Jeff. What are we going to do? My two girlfriends are alone up there! The car got stuck in a mud wash up on the cliff road. They've been waiting for help. I—I thought my other, er, friends would have gone back for them by now," Faith choked out.

Jeff sent her a quick, laserlike glance. "The ones you were running away from?"

She nodded, holding his quick gaze. Worry and

fear coiled together inside her.

Jeff gazed back down the highway. The headlights of the truck shone a long way ahead, lighting up bushes and scrub at the side of the empty road. Ahead, there was a wide turnoff. He slowed and steered carefully into it.

He parked, but once again kept the engine running. Turning slightly, he held Faith's gaze with his own. His eyes were filled with concern. "It would take us at least a half hour to get back where I picked you up. And there's no way I can make it up on the Kanabi road. Not in this rig."

"But we have to! There must be something we can do. Warn them! KC and Courtney are trapped up there. Who knows what Lance Putnam will do."

Jeff stared at her, his forehead wrinkled in concentration. He drew his hand slowly through his hair.

The CB squawked again. *"There they are! Revenge is oh, so sweet . . ."* The voice cut off suddenly, and Faith felt terror rise in her throat.

"Okay," Jeff said, rubbing his chin roughly with the side of his hand. He stared down at the dials on his dashboard. Suddenly, a dawning light flashed in his eyes. "Not to worry, Faith," Jeff said softly. He grabbed the microphone from its cord and flicked the button on the side. "I have an idea."

Seventeen

"Wait a minute, KC!" Courtney screamed, trying to focus down the winding road where headlights approached them. "That's not Ted's Jeep. Do you think it broke down?" Courtney sent KC a worried glance. Alarm flickered inside her.

KC peered through the diminishing light. "I—I don't know. I don't recognize—"

Courtney held her breath as a car disappeared around the bend just below them. She wondered why anyone would be out for a ride through the cliff area at night. She wouldn't feel safe climbing in the car with just anybody. Especially after what the Del Oro Spa manager had said about the lowlifes who drifted through the region.

The car reappeared around a bend in the Kanabi road about a half mile away. Courtney saw a flash of cream-colored paint. Below, another car appeared, moving fast up the mountain road in the first car's wake.

Courtney gasped. *That car!* she thought desperately. *I recognize that car!*

She knew KC was staring at her.

"What? Courtney, what's wrong?" KC insisted, fear making her voice ragged.

"Listen, KC." The sleek, cream-colored convertible eased around the bend in the road. "I—I think this may be Lance Putnam and his friends."

"What?" KC hissed. Her face was white in the shadows, color draining quickly from her cheeks. "Oh, God!"

Courtney scanned the hillside behind them for a place to hide. Only bare cliffs ran all the way along a ridge. Flat. Unwelcoming. Barren. They probably led to the cliff dwellings, which were supposed to be up around the next bend. Courtney swallowed, her parched throat closing over her panic. She looked to the side of the road where the turnoff ended. Beyond the flat, muddy patch of drying mud, the plateau dropped down for hundreds of yards through sagebrush, thorny cactus, sharp-limbed trees, and jagged rocks. There was no escape that way. They'd fall for sure, or get ripped to shreds.

Courtney darted a look back toward the ap-

proaching cars. There was no time. She could hear
the engines now, and laughter. The sports car flashed
its headlights across her face, then slowly, almost silently, it pulled behind Courtney's convertible. The
engine stopped, and a horrible stillness descended
over the mountainside. The light was almost gone as
the sun dropped below the horizon. There was a
vivid orange afterglow shining across the sky. It lit
the cliff behind the car with an eerie luminescence.

A tall, muscular blond guy eased out of the driver's seat. Courtney swallowed hard. It was Lance
Putnam. He was dressed in jeans and a dark-colored
long-sleeved sweater, and there was a thin smile on
his lips. From the passenger's seat rose the dark-
haired guy from Pinky's who'd defended Lance.

"Well, Jake. What have we here?" Lance Putnam
said as he strolled casually toward Courtney. She
backed away. His mouth took on an unpleasant twist.

Jake grinned and stepped toward KC. "Some
damsels in distress. Looks like we need to give them
some aid." He made a vicious sound that could have
been a laugh. The other car that been following
pulled in behind the convertible, its headlights flashing against the cliff wall. Three guys climbed out
and walked slowly up the slope toward them.

Courtney tried to keep calm. True, Winnie
hadn't been able to get away from Lance without
Ted punching the guy in the nose. But she was not
Winnie. She had more experience. And she knew
what this guy was capable of.

"We're just waiting for Ted to return with the tow truck. He'll be here any minute," Courtney managed. Her dry throat closed over the words, and needles of fear sliced through her. She was proud of herself. Her voice didn't even shake.

"Will he? You sure about that?" Lance whispered, stepping closer across a patch of caked mud. Courtney could see the black-and-blue bruise on his cheek from the fight with Ted. It made his smooth face look twisted and mean. "And where's little Ms. Winnie?" He reached out one hand and flicked Courtney under the chin. When Courtney didn't answer, he nodded his head. "Flo told me all about your trip up here. But she said you were bringing the whole crowd." He looked around in an exaggerated way, a look of mock surprise on his face. "I don't see anyone else."

"They're bringing help. They should be here any minute," Courtney bluffed. She was aware that Jake was moving close to KC.

"Right." Lance smiled. His face shone in the dim shadows, and the three guys behind him laughed. She remembered the way Lance and his gang had looked like hyenas in the parking lot of Pinky's. Now their glittering eyes resembled wolves'.

"Well, I don't think they're going to get here in time, do you, boys?" Lance said half over his shoulder.

"Nooooo!" the others crooned. Courtney backed up another step, and felt the bumper of her car jab into her legs.

Lance smiled menacingly at Courtney. "I didn't

appreciate what Winnie did to my car. I think you girls need to be taught a lesson. And I think we'll start with you," he said in a cold voice. "I think we'll send a little message. A message your little friend won't forget." He leaned forward, pressing Courtney's body against the hard surface of the car.

The guys behind Lance moved in, and Courtney felt hot, nauseating panic rise inside her. "Run! KC!" she screamed, tensing her muscles and shoving forward suddenly, trying desperately to catch Lance off guard. She collided roughly into him. It felt as if she'd just connected with a solid brick wall. His hands clamped around her arms, and he pulled her against him tightly.

"Look out!" Jake called, lunging past Lance toward KC. Courtney couldn't see her, but she heard a sudden intense struggle, then saw Jake dragging KC back. The three other guys moved forward as one, ringing Courtney and KC. Courtney was aware of their eyes, and smiling mouths as they strained forward.

The panic gripped her more tightly. She had to move, she told herself. She had to get away. Tightening her muscles suddenly, she clenched her arms and twisted her body to one side. Her right foot stabbed out, and her hiking boot sank into Lance's leg.

"Ooof!" he groaned.

Lance yanked Courtney against him even tighter, his fingers digging into her arms. "And you won't forget this evening, either," he whispered. Then his mouth came down hard on hers.

*   *   *

Ted was desperate.

The highway flowed out in front of him like a gray snake, a pale-yellow center line streaming down the middle. He'd been following the truck for miles, but somehow, he'd lost it. The road and the white pool of his own headlights lay before him, frustrating his search for Faith and the truck she'd escaped in.

"We've lost them!" he shouted.

"But they couldn't have just disappeared. I mean, that truck was the size of a drive-in bank!" Winnie moaned.

Ted slammed his hands on the steering wheel. "I can't believe she went off with a trucker!"

When he'd watched Faith climb into that truck cab, he felt as if he were watching someone else's life. Faith couldn't just walk away from him like that. Could she? Endangering herself just to prove a stupid point? To get back at him for flirting with Winnie? It was like a curtain had been pulled back on his life . . . and he felt guilt and regret at what he saw.

But when he'd tried to follow the truck, speeding down the highway in its wake, he finally realized that Faith had left, that she'd rather risk riding with a stranger than staying with him. And Winnie.

Suddenly, he saw an isolated blue sign with a silver phone on it. Underneath sat a booth with all its windows broken. He shot a quick look at Winnie. She nodded. Her face was pale and strained. They hadn't spoken much as they drove. He knew how she felt. Words seem to stick in his throat when he thought about Faith.

He prayed the phone still worked. It looked as if everyone within a hundred miles took potshots at it. "All right. Plan B," he muttered. He steered the Jeep off the side of the road and hopped out. "You have any change?" he barked at Winnie.

Ted jogged to the booth and yanked out the tattered phone book that was attached by a rusty chain under the little shelf. He started dialing numbers. He punched quarters into the phone, called emergency numbers, the police, the sheriff. He called rescue squads as far away as Las Altas. A half hour later, he was still punching quarters into the pay phone. "Are you sure?" he asked. His voice was hoarse from talking. "That's the right license number. I'm sure of it." He was talking to a woman from the transportation department.

"I'm sorry, sir. But if the driver has done nothing illegal we can't trace his registration."

"But my girlfriend went with him!" Ted yelled.

The voice on the other end paused for a moment. "I'm sorry." *Click.*

Ted banged the receiver down so hard, the phone booth jumped.

"I can't believe this!" he wailed. "I can't believe no one can trace this guy. I can't believe I let her go."

He pounded once on the metal frame of the booth. Winnie stared at him from the dim interior of the Jeep. All he could see were two wide eyes, and the flash of ruby red as her bowling jacket caught the headlights of a passing car. Ted felt a sudden flood of guilt. It was overpowering. Tears stung his eyes, and he brushed them away angrily. Why did he *always* do this? Why couldn't he get it right? He was always screwing up a good thing, and Faith was the best thing to ever happen to him.

He heard a scuffle of footsteps, and turned to see Winnie crossing the dusty patch of roadside. She stepped up to him and cocked her head to one side, her mouth curving down in an unhappy frown. "Hey, Ted," she said, her voice filled with grief. "I know how you feel."

"Do you?" he mumbled. He crossed his arms tightly against his chest.

He didn't believe anyone else could possibly feel the utter hopelessness he felt.

"I always screw up everything," she went on in a flat voice. "Hurricane Winnie, that's what you should call me. Everything I touch turns into total, utter, complete chaos." She jammed her hands into the side pockets of her bowling jacket, hunching her shoulders in a tight shrug.

Ted looked at her for a minute, then eased forward past the narrow frame of the booth. "Well, feeling sorry for ourselves isn't going to get us anywhere. We can only pray Faith is all right. I guess we better track down a tow truck and see if we can pull Courtney's car out of that mud."

He trudged toward the Jeep, crawled into the

driver's seat, waited for Winnie to climb in, then started the engine. He turned the Jeep west, back toward the Kanabi cliff dwellings road. Away from Faith. He felt a black emptiness bigger and wider and darker than any the desert could offer.

"Get away from me!" KC screamed as Lance slid his hand under her shirt. His fingers were sticky on her bare skin. Jake grabbed her shoulder and pinned her back onto the ground. She felt the caked mud slide against her. Courtney was screaming, too. Two of the other guys were holding her between them. KC kicked out with her foot, and tried to pull away from Lance's probing hands.

"Let her go!" Courtney yelled, kicking out at the guy holding her.

"You'll get your chance, baby," Lance muttered, trying to get his weight on top of KC. All KC could think of was not letting him wedge her against the ground. If he did, she'd be doomed.

She kicked up with her knee just as Lance moved onto her, and he swore loudly. "You bitch!" he yelled, his hands moving up her shirt.

KC yanked hard against Jake's hands as they pressed her harder against the ground. His fingers dug into her skin, and she cried out in pain. Then, suddenly, the pressure eased, and Jake and Lance charged up. KC struggled forward. *Oh, no!* she thought. *They're going after Courtney!*

Courtney stood there, staring at KC, her eyes

wide and frightened. It seemed suddenly as if everything had stopped. Lance and Jake were standing close together, talking. The other guys huddled around them tightly. KC frowned in confusion, clutching her arms across her body. She was trembling so violently, she couldn't stand.

Then KC heard it.

A siren. She heard a siren, bouncing off the walls of the cliffs behind them, echoing through the evening.

The police! she thought. Could it be the police? Way up here? Had Ted and Faith and Winnie finally reached help?

Courtney ran to KC. "Are you okay?" she asked desperately.

KC nodded. Chills rolled over her, and she was weak. She sank to the ground. Courtney slid down beside her.

Lance and his friends tightened their huddle as the siren got closer. They cast worried looks at KC and Courtney. KC didn't care. All she cared about was that the police were coming. They could tell them about Lance and his horrible gang. KC let out a ragged sigh. She'd finally get off this mountain.

The siren was drawing closer, and as KC watched, the guys fell apart and began strolling around the pullout area as if they were enjoying the scenery. Within a couple of minutes, a police Jeep sped around the last bend and came to a roaring stop just behind the last car in the little line.

It really was the police! KC felt weak with relief.

A policewoman with short, curly dark hair got out and cast a quick but thorough look around the group. Her partner joined her.

Courtney let out a long, slow breath. It wasn't Joe. This guy was short, stocky, with round gray eyes and a friendly smile.

"Well, Mr. Putnam, isn't it?" the officer said, a big smile on his round face. The insignia on his hat matched the seal on the door of the Jeep.

"Howdy, Sheriff Cook. It's been a long time," Lance said in a smooth voice. KC stared at Lance in the growing darkness. He'd switched from savage to suave in the bat of an eye.

The policewoman eyed KC and Courtney. They sat side by side, their backs against the convertible door. "What's been going on here?" she said. Her voice was sharp.

KC opened her mouth to speak, but Lance Putnam spoke quickly, "A little party, Officer," he murmured. "We're legal."

Sheriff Cook nodded, pointing to his partner. "This is Officer Fremont. State Police. We were heading back from a trial in Phoenix when—"

"Can I see your license?" Officer Fremont interrupted, eyeing Lance.

Lance grinned. "Of course, Officer," he crooned. KC watched in amazement as he slid his hand to his back pocket and drew out his wallet. If she hadn't known better, she could have sworn he hadn't a care in the world. He was acting as if he'd been enjoying a quiet evening on the hillside, watching the sunset.

Officer Fremont examined Lance's license carefully. KC noticed the other guys exchanging worried looks. Jake had dropped back toward the cream convertible and hovered near the door.

"We got a call from a trucker saying two girls might be in some trouble up here." Officer Fremont cast a curious look at KC and Courtney. Then she turned to look directly at Lance. "You know anything about that, Mr. Putnam?"

Lance laughed lightly. He looked straight into the officer's eyes, shaking his head slowly. With one hand, he casually brushed the dust off his jeans. "No, ma'am. Actually, we were just getting ready to head out. Just spotted a western diamondback. Thought it'd be a good time to relocate the party. Freaked the girls out a little."

He cast a sharp look back at them, and KC froze. The sheriff reached forward and patted Lance on the arm. "How's your daddy? Haven't seen him in a while."

The policewoman gave the sheriff a disgusted look.

"Why, he's just fine, Sheriff," Lance purred in a singsong voice. "He'll be pleased you asked about him. I'll make sure I let him know, too."

KC's jaw tightened. The message was clear. *Be nice to me, and I'll make sure my dad's nice to you.* "The only trouble, Sheriff, is Courtney's car here. A gully washer sort of did a number on those tires."

Lance laughed and pointed to the mud-encrusted tires. The sheriff laughed, too. The policewoman crossed her arms.

"Well, boys," the sheriff chuckled, "we'll take care of it, if you want to be on your way. Looks like a false alarm," the sheriff finished, giving Lance a sunny smile.

"Now, wait a minute, John," the policewoman began. But she was cut off by the sheriff.

"Officer Fremont here is new to the area, Lance," the sheriff went on deliberately. "She doesn't know all the ropes yet." He sent Lance an apologetic smile.

Lance nodded, and a charming smile lit up his face. KC swallowed hard over her dry throat. She didn't believe this! He looked like a fraternity president greeting new pledges on a Friday night. He held out his hand toward Officer Fremont, his manner silky and smooth. Reluctantly, Officer Fremont shook it slowly.

"Welcome." He beamed. "I hope you enjoy the area. I guess we'll hit the road, then. Good night, Sheriff Cook. Officer Fremont." He turned, and KC gasped as she saw the smile vanish. A cold, angry expression settled onto his features. "Good night, uh, Courtney. KC. See you soon. I *hope*."

KC swallowed in fear, but as he turned and walked toward his car, the fear was replaced by a surge of relief. Lance and Jake climbed into the sports car, and the other three guys piled into their car. Within minutes, the two cars disappeared down the road, and the sheriff nodded and rubbed his hands together. "Now, ladies," he said, examining the back tires of the car. "Looks like you could use some help."

KC and Courtney struggled up. "Oh, thank you, Sheriff," KC blurted, steadying her cramped legs against the side of Courtney's car. "They—they—"

The sheriff raised his hand. "Now, now. Let's see what we can do to get this old beauty out of the mud."

KC shot Courtney an angry glance. Courtney shook her head slowly. It looked as if the power of the Putnams had done its work again.

"Let's winch it to the rear axle, John," Officer Fremont said in a matter-of-fact voice. "Are you sure you're okay?" The officer walked toward the trunk of Courtney's car and stood staring at them for a moment.

KC nodded, feeling limp. "Yes, thanks. Just a little tired and thirsty. We've been out here all day."

Officer Fremont's eyes opened wide. "Well, no wonder you look so strung out. There's some water in the Jeep. If you could open the trunk, I'll make sure John here doesn't rip the back end of your car off."

The sheriff laughed. "I've been pullin' cars out of these gullies since before you were born."

Officer Fremont gave the sheriff a patient smile, while Courtney clattered her keys into the lock and flipped open the trunk.

Suddenly, KC was aware of silence. Utter silence. Even the breeze rustling through the pine trees and sagebrush had stopped for a moment.

What was wrong? She spun back to look at Courtney and froze.

Courtney turned slowly to look at KC. Her eyes were wide with shock and fear.

The parcel! She'd forgotten about the parcel! Her breath clogged tightly in her chest. Maybe the officer would ignore it. After all, it just looked like a regular box she could be mailing to anyone. The breeze picked up again, whistling through the pine trees. The air was filled with the biting scent of pine and sage. In the distance, a coyote howled. Maybe she wouldn't even notice it, KC thought.

Officer Fremont turned her head slowly toward Courtney as KC hurried to her side. "Excuse me, Courtney?"

Courtney executed her best sorority smile. "Yes, Officer?"

"What is this?" Officer Fremont spoke, then reached into the trunk and pulled out the parcel. Courtney hesitated.

"Souvenir paperweights," KC said quickly.

At the same time, Courtney said, "Turquoise jewelry."

They stared at each other, matching expressions of horror on their faces. Officer Fremont cocked her head to one side. "Oh, really. You girls better get your stories straight. Hey, John."

The sheriff appeared from under the car. "What? I got it—" He stopped when he saw the box.

"A search, I think," Officer Fremont said calmly.

The sheriff nodded. "Absolutely."

KC felt frozen. The fear that had disappeared when Lance drove away came back and slammed her in the chest. She felt sick. They were in real trouble now. What would happen to them? What if it was drugs or forged money or some other kind of loot? KC swallowed again, her throat closing over her breath so tightly that she felt as if she were suffocating.

Horror-stricken, she watched as the officer took out a penknife and sliced open the wrapping. She was being meticulous about the edges. Making sure not to destroy any evidence, KC thought miserably.

The box opened, and the officer sunk her hand into fuzzy wrapping material. KC held her breath. The officer pulled something out, moving slowly, gently. In her hand was a dark-brown, ridged piece of pottery.

KC let out her breath thankfully. What a relief! It was just an old piece of some ancient pot. Grady was an anthropologist. Of course he'd be passionate about crusty bits of clay!

KC grinned at Courtney, but the grin froze on her face when she caught sight of the officer's expression. The woman looked like one of those thunderclouds that had passed over earlier in the day. Her eyes were filled with hostility, and they were looking right at KC.

"What's wrong, Officer?" KC managed.

"Ever heard of the Antiquities Preservation Act?" The woman's voice was like ice.

"N-no."

"Well, the law prevents anyone from removing antiquities from their place of origin. This piece is an artifact, in case you didn't already know that."

"B-but . . ."

"It's early, too. Before the migration, by the look of it. And you're trying to remove it. Right?"

KC's chest tightened painfully. It felt as if the world had just collapsed on top of her. Trust? She felt the fragile chips of trust shatter inside her again. Like the fragments of the old, fired clay, crumbling into bits before her eyes.

The sheriff and Officer Fremont exchanged a long look. KC could see some kind of agreement pass back and forth between them. The cold night air dried the sweat along KC's neck.

Officer Fremont turned slowly toward Courtney and KC. "You're under arrest," she said bluntly. "Both of you."

Eighteen

*I*t was like being in a moving cocoon, Faith thought. The road passed under them like a flashing, gray conveyor belt. From her seat in the cab, Faith felt as if she were gliding above the road, above her worries, above her anger at Ted and Winnie. Above everything. Jeff Warshasky guided the long rig expertly along the highway toward Las Altas so she could get a direct bus back to Springfield. And she felt as if she were flying.

She shot Jeff a quick glance in the darkened cab. They'd talked about books they'd read, movies they liked, places they wanted to go. Jeff's gray eyes shone with happiness, and he hummed a tune along with the country-western tape that was playing softly. He tapped long fingers on the steering wheel. Faith smiled. "So, you'll be able to get the truck back to your dad by ten o'clock tomorrow morning? You're sure?" Faith asked. She wouldn't want his offer to take her to Las Altas to get him into trouble.

Jeff grinned at the windshield. "Are you kidding? This rig can really move when I want it to. Five-hundred-horsepower engine."

"Really?" she asked, wondering what exactly that meant.

He laughed and drew his hand threw his curly hair. "That means powerful," he said, sending her a warm look. "I'll get back to Verde Flats in record time. Then I'll haul those precious computer desks to the moon if I have to."

Faith nodded and laughed, feeling his warm smile wash over her. "I think your dad said Tucson."

They'd chatted easily about Jeff's life on the road, about how much truck drivers enjoy driving, and Faith found herself envying his freedom. He was always moving, seeing new places, new people. He told her about a crowd of Japanese travelers near the Grand Canyon. They'd never seen a truck like his before and wanted to look inside, so he gave them a guided tour. They'd crawled all over the cab, even taking pictures of the steering wheel. Jeff laughed at the memory. He laughed a lot.

His whole life seemed like that, generous, good-natured, and fun.

Suddenly, Faith didn't want to go home. She'd

come on this trip to try to capture something. She wasn't even sure what it was. But she knew it still eluded her, drifting just beyond her vision like one of those desert mirages. She might not be able to define it, but she knew she wasn't going to discover it by going home, by running away.

"I'm not sure I want to go home," she said into the darkness.

Faith could feel Jeff pause, his breath sort of hanging in the air. "What do you want, then, Faith?" Jeff asked softly. The truck rolled forward, the tires humming their low-pitched whine, the headlights piercing the murky blackness on either side of the road.

"I—I don't know. I just know I don't want to leave, not just yet. I'm still trying to find something. Something really special. Maybe even extraordinary. A few hours, that's all. A few hours I'll always remember," she said.

Jeff nodded in the dim light that his dials cast on his face. Faith watched as a slow smile grew. He turned and gave her a soft look, his eyes full of tenderness. "I know. And . . . I think you deserve it. There's an area to the south, sort of a small version of the Painted Desert. The rocks lie all over the place like the bones of some giant. And they're iridescent. At night, they send off these amazing colors," he whispered. "Want to see it?"

"Sure," Faith heard herself saying. "I'd love to."

"Okay." Jeff nodded, another brilliant smile lighting his eyes. "The turnoff's just east of here, right before we get to Las Altas. We'll be there in time for the last of the sun. You know, when the colors sort of explode above the horizon."

Within a half hour, they'd made it to a flat, open expanse of rocks. Faith crawled out of the cab, stretching her legs down toward the ground about five feet below her. She was feeling sort of numb and cramped. But as she climbed down, the heat from the ground coiled up her legs, relaxing her, soothing her. She turned toward the flat area beside the truck.

Brilliant azure, emerald, and sapphire-colored stones lay scattered across a plain of whitish dirt. The heat of the day still shimmered in the air, and Faith took in a low, deep breath. The petrified minerals, trapped in large stumplike blocks, gleamed and shone like huge gems scattered across a table.

There were lavender-colored rocks and ones that looked like bronze. Faith sat on the wide step of the cab and stared. "It's as if a rainbow fell down here to rest," she murmured, spellbound by the extraordinary beauty of the rocks.

Jeff had crossed in front of the truck and now sat down beside her. A deep-rose light lined the horizon in a wide band. Then it turned to gold. Then bronze. The rocks began to glow and vibrate with colors.

Faith watched silently, feeling a deep calm meet her. Her heart seemed to open, and her worries faded away like the setting sun. This was what she'd been waiting for, searching for. One spectacular sunset. A color and light show beyond her wildest dreams. A quiet comforting silence surrounding her, allowing her to have her dreams. An open space.

Jeff slipped his arm around her shoulder, and she leaned back. He didn't speak, and neither did she. The light changed again and the rocks continued to shimmer with their own special magic.

This was what she'd hoped to find. Her spring break with Ted was supposed to have felt like this, this wonderful, this unforgettable. This feeling she didn't want to lose.

A real jail cell. KC couldn't believe it.

The smell of dirty clothes and alcohol pervaded the air of the tiny two-room jail. KC stared at the small window above her head where the stars burned brightly in the night sky. They looked like a painted backdrop to the miserable cell.

Officer Fremont had driven KC and Courtney down the mountain after the police Jeep had pulled Courtney's car out of the gully. Sheriff Cook drove the convertible. And now KC lay on a narrow cot crammed against the wall of a jail cell.

Her jeans were caked with mud, and her shirt was torn. Across from her, Courtney looked just as bad. There was a long tear running down the side of her expensive slacks. Dust and grime covered her cotton blouse.

Beyond the barred door of their cell, there was a small open area and another door leading to the outer office where Officer Fremont was filling out a report. KC stared up at the dirty ceiling where one bare lightbulb shone. Her muscles felt like lead, and her clothes were sticky and stiff.

The outer door creaked open, and KC raised herself on one elbow. Officer Fremont was heading for them, her hat on her head and a notebook in her hands. "You'll spend the night here, while we get the evidence analyzed. You'll have to be charged in the morning. The judge went on a fishing trip."

KC struggled up off the cot. She shoved her hair back off her shoulder and crossed to the bars on the door. She gripped them with shaking fingers. "But, Officer, someone gave me that package. It's not mine!"

"So you say. But as you refuse to say who gave it to you, you'll have to be charged as the owner. Unless you want to tell me now who gave it to you? Well?" Officer Fremont's gray eyes bore into KC's. KC looked away. "I didn't think so," the officer snapped. She scribbled a note in her book. KC had a sinking feeling in her stomach that the list of charges against them was getting longer by the minute.

"It was in your possession, young lady. And that's all that matters," Officer Fremont said in an expressionless voice.

"But it should be taken to Las Altas," KC said desperately. "It's important!"

Courtney rose from her narrow cot and joined KC at the front of their cell. "Maybe you could call someone, verify that she's telling the truth," Courtney said wearily.

Officer Fremont set her jaw. Wordlessly, she shook her head.

"Listen," Courtney went on. "My father will be furious when he hears what you've done. Locking us up like a pair of criminals. I need to call him again. There was no answer in his office before. I'm sure he'll send an attorney from Santa Fe or Tucson."

The policewoman let a little smile curve her mouth. "At ten o'clock? I don't think so. Important parents and friends can't help you. The law's clear. You've been caught transporting protected objects." She sent a quick, serious look at KC, then turned on her heel and walked out.

"Please!" KC called after her.

Courtney huffed out a breath and collapsed onto her cot. "Oh, KC. I can't believe this. It's a nightmare!"

KC fell onto her cot and jabbed her hands behind her head. She felt so alone, so desperate, so empty. Emptier than she'd ever felt. Even when Brooks died and people suspected her, it didn't feel like this. This was black and deep and scary. Back then, she knew she was innocent. But this time, she was guilty . . . she guessed.

And just when she'd actually made a step forward—a step toward trusting someone. Of trusting Grady. And this is where it landed her. Not just humiliated and betrayed. But in *jail*!

"I can't believe there was stolen pottery in that box. I can't believe it!" KC shouted, yanking her hands from behind her head and slamming them against the wall.

Courtney leaned up on one elbow and faced her. KC looked at her sadly. And her trusting Grady hadn't just landed her in this mess. Courtney was in it with her.

"Well, the evidence speaks for itself," Courtney said. There were dark circles under her eyes, and her hair was sticky and flat.

KC flopped back onto the thin mattress. "Yeah, I guess it does. I just keep telling myself that Grady wouldn't do something like that. Wouldn't set me up. But I guess he did." KC felt heavy despair pressing on her, weighing her down. "I thought I could trust him," she added miserably.

Courtney sniffed, brushed her bedraggled hair away from her face, and leaned back against the wall.

KC rubbed her hands across her face. "I don't know why it was so important to get that piece of pottery to Dr. Sanchez in Las Altas. It doesn't make any sense."

Courtney leaned her elbows forward on her knees and plunked her chin into her palms. "Maybe he was going to sell it. I think there's quite a black market in artifacts."

KC felt the questions rolling around in her tired brain. "And what happened to Faith and Ted—and Winnie?" she asked suddenly, pushing away the thoughts of Grady's betrayal. She sat up and faced Courtney. "I can't believe that they'd just leave us out there, either." KC shook her head.

"I don't know, KC. I guess the Jeep broke down. All I know is I want to get out of here," Courtney murmured, curling herself sideways again to lie down.

In the outer office, voices murmured. KC heard the clanking of keys and the scrape of a chair. She stood up and paced across the small cell. Her head was beginning to throb and her eyes burned.

Somewhere beyond the door that led to the outer office, a man's voice called out. Then there were more sounds of activity. Chairs thumped. A door slammed again. Footsteps bumped across the floor, back and forth, back and forth.

The door leading into their little room creaked open and KC heard footsteps draw near, then stop. She heard Courtney gasp. KC turned to see who stood there. It was the officer from the spa! He was dressed in the same khaki uniform, his badge shining on his pocket, the gun positioned at his belt. He stared at Courtney, a horrified look on his face.

KC glanced quickly at Courtney. She stared back, all the color draining from her face. She looked as if she was about to faint.

"Interesting prisoners we're getting these days," he said, his voice cold.

Courtney wrinkled her forehead. "Joe? What are you doing here?" she whispered.

Joe pulled back his shoulders. His blue-black hair shone under the harsh overhead lights. "My shift. I get to watch you. According to the report, you're pothunters. Stealing rare and precious antiquities to sell to the highest bidder." His voice had grown sharp, and his eyes were like two black pieces of coal. KC swallowed hard. Grady had mentioned pothunters, hadn't he? That first night when she met him back at the Cactus Cottage Motel, when they'd talked under the stars. It seemed like a lifetime ago.

Officer Fremont's voice called from the outer office, "Joe! Sign in so I can go home! I locked up the evidence. Come on!"

Joe nodded brusquely to Courtney and walked out.

"I can't believe this!" Courtney wailed. KC watched her. Tears pooled in her eyes and slid down her cheeks. KC struggled against her own tears.

Outside, a car engine revved and sped out of the dusty parking lot surrounding the small jail. A deep and heavy silence fell, and KC collapsed on the cot again. She might as well try to get some sleep. She was weary all the way to her toes. What were they going to do? And what would Grady think when he found out that she'd never made it to Las Altas?

Suddenly, the door swung open again to the outer office. Footsteps hurried to the cell.

"KC Angeletti, right?" Joe whispered.

KC struggled up to face Joe. "Yes?" His face was filled with concern and urgency instead of coldness.

Joe looked left, then right, then quickly pulled an envelope out of his pocket. It had already been opened. "Here. This envelope was in the box. It's addressed to a Dr. Carlos Sanchez, but I think maybe you should read it."

KC grabbed the envelope through the bars. She stared at Joe, but he wasn't looking at her. He was staring at Courtney, the cold expression gone. In its place was a soft, sort of sad look.

Courtney's tired cheeks were washed with a pale blush. Their eyes locked, and then Joe hurried out the door again. Courtney smiled slowly, then turned her head toward KC. "What is it?" she asked.

KC's fingers trembled as she slid the letter out of the opened envelope. Her eyes passed quickly over the paper. "It's a letter to Dr. Sanchez, all right," KC said. She felt a sudden stab of excitement and curiosity.

"*Dear Doc,*" she read out loud. "*Our suspicions about the Las Altas end of the cave formations is right on! But it's urgent, I repeat urgent, that you call a meeting of the Antiquities Preservation Society and propose setting aside the whole sector. The Mesa Alta caves are in danger. There is one cave that is filled, I mean filled, with potsherds and fragments. But further in, there is a perfectly preserved cavern, stuffed with artifacts. I found it by accident.*

"*There is a gigantic problem. The Putnam organization is already doing preliminary blasting. There is a small vein of gold running through the roof of one of the outer caves. The Putnams want it. They'll blow up the whole mountain to get it, too. You and I know it. They've done it before. Unless we do something, this major discovery will be blasted to oblivion before we can even catalogue it, let alone preserve it.*

"I found the fragments just about a week ago. They are the evidence we need to take to the Department of the Interior and the Society. I had a whole collection of different pieces, but Lance Putnam and his buddies followed me one night and roughed me up when they discovered where I'd been working."

KC looked at Courtney, who'd sat up straight and was staring at her from her cot, her brown eyes huge. "My God, Courtney!" KC gasped. "The night I was supposed to meet him at Casa Linda. Remember? He didn't show up. Those goons from Pinky's beat him up!"

Courtney nodded quickly. "I remember."

KC went back to the letter. *"I had to go back and get another piece, missing an important appointment."*

KC's heart zigzagged. That's what he was doing. She thought he'd stood her up, left her out there with the cliff dwellings and the ghosts and the owls. But he hadn't stood her up at all. He was getting the precious piece of pottery to send to Dr. Sanchez. Trying to find something to preserve.

"I was afraid Lance would follow me, so I couldn't bring this piece along myself. I've sent along the fragment with the only person I can trust, the only person who understands the importance of what we're doing here. KC Angeletti."

KC let her eyes meet Courtney's. He trusted her. More than anyone. She felt as if the blazing desert sun had just been turned on full blast in her heart.

Nineteen

"Faith, I can't believe I did this to you," Winnie said to herself as she dangled her feet over the side of an immense chasm. Across a black pit of space rose the block shapes of cliff houses crawling up the side of the mountain. They were lit up by the Jeep's headlights.

Ted and she had driven back up the Kanabi cliff dwellings road. They'd given up finding Faith, so they'd decided to go back and help KC and Courtney. But KC and Courtney weren't where they'd left them, so Winnie suggested checking out the Kanabi ruins.

She could relate to ruins. After all, wasn't that what was left of her friendship with Faith? Winnie squinted slightly against the glare of the headlights.

She and Ted sat on the edge of the canyon that separated the parking lot from the huge cliff settlement. It was immense. The houses ran five and six stories high. Giant blocks of golden bricks marched up the side of the canyon like some adobe Lego construction.

"Do you think KC and Courtney got that car out by themselves?" Winnie asked Ted, her voice flat. "I mean, where could they have gone?"

She gave Ted a quick glance. He looked worried too, as he sat staring at the desolate houses and rooms with an unfocused gaze.

"I don't know, Winnie!" Ted burst out. "I—I don't even know where Faith is! How am I supposed to know where KC and Courtney went? This country swallows up people whole."

Winnie nodded grimly. This whole mess was *her* fault. It wasn't Faith's fault for being uptight. Or Ted's for picking up on her signals. Or anybody's fault. It was *her* fault. She stared at the empty black windows of the cliff houses. They looked like accusing eyes. She bit her lip.

"I should just jump off this cliff," she muttered. "All I seem able to do is screw everything up. All I seem to do is throw myself into situations where other people get shattered."

The silence hung in the air. Ted crossed his arms and remained silent. He was probably mad at her, too.

"Listen, Ted," Winnie went on. "I'm sorry if I sort of dragged you into my mess."

The crickets chirped loudly from the trees beside

them. In the canyon, an owl hooted. Through the headlight beams, Winnie saw bats swooping. They squeaked as they dove for bugs.

"Sometimes, I don't know why I do things. I just *do* them. And I guess I don't think ahead. I don't think about other people," Winnie said.

Ted shot her a quick look. His mouth was set in a hard line. "Hey, Winnie. Don't beat yourself up. It was as much my fault as it was yours." He struggled back from the side of the chasm and stepped back to lean against the Jeep. Winnie looked up at him. His face twisted in agony. "I didn't exactly ignore you, did I? I can't believe myself! I do this kind of thing all the time! You'd think I'd learn. You'd think I'd get a clue!" He turned and pounded his fists on the hood of the Jeep.

"I just can't believe it. I can't believe I reacted the way I did." He put his head down on his hands.

Winnie felt a swirling chaos inside her. Ted could shout all he wanted about it being his fault. But it wasn't. She knew it. She'd started it. She'd kept it up. She'd pushed until he responded to her. That was all there was to it. And her best, most loyal friend in the whole world paid for it.

"I will never forgive myself if anything happens to her," Ted went on. "All I can do is pray she's okay." He hung his head. "I know she'll never forgive me."

Winnie scooted back away from the cliff. She tugged her bowling jacket around her. The night air chilled her all the way through to her bones. She crossed to Ted. "She might. She's the most forgiving person in the entire world. Maybe she'll forgive you," Winnie whispered. Her voice shook. "But me? No way. I'll *never* be able to make up for what I've done to her. I've done something no real friend would ever do." Winnie brushed her hand across her eyes.

Ted looked up, and Winnie could see tears shining in his eyes.

"I know," he whispered.

Winnie glanced back across the canyon toward the cliffs. They seemed so sad. They were like a mockery of a living village. Winnie sighed a deep, ragged sigh. Her flirting with Ted had made a mockery of her friendship with Faith. She saw that now.

And Faith? Would Faith ever be able to talk to her, to joke about her junk-food binges and her tacky jewelry? Would she ever go for a manic Winnie jog again? Or a midnight run to the snack bar for corn chips and Twinkies?

Winnie felt the slow trickle of tears down her checks, and she brushed them away with her satin sleeve. She'd beg her if she had to. All she knew was that she'd do anything, anything at all to make it up to Faith.

"Well," Winnie said slowly. She gazed out across the cliffs. They sent deep shadows into the crevices of the ancient town. "We should go to Las Altas. Don't you think? I mean, that's where KC's grandmother lives. And she had that box to deliver. And . . ." She hesitated, looking into Ted's weary face. "The truck Faith got in was headed east."

Ted shook his head. "Faith may be back in Springfield for all we know." He climbed in the front seat and slapped his back against the seat. Winnie crawled into the passenger seat, curling sideways to face the driver's side.

"Yeah. I guess she could've headed home," Winnie said, trying to get comfortable.

Ted flicked off the headlights and the quiet darkness enveloped them. "Okay," he said. "Tomorrow, we head for Las Altas and the university. We see if we can track down KC and Courtney." He paused. "And we pray like crazy that we find Faith. If she's not there, we head back to Springfield."

Winnie nodded, pulling a sleeping bag from behind her and tossing it over her legs. The night air was getting cold. The owl in the canyon hooted again. "Okay. Sounds good," she said. "I'm going to try to get some sleep. See ya in the morning." She hunched her shoulder into the seat.

"Yeah," Ted said. He reached back and grabbed Faith's sleeping bag, held it in his hands for a few minutes, then slowly tucked it in around his legs, holding the top against his cheek.

Winnie sniffed as she closed her eyes.

Courtney felt as if she was drifting. Then, slowly, her feet began to slide into dark, sticky mud. Deeper and deeper she sank. Snakes hissed from the sides of the dry streambed. The mud closed in. It crawled up her legs. It was slimy and hot. Suddenly, it cracked open, and she was free. She had to escape the mud. Plunging forward, she stumbled and slid over the parched ground. She saw her car. She climbed in and sped off toward some tall mountains, blazing fiery red in the hot sun. Behind her, she heard screams and shouts. A tangle of guys in a sports car sped after her. Closer. Closer. Her car slowed. Suddenly, they hurled gold nuggets at her, denting the convertible. One hit her in the back of the head. She screamed as the car swerved.

"Ahh!" Courtney opened her eyes. She was gasping for air. What? Where? Sweat poured off her forehead. She was sticky and hot. Where was she? It was dark. She drew herself up onto her elbow and looked around, blinking. Across a small space was another cot. KC. Jail.

"Are you okay?" a concerned voice called in the darkness.

She flinched, startled, then squinted through the dimness toward the cell door. "Joe?" Courtney rasped. A dim figure stood in the area outside the cell.

"Yeah, it's me. Are you okay? You screamed."

She crawled out of the cot. Her muscles ached, and her clothes were stiff with mud. She felt grimy and miserable.

"I—I had a dream," she whispered. She reached the bars on the door. They shone with a horrible metallic gleam. Her dream had frightened her. Her heart thudded in her chest. "Oh, Joe," she murmured, reaching her hand through the bars.

He grabbed her hand tightly, holding it firmly in his. His skin was cool and dry. She drew up the palm to her face and laid it against her skin. She remembered how his hand felt in hers when they danced at Pinky's. She remembered the intense, intelligent look in his eyes.

His other hand came up and stroked her hair back from her face. The bar stopped his hand, and Courtney leaned closer, resting her forehead against the metal.

"Oh, Joe," she wept. "I'm so scared." All her confidence had vanished. Her competent ease couldn't stand up to the thirst and hunger she'd felt earlier, or to Lance Putnam and his goons, or to being locked away in a dingy jail. She used to think she could master any situation. But now, she was just weak and vulnerable. "How did all this happen? Why do I suddenly feel as if I'm falling apart?" she whispered.

Joe brushed his hand across her forehead gently. She looked up into his dark, shining eyes. He smiled at her. The same soft smile he'd given her at Pinky's. "Things happen, that's all," he murmured. "We don't all have to be strong every second." Her tears dripped onto his hand. "You can't plan on being afraid. It just hits you. Suddenly. When you least expect it, when you least want it. It jumps into your life so fast, you don't even know what it is until it's got you."

Courtney searched his face. She brushed her fingertips across the scar on his cheek. His eyes glittered intensely. It was that look again, the look that seared right into her soul. She held his gaze, nodding shakily. "I didn't think you'd understand," she whispered.

Joe gave her a lopsided grin. "Why? 'Cause I'm a cop? You believe that stupid stereotype? That cops are thickheaded grouches with guns?" He brushed a tear off her cheek with his thumb. "I joined the force to help people, Courtney. To bring them together if I could. To make a difference. I don't want to push people around."

Courtney nodded, waiting. "And?" she encouraged.

"Fear is surprising, that's all. It shows up at inconvenient times. Like the other night at Pinky's."

She stared at him. "What do you mean?"

"Well, I'm just starting out, you know. I got scared. But now . . . now, I don't know. I guess I don't feel good about caving in to Lance Putnam, that's all."

She watched the shadows on his face. How could she have thought he was a coward? *She* wasn't a coward. She didn't consider herself someone who collapsed in a crisis. Yet, here she was, weeping all over the place. Feeling as if she'd never get her strong, confident self back.

Suddenly, Courtney was ashamed of herself. She'd taunted him at the spa, mocking his inability to act at Pinky's. And here he was comforting her. Making her feel better. His fears were just as real and just as scary as hers.

She pressed her face against the bars. He drew closer. She brushed his lips in a feathery kiss. He flinched, then moved closer, letting his lips meet hers. Heat crinkled her skin. It was strange, Courtney thought, feeling so close, so safe, with cold bars touching her cheeks.

She paused for a moment, pulling back, languishing in the sensation his kiss had sent through her body. A thought came snaking into her brain. "You know you don't have to cave in to Lance," she whispered.

"What do you mean?" he asked, his voice edged with curiosity.

"You read Grady's letter, didn't you?" she asked. "You know he's telling the truth. The Putnams are exploitative, greedy bullies. You can do something to stop them. The blasting in that cave could start at any moment. Maybe KC and I can stop it. If—"

Joe was staring at her, his eyebrows drawn together. He drew his hand back from her face and backed up from the bars. "If?" he repeated.

"If you let us out," Courtney whispered.

"WHAT!?"

"Shhhhhh!" Courtney said, raising her finger to her lips. "Listen. We can get to Las Altas and warn Dr. Sanchez. Maybe we can stop them!"

Joe stared at her, his eyes like onyx. He waited for an instant, then reached for his keys at his belt.

Courtney beamed at him.

But then, suddenly, he froze. "I—I can't. I can't let you out." His breath came out in a long gasp. "Listen, I'm a cop. I believe in the law. I can't just ignore it when it suits me. I want to help you," he said, his voice desperate. "B-but I can't."

"Please, Joe. It's the only way." She caught his gaze in her own. "Do it for me, then. Please. Please!" She watched as a flicker of confusion and despair raced across his face. Then slowly he shook his head.

"I can't, Courtney." He gave her an excruciatingly sad look. "Not even for you."

Twenty

The inside of the Las Altas Truck Stop was filled with the scent of sizzling bacon, fresh coffee, and grilling steaks. Waitresses sang out orders. Truckers talked in low voices. Families in booths chattered over breakfast.

Outside, the morning sun blazed brightly on the mountains that rose majestically above the city. Faith sat in a red leather booth, sipping some coffee. She was wearing her same old, plaid flannel shirt and jeans, but she felt new and fresh and different. They'd pulled into Las Altas a short time ago after spending the entire night watching the stars and the rocks and the desert.

Across the table, Jeff stuffed a forkful of pancakes in

his mouth. He chewed, then washed down his mouthful with a gulp of coffee. "Why is it that whenever I stay up all night, I crave pancakes?" He grinned at her.

Faith cut up her own gigantic stack of fat, steaming pancakes and shrugged. "Search me. I get the same craving. Whenever we do a theater project back at the university, we end up pulling an allnighter. We *have* to get pancakes in the morning."

Jeff nodded, then slurped his coffee again. They were seated in the section reserved for "professional drivers," and around them sat all ages and sizes and types of truckers. Women and men, short, tall, fat, thin, young, and old. Faith realized that there didn't seem to be a "typical" truck driver.

"This was so fun," Jeff went on. "I'm really glad you were standing out on that highway with tears running off your nose."

Faith reached over and batted him on the head with her napkin. "Thanks a lot. I probably looked like a walking faucet."

Jeff nodded, his eyes twinkling merrily. "A little. But, just think if you hadn't gotten steamed at Ted and Winnie, we never would have met."

Faith and Jeff had talked all night. She'd told him about her so-called dream of a romantic vacation with Ted, and about Winnie's behavior. He'd listened, offering her sympathy and understanding. Faith smiled at him now as he ran his hand through his tousled, curly brown hair. They'd never had a lull in the conversation. Or a pause. Or awkwardness.

Faith thought for a moment about Ted. How occasionally, during lulls in their conversations, he'd sweep her into his arms, whether or not she wanted to be swept. And with Ted, there was always that nagging fear, that just around the corner someone was going to come along and take him away, for good. There was always worry. It made it exciting . . . and exhausting.

Jeff was different. Very different. No worry. No anxiety, no holding her breath. Jeff had given her something completely new. Something she'd never experienced before. A refuge, a resting place in time. With a new friend.

"Yeah, we never would have met," Faith said. She stared at him. She wanted to memorize his face, his gestures, his smile that lit up his eyes. She'd never forget the way he'd helped her. "So I guess I'll thank Ted next time I see him," she said, grinning.

Jeff choked on his coffee. "You don't have to go that far!" He reached out and took her hand. "Listen, I just want to say that I really had a super time. I think you're great. And when you see Ted, you can sock him in the eye for me."

Tears were gathering in Faith's eyes, and she squeezed Jeff's hand. He was looking misty, too. He sniffed, grabbed a napkin, and wiped it quickly across his face. He fumbled with his sleeve as he groped to look at his watch. "Let's see. It's five. The bus leaves at noon. There's plenty to see in Las Altas, though." He grinned at her. "If you can keep your eyes open."

Faith laughed. "Sleep? Who needs it. You're talking to a theater major here. Five more cups of coffee and I'll be ready to go. I guess I'll spend the morning walking around town, then catch the bus back to Jacksonville. I ended up with a great spring break, thanks to you," she said softly. "It certainly wasn't the vacation I expected, but I'll never forget you, Jeff. I promise."

"Good. I'll never forget you either, Faith. So far, you're the only one who has seen anything in my woodwork except potential homes for termites," he said.

She laughed. They rose, paid their check, and drifted out of the busy truck stop. It sat along the side of a secondary road that led to the highway. Trucks and cars sped past, sending dust, fumes, and diesel smoke into the morning air. The sun sat on top of the mountains, and the pale-yellow light streamed across the asphalt. The road was lined with fast-food places and filling stations. Faith gazed around her. She didn't want to lose what she'd found with Jeff. She didn't want to lose any of it.

Slowly, without speaking, Jeff took her hand. She turned, a question in her eyes. Jeff stood and held her gaze for a moment. She could see the slow smile light up his eyes, reaching across his face. She felt her blood sort of hum and buzz as he drew closer to her. When his lips found hers, a driver whistled loudly from the parking lot behind her. Cars honked their horns. A truck pulling out on the road blasted his diesel horn. But Faith didn't care. She threw her hands around

Jeff's neck and kissed him back. His lips were different from Ted's, softer, warmer, so right, so perfect, and so, so safe.

"Ugh," KC groaned as she tried to find a comfortable spot on the iron-hard mattress. She opened her eyes, blinked, then rubbed them roughly. She was lying on the jail cot. She felt bruised and sore, and the cot was beginning to feel like a medieval rack. Spanish Inquisition. Winnie would make a joke about it. KC felt like crying.

The pale dawn light slid into the room. The dingy white walls looked even worse in the daylight, smeared with mud and yellowish stains. Across the small space between the cots, Courtney slept. Even in sleep, her face looked pale and worried.

KC looked up at the ceiling. It was dirty, with gray spiderwebs hanging in the corners. She thought about the letter Grady had written to Dr. Sanchez. She was the only person he could trust! Part of her felt joy at the idea that Grady, a total stranger, could see parts of her that her own friends couldn't see. She knew she was loyal, honest, and determined. And Grady had known it right away. Inside the case of ice that had been surrounding her heart, there were little slivers of heat and light. Grady trusted her. More than anyone.

But mingled with the joy of the realization was dark, solid fear. She'd let him down. True, the events that had landed her in jail weren't her fault, but he was relying on her to save those ancient caves, the dwellings and the artifacts of those people he cared about. That she cared about, too. The ancient ones who had gone before. Tears filled her eyes. The ancient ones . . . the vestiges of the things they cherished and carved and formed would be blasted away by Lance Putnam. It made her feel sick.

Today, an officer would drive them to Las Altas to be charged with stealing a piece of pottery. KC shook her head against her pillow.

The door to the cell area creaked open. KC looked up. She was shocked to see Joe. He wasn't looking at her, though. He stared at Courtney, a soft look in his eyes.

"Courtney," he whispered.

KC stretched across the narrow space and shook Courtney's arm.

"Hmmm?" Courtney pried open her eyes, squinting against the sunlight. "What?"

Joe jangled a key, moving to one side of the cell door. KC frowned at him. What was he doing? He fumbled at the door, and something clanged, metal against metal. He was unlocking their door? But why? Was it time to go already? Was he bringing them breakfast? At sunrise?

"Joe?" Courtney muttered, struggling to her feet. He stepped into the cell in a quick movement, and swept Courtney into his arms in a fierce hug. Courtney's eyes widened in surprise. "Joe?" She hugged him back.

"You were right," Joe whispered. His voice was intense, tight. "I was wrong. I've been thinking about this all night. I did go into the force to help people. I didn't go into the force to let people like Lance Putnam push everybody around. And if stealing antiquities is a crime, you can bet blowing them up is a bigger one."

Courtney flung back her head and looked him straight in the eyes. "What? Are you kidding, Joe? Are you *sure*?"

Joe nodded curtly. "I'll take responsibility. But I want you two to get to Las Altas and warn Dr. Sanchez." He sent KC a quick glance. "I'll drive you there myself. Here, I brought your backpacks. We've got to go. I left a report for the next shift coming on."

KC felt half paralyzed as she quickly collected her things. *What about Grady?* she asked herself. She wondered frantically what had happened to him. Little spasms of fear pulsed through her even as she followed Courtney and Joe out of the cell area and into the outer office. He was still waiting up in the Mesa Alta cliff area for the experts to stop the destruction of the caves, the experts, she thought miserably, *she* was supposed to bring.

They crossed the tiled floor of the tiny station and hurried out the door into the bright parking lot. KC squinted at the blazingly clear light. Courtney hurried to the patrol car parked in front of the jail. KC hesitated.

Joe opened the door of the car. "KC?" he asked, a frown wrinkling his forehead. "We've got to hurry."

KC glanced across the parking lot toward Courtney's convertible. She looked quickly at Joe, then at
Courtney. "Listen. I want to find Grady. He can
help. He knows right where the caves are. I could
bring him in Courtney's car."

Joe and Courtney exchanged worried looks.
"But do you know where he is?" Joe asked.

KC bit her lip. "I can find him," she said with a
sudden burst of confidence. "I know I can."

Joe nodded and climbed into the driver's seat.
He grabbed his sunglasses off the dashboard and
slid them on. "The plaza at the center of Las Altas is
a good place to meet," he told KC. "Courtney and I
will find Dr. Sanchez, then swing around to the
plaza to find you. There's a café called La Cantina.
We'll meet you there." He looked at his watch. "At
noon. Got it?"

KC nodded quickly. Courtney reached into her
pack and yanked out her keys. Leaning across the
front seat toward Joe, she held them out to KC. "Be
careful, KC. With yourself . . . and with my car." She
smiled weakly. "And good luck."

The plaza, Faith thought happily. Bustling,
crowded, hot. Filled with the smell of food cooking
in outdoor restaurants, the sound of the breeze in
the tall cottonwood trees, the fountain, the cars.
Crowds of people surged along the sidewalks, talking, laughing, shopping.

Faith strolled along the north side of the square

beside a long, low red adobe building with a wide, wooden portico. Underneath it sat Native Americans with dolls, necklaces, rings, brooches, pottery, beads, all laid out on black velvet. Turquoise and silver glinted in the shade, and the murmur of voices, customers questioning, vendors selling, mingled with the morning breeze.

She felt happy. The sensations that Jeff's kiss had stirred inside her still lingered, and as she examined a silver and turquoise necklace, his smiling face, his laughter, his soft voice enveloped her like a comforting blanket.

She smiled at the old woman sitting on the ground by the jewelry, then headed across the street. Along the western side of the plaza were more shops. She went inside the Sonora Gallery. It was filled with native crafts and artifacts. Blankets and bleached cows' skulls hung on the walls.

In the case by the door sat primitive objects and carvings, mostly fat animals carved out of stone, pots, and beads. They looked like stuff that archaeologists dug up. It reminded her of KC and Grady, and KC and Grady reminded her of Ted and Winnie.

Ted and Winnie. For a moment, she wondered where they were. If they missed her. If they cared enough to wonder where she'd gone. She knew she didn't care. She didn't care if she ever saw either of them again.

Bristling disappointment prickled her insides as she moved along the glass case toward one filled with more turquoise and silver jewelry. The worst part about the whole thing, she decided, was that Winnie had been the one to lure Ted away. Winnie, of all people.

Faith stared at a huge squash blossom necklace. Big pieces of turquoise were nestled in intricate silver crescents. Each crescent was attached with a delicate loop to another crescent, each individual, each different. Together they formed an astonishingly beautiful whole. In a way, they reminded her of Winnie.

They'd been through a lot together. Their friendship was like one of those necklaces, Faith thought. Twining together their differences. But now? Now what they had was destroyed. It was as if Winnie had come through and yanked them apart. Pulling apart the precious and fragile creation. And for what? To get noticed? To make herself feel good? She wondered if Winnie even knew. Well, Faith knew one thing at least. She would never, ever forgive her.

Faith walked out of the shop into the blazing heat of the square. She glanced at her watch. It was almost noon. The bus taking her home was going to leave soon. If she wanted iced tea for the ride, now was the time to buy some. She spotted a sign on the corner in front of her. The Ocatilla Café. She hurried toward it, pushed open the door, and slipped into the cool interior.

After placing her order, she took a seat in a small booth. A ceiling fan hummed, and even in the air-conditioned building, she could feel the waves of heat pulsing against the windows.

As she sat there, watching the streams of people pass by the window, a young man with red hair burst through the front door and headed straight for the phone booth nestled in the other corner. Faith watched him, puzzled.

He looked familiar. Reddish hair, freckles, brown eyes. She didn't know anyone in Las Altas. Why did he look familiar? He stabbed a quarter into the slot and punched in some numbers.

The waitress brought over her iced tea to go. Faith paid her, then rose to leave. As she stepped toward the door, she heard his voice hissing into the receiver.

"I tell you, Lance. It's all set. No, no one knows about it. Are you kidding?"

Faith drew in a sharp breath. Lance? Lance Putnam? Quickly, Faith stepped to the postcard rack beside the door and pretended to examine the display.

"But we have to go. Now!" the redhead insisted.

She peered past the postcard vistas of mountains and canyons, the joke cards of jackrabbits with antelope bodies. Suddenly, in a blinding flash of recognition, Faith knew who he was. The redhead from Pinky's. Lance's buddy who was with him in the parking lot.

"Yeah, I followed the cave snoop here, to Las Altas. Jake and Paul are keeping an eye on the cave," Lance's buddy said, dropping his voice. Faith leaned forward to hear. "After we roughed him up, we took the evidence. Yeah, you know. Pots and crap. I've been following him to make sure he doesn't contact the authorities. I thought I lost him for a half hour yesterday, but I got back on his trail."

There was silence while the guy listened.

"Nah. No problem. I caught up with him at Flo's." The guy laughed again, and shivers went up Faith's spine.

Faith bit the inside of her cheek. Flo's? That was where KC had gotten that package from Grady. Could they be talking about Grady? Was Grady the cave snoop? Had they really beaten him up? Faith frowned.

"He won't want to keep going after what I said I'd do to him if he kept going back to the Mesa Alta section. Oh, I'm sure of it, man. But if you want that gold, you have to start blasting now!"

Faith sucked in her breath. Gold? Jeff had mentioned something about the Putnams. About how they wanted to blow up the whole desert just for a few bits of gold. How they were always racing to get into areas to dynamite them before the historians got there first.

"I'll meet you at the Mesa Alta caves."

Faith dodged quickly around the rack and turned away from the phone to examine the wall over the booths. She heard the whoosh of the door, and she spun back. Lance's friend was gone. She let out her breath. Crossing to the wall beside the phone booth, Faith quickly searched the large map that hung there. She stuck her finger on Las Altas, then let it move west a little way until she found what she was looking for. Mesa Verde caves. The cliff lines ran all the way to Gold Hill and beyond. There was a state road that led to just south of the caves, then a dotted line showing a dirt road to the cliffs themselves.

Faith stared. What should she do? She had to tell someone, warn someone. Those jerks were going to blow up an historic site and no one knew it! She raced outside, still clutching her tall cup of iced tea, her eyes frantically searching the plaza. The heat blasted into her face.

She could get a taxi. Tell the driver. Maybe the driver could take her out to the caves. They weren't that far from town, and she had a little money left. Suddenly, she stopped and stared. Parked across the plaza, its top down, with supplies and equipment tied securely in the back under a tarp, was Ted's Jeep!

Ted and Winnie were in Las Altas! Faith scanned the square, but neither Winnie nor Ted was in sight.

Well, too bad. They'd just have to figure it out on their own. Fumbling with her cup, she stuffed her hand into her pack. Her set of Jeep keys clanged in the bottom. She ran down the sidewalk and climbed into the Jeep.

Faith jammed the key in the ignition, started the engine, and pulled out. Recalling the layout of the map in her mind, she sped out through the city traffic, west, toward the Mesa Alta caves.

Twenty-one

There was nothing else in the world like the sun in the desert. If KC had learned anything this spring break, she'd learned that. It was harsh and hot and unforgiving. KC wiped her arm across her forehead. Sweat dripped down her back under her shirt. She was heading toward Las Altas, and the road was flat, monotonous, and gray.

She felt frustrated and tired. She'd spent the morning driving part of the way to the Kanabi cliff dwellings, thinking Grady might have gone up there. The road was deserted.

Then she'd gone to Flo's and hung out in the parking lot. She'd even driven back to the Cactus Cottage Motel, thinking he might be trying to track her down through the motel. But the manager said that he hadn't seen anyone who fit Grady's description.

She tried to ignore the heavy sense of fear that added to her weariness. What if Grady had left the area? Maybe he decided the risk of getting roughed up again by Lance Putnam wasn't worth it. Or what if . . . She wouldn't let herself think about the alternative. As she headed east, as the sun fried the back of her head, the tendrils of terror that she'd kept at bay all morning returned. What if he was dead?

She passed signs pointing south to someplace called Quinta Junction. There were Spanish names. Senitas Valley. Puerco Flats. Verde Flats. There were Indian names. Towaoc. Hualapai. Wapatki. And between them, distances that stretched along endless roads.

She sped toward Las Altas, passing small settlements of run-down houses at first. Then the closer she got to her destination, the larger the settlements became, until one town began to run into another. And she had to slow the big car through busy intersections, past shopping centers and residential developments. As she crawled through traffic toward the center of Las Altas, she nervously glanced at her watch. It was noon.

The streets stayed crowded, jammed with vacationers enjoying the museums, galleries, Spanish churches, and restaurants. Signs pointed to the Mission Church, to the University of Las Altas. The stadium. The administration complex. The theater. Finally, she squeezed the car into the plaza and sat, stalled in a traffic jam.

She inched the car around the plaza three times, the heat baking her ferociously. At last, she gave up trying to find a place to park and pulled into a shaded side street. She'd walk back to the plaza and hope she didn't miss Joe and Courtney during her detour. Two blocks farther, she found a parking place in the shade. She climbed slowly out, feeling the sweat trickle down the backs of her legs as she straightened. She turned toward the plaza again where the crowds surged through the streets. It looked like a disturbed ant hill. Behind her, the street where she'd parked led off into what looked like a residential district filled with small, well-kept, adobe houses.

The sun beating down on the asphalt sent waves of hot air into her face. KC scraped her hair back off her face. She stepped toward the plaza. It was after noon. Maybe Courtney and Joe had been delayed at the university. Perhaps Dr. Sanchez wasn't available. After all, it was spring break. Maybe he'd gone on vacation.

She puffed a breath upward to cool her forehead. Grady would have known if Dr. Sanchez wasn't there, she told herself. He wouldn't have written him that letter if the professor had been away on vacation.

KC hesitated. A cool breeze fluttered from behind her, from the quiet street. Its cool, rustling tree limbs whispered to her. Curious, she glanced up at the street sign.

Hermosa Street.

It was familiar. Had something drawn her there? Why had she ended up here, away from the plaza, in this quiet side street? *Wait a minute!* she thought, flinching a little in astonishment. Her grandmother's letter. Her grandmother lived on Hermosa Street, she was sure of it. KC fumbled in her pack and retrieved the tattered letter—341 Hermosa Street.

"Oh," she whispered. KC turned away from the plaza, then walked quickly up the shaded sidewalk. The fresh, fragrant air blew against her cheeks.

Within a few minutes, KC had found it. It was a small, whitewashed adobe house, its front yard filled with deep red daylilies and white daisies. Feeling as if she were moving through a dream, KC followed the narrow path to the front door. Bees hummed around her, dodging in and out of the explosion of blossoms lining the path. KC felt shy and tentative suddenly, and even though she knew the woman who lived in this house was her mother's mother, she'd never met her or spoken to her. She knew nothing about her. She could be anyone.

KC raised her hand and knocked lightly. She tried to control the sense of urgency rushing through her. A sense of facing some part of herself.

It took only a few seconds until the door swayed open, and a small, plump woman stood before her. She was dressed in a long, dark-blue dress, and her eyes were brilliant and black. Her mouth curved softly in a deeply tanned face lined with wrinkles.

KC's voice clogged in her throat. "Mrs. Quintero?" she managed.

The dark eyes gleamed. "Yes," the woman said. Her voice was rich and smooth as honey. "I am Maria Quintero."

She studied KC intently, staring up into her eyes. Then, slowly, Maria raised her arms and held them wide for KC.

KC stepped into her soft embrace and returned her hug. Tears spilled out of her eyes as she clung to the soft shoulders of her grandmother. She'd found her. At last. She felt as if she'd come home.

"There," Maria said, pointing to a photograph, "there is your mother. Beverly was ten in that picture. That shaggy pony she's with, the one chewing on her sleeve, he followed her everywhere. Just like a big dog."

KC smiled at the yellowed picture. A slim, dark-haired girl stood in front of a low wooden porch. She hung on to the reins of a shaggy pony. The girl looked just like KC had when she was ten. KC felt a strange connection to her. The little girl was squinting into the sun, and KC saw that the knees of her jeans were worn out. *Just like mine always were,* she thought.

The trees lining Hermosa Street shielded the house from the afternoon sun. KC sat on her grandmother's sofa, holding a thick photo album with a tattered, dark-brown cover on her knees. In front of her, on a wide, low table, sat her cup of tea. Beside her, Maria was smiling and pointing to the photographs.

"This was your grandfather. Manuel Jefferson Quintero. He was born in Las Altas. His mother was from Mexico City, and his father"—she laughed a little—"his father was from Boston. They were very different, fiery. They taught Manuel to be proud of his heritage. Proud of what he accomplished. He was a good man."

KC gazed at the picture. A tall, white-haired man stood beside a chair, staring straight at the camera. He held himself erect, shoulders back, head high. He looked a bit stiff, as if the dark suit he was wearing was uncomfortable. But behind his dark eyes, there gleamed just a hint of a smile.

KC glanced at Maria. Her hair was very long, worn in braids down her back, and her cheekbones were high and prominent. She wrinkled her face into a smile. "I am Altaverdi. We still herd the sheep and weave the blankets and craft the pots. We still do what our ancestors did. We still dislike change." Her smile broadened. "But Beverly, your mother, wanted the big city and the bright lights. She got into trouble. I couldn't help her. She had to go her own way. Down her own path."

KC remembered when her birth mother had visited her in Springfield. She'd told KC the story of how hard her life had been, how she'd had to give KC up for adoption. She'd had no choice. No choice at all, she said.

The photograph stared at her. Her grandfather. Her grandmother. Beside her, KC could feel Maria's dark eyes studying her face. "You look like Beverly," she said finally. "But you also look like yourself."

"Sometimes," KC murmured, "I don't know who I am. Other people hurt me, or—or maybe think bad things about me, and I feel bad about myself, too. I wonder. Maybe they're right. Then I think I can do everything on my own. Be a success. Organize and plan and accomplish."

Maria reached out and took KC's hand. Even though the skin on her own hand was dark brown from years of working in the sun, the skin was soft and warm. "Do you really believe those other people? Those who doubt you? Are they right about you? About the world?" Maria asked.

KC shook her head slowly. "*No*. But fighting against their opinions can take a lot out of me."

Maria's head nodded, and the soft, wrinkled hand patted KC's smooth one. "It is a struggle to stand up for what you are. For what you believe. That is true. That has always been true. And, in some ways, we are, each of us, always on our own." Maria covered KC's hand with her other hand, holding it in a soft clasp, protected as though it were inside a shell. "But that does not mean we need to be alone. Perhaps now you will know more clearly who you are. Perhaps now you will always see us, the Quinteros, my family, as well as the Angelettis, as yours. And know you need never be alone. You are independent, yes. I can tell. I can see. Be patient with who you are. It is a good way to be." Maria gazed into KC's eyes, and KC could see the dark, glimmering lights flickering in them.

Maria squeezed KC's hand. They sat in the cool stillness, holding hands, and KC could sense through her palm the pulsing heat of a glowing power and strength. It was as if Maria was sending something into her, through her, and KC began to relax. KC felt sure, quiet patience. The past called to her. Slowly, KC realized who she was *did* matter. The voices she'd been touched by all through the trip suddenly made sense. The tingling sensation she'd felt at the cliff dwellings and at the museum rippled across her skin. The voices were steady and simple. They were like the beat of a drum or the color woven into a blanket. *This is your past. This is who you are. You must never let it go. You must never forget it.*

Part of me came from those deep cliffs, KC thought.

"We ranched in the outlying land east of Las Altas," Maria spoke softly. "It was hard work, but it was good, too. We knew what we wanted to build. And we built it." Maria smiled again, the deep crevices in her face lighting up. "We also knew we wanted to survive."

"Were you far away from people and stores and cars? Was there anybody nearby?" KC asked.

"No one for miles and miles. We drove into town here for supplies and to get the news. Now and then, we'd need a doctor. But not too often. We moved once. To Portland. That's where Beverly . . . well, she had her own journey to travel. When she got accepted into college, we came back to the ranch." A flicker of sadness swept across her face. "After Manuel died, I sold the ranch." She smiled again at KC and gazed around her slowly, at the woven blankets on the walls, the smooth, black pots lining the shelves that ran from floor to ceiling in the small room. "This is my home now. This is enough." Maria sighed, and closed her eyes briefly.

"If you're tired, I could come back later," KC said. "I'm supposed to meet my friends somewhere." She gestured vaguely out the front door. Part of KC wanted to stay there forever, to stay in the shelter of the past and in her grandmother's soothing company. But she knew, too, she had to find the others soon.

"Yes, that would be good. I get very tired. Come back to see me. We will speak again," Maria said.

They rose together. "It has been good, KC. How relieved I am that we have had this chance to see each other."

KC was going to shake her hand, but instead she bent down and gave the woman a tight hug. Tears stung her eyes as she drew back.

"I'll see you again soon," KC whispered, then, collecting her pack, she headed out the front door.

KC stepped along the path, feeling the overwhelming sense of having found a new beginning. The cool air under the trees brushed her face, and she smiled. The birds chittered in the leaves above her head, and the garden flowers danced in the breeze.

KC made her way toward the front gate. The hinges creaked a little when she opened it, as if it were saying good-bye. Suddenly, from the left, came the sound of squealing tires and clattering gravel. She turned quickly to see a beat-up pickup truck careening around the corner from the center of town. It roared up the quiet street, braking loudly as it approached her.

KC held her breath. The quiet of the street had been shattered. She pulled back her shoulders and stepped forward to give the driver a piece of her mind. Then she looked up. *That truck,* she thought. A flash of recognition flamed through her. Rust spots. Dents. Dust.

"Grady?!" KC screamed.

The driver pulled next to the curb, then jumped out of the seat. His footsteps pounded on the street. Then, suddenly, she saw him. His auburn hair and beard, his bruised cheek, green eyes. His rumpled trousers with their bulging pockets, a faded red shirt. With a rush, he was in KC's arms.

"KC, I found you. I can't believe it!" he breathed. His body clasped hers tightly.

"How did you know I'd be here?" she asked against his shoulder. She could feel his pounding heartbeat through his shirt.

"I read the letter in your pack. Remember? Back in the cave? I made a note of this address in case I needed it. Oh, KC. I am so relieved." His arms tightened around her, and she breathed out a contented sigh.

Then she remembered. She drew back, brushing her fingertips along the bruise on his cheek. "Your pottery. The package. The police took it," she said quietly.

"The police? Oh, no!"

"I read your letter to Dr. Sanchez, too," KC added.

A moment passed before he said anything. They stared at each other. KC could feel his disappointment, his sudden intense crash into gloom. Finally, Grady broke the spell. "Now you know. But there's more. I'm running from Lance and his buddies right now. They've been following me. I can't get to Dr. Sanchez. I can't get to him to tell him about the Mesa Alta caves. They're going to blow them up any minute, KC! There's nothing we can do!" His voice was desperate, and suddenly his face looked weary and defeated.

"The caves? You mean all those things you found? There's no way we can stop them?" KC asked, ducking a little to look into his eyes "We have to do something!"

Grady shook his head. "I don't see how. All those artifacts are going to be blasted to bits. I can't believe it."

KC caught Grady's gaze and held it. "You tried, Grady. You tried really hard."

"And you must try even harder," a voice spoke from behind them. Maria had come out onto the porch, and was standing like a small statue, holding a cane. "If there are caves in danger, *you* must save them." Her voice vibrated with intensity. "Our past tells us who we are. Connects us to those who have gone before. If we destroy the past, we destroy ourselves."

KC grabbed Grady's hand and dragged him to the truck. "Come on, Grady. We have to try. If we don't do it, no one will!"

She jumped into the passenger's side, while Grady started the engine. KC waved to Maria. "We'll do it, Grandmother," she called.

From the porch, Maria stared at KC. KC could see tears in her eyes. A streak of sunlight poured across her face, making KC think of the ancient masks in the museum.

"I just hope we get there in time," Grady said as he pulled away.

"She's medium height, blond hair, green eyes. She's wearing blue jeans and a red-and-blue plaid flannel shirt," Ted said to the woman behind the counter in the Las Altas Trading Post.

Winnie stood behind him, fidgeting with her spiky hair. This store was the fifth they'd tried, and so far, no luck. They were searching for Faith in every store in Las Altas. Not one person had seen any sign of Faith. She couldn't believe she had simply vanished into thin air. And Ted was not giving up. He was determined to track Faith down.

"Sorry. Doesn't sound familiar," the woman said in a flat voice. "But we've been swamped all morning. I wouldn't know if the President of the United States himself walked in here."

"Long braid? All the way down her back?" Winnie added, her brown eyes concerned.

The woman shrugged. "Sorry."

Winnie and Ted left utterly defeated. By now the entire plaza was crawling with people, some shopping, some just strolling around looking. Tourists in polyester slacks and sleeveless shirts mingled with well-dressed women wearing designer sundresses and white straw hats. It suddenly seemed to Winnie that the whole world had just decided to meet for lunch in Las Altas.

Ted surged through the crowd, ignoring the dirty looks he was getting from people he shoved out of the way. "Ted, this is ridiculous!" Winnie said, trying to calm him down. "We'll never find her in this mob!"

On one corner a quartet of guitarists strummed Spanish folk tunes, and all along the sidewalks, vendors haggled with shoppers over their wares. Flowering pots of geraniums swayed in the breeze. Ted ignored her. He continued to press through the mass of bodies. Winnie got jabbed by an elbow and poked by a gigantic purse as she tried to keep up.

She finally made it to the corner where Ted was surveying the crowds. "Maybe we should try that café over there," he said, pointing to La Cantina, a small diner-type restaurant beside an art gallery.

Winnie sighed. Her feet hurt, and her muscles ached from sleeping curled up like a pretzel in the Jeep. All she wanted to do was collapse on some cool bed and sleep for two weeks. "Maybe we should just head back to Springfield," she said.

Ted nodded slowly, his mouth curved in an exasperated frown. "Yeah. I guess you're right. If she had been in town, there's no way any of these people would remember. Look at this place!"

Winnie grabbed Ted's arm again. "Let's get back to the Jeep, pick up some food, then drive home." She pulled Ted toward the side of the plaza where they'd parked the Jeep. "It's only twelve hundred miles," she went on. They shoved their way through a small group of students all speaking in German, and stopped short.

"Wait a second," Ted muttered. "Isn't this where we parked the Jeep?"

Winnie nodded. They had parked in front of the Ghost Dance Gallery, but there was no Jeep in sight. Only a dark sedan.

"Someone must have taken it," she said simply.

Ted's eyes bulged. "Someone's stolen the Jeep! This is turning into a nightmare!" Several people approaching the plaza turned around and crossed back across the street when they saw Ted's face. She couldn't blame them. He looked as if he wanted to kill someone.

"Calm down! Maybe we were parked too long, or something. Maybe it was towed by the police," Winnie reasoned in an attempt to soothe him.

"Yeah, okay," Ted muttered, still glaring at the sedan. "Let's find the police."

He made a quick survey of the street. "There's a

phone booth. I'll call." He darted out into the traffic, causing a motorist to honk his horn savagely.

Winnie glanced back and forth before stepping out, unwilling to get run over by a desperate driver eager to get to the other side of the square. Her foot stopped three inches from the curb.

She looked to the right just as a blue and white police cruiser eased slowly around the opposite corner, trying to get into the square. Winnie stared at it for a second. Maybe it was a hallucination. After all, she was pretty tired. But no, it stopped, then started, then stopped again, just like the rest of the cars all trying to inch their way from one side of the plaza to the other.

"Ted!" Winnie yelled. "Over there!" She pointed frantically toward the white and blue car. Ted was too far away to hear.

"Hey!" she shouted, waving her arms at the cruiser. "Hey, police! Hey!" She wondered if she should scream fire or something. She jumped into the street, and the cruiser hesitated before swinging into the line of traffic. She made a leap for the door. "Hey, Officer," she began, rattling the door handle. It was locked. The words stuck in her throat. On the front seat, beside a familiar dark-haired man, sat Courtney. In the backseat sat an old man, with thinning gray hair and a pair of glasses. He was wearing a cotton shirt and jeans.

"Winnie!" Courtney screamed. The driver rolled down the window quickly.

Winnie blinked and opened her mouth. "Courtney? What are you doing in there?"

The driver, Winnie now realized, was the guy who'd pried Ted off Lance Putnam that night at Pinky's. Courtney leaned across his lap. "What are *you* doing here?"

Winnie felt a flood of relief. "Oh, God, Courtney! We're looking for Faith. And someone stole the Jeep!"

Looking up quickly, she saw Ted searching the street for her. His face was panic-stricken. When he finally caught sight of her, she waved frantically. "Over here, Ted! Come on!"

He charged across the street and reached her side. "We don't have time to report the theft right now," Joe said. "We're headed out to the Mesa Alta caves to stop Lance Putnam."

Ted gave Winnie an excited look. "Let's go!" he said, yanking open the back door and diving into the cool interior of the car. Winnie followed him.

Joe turned on his flashing lights, and was out of the plaza in three minutes flat.

Twenty-two

"**B**eautiful," Faith said as she gazed up at the tall, square cliff dwellings. The sun beat down on her head and shoulders.

She discovered that the dirt road she'd followed from the state road led to a small canyon, then stopped. She'd parked the Jeep behind some tall, scrubby chaparral bushes, then walked into the narrow valley with its red rock cliffs rising on both sides. About a hundred yards farther the first cliff houses appeared. She was standing in the sun, feeling the sweat sliding down her spine, staring at them.

Quickly, she hunched out of her flannel shirt and tied it around her waist. Her cotton T-shirt felt cool against her skin.

Her pack hung on one shoulder, and as she headed deeper into the canyon, birds trilled their songs in the bushes. To her left rose bigger cliff houses, piled one on top of the other. The golden stones shone like amber. Loose stones crunched under her shoes.

At the far end of the narrow valley sat a pile of rubble. It looked as if part of the cliff had collapsed suddenly and cascaded into a heap. She headed for the pile. It might be a landslide, she thought, caused by erosion or a tremor of some kind. Or it might be the result of what Lance Putnam and his friends were up to. Could they really be blasting away at this magnificent hillside? Faith glanced up. The dwellings reached up the side of the cliffs, blending miraculously into the reddish stones.

Faith picked her way carefully through the scattered rocks and cactus lining the base of the cliff. Beside her, she felt the silent presence of the houses, with their dark windows watching her. The ruins felt lonely. Kind of eerie. Faith climbed over a boulder and peered into the empty, roofless chambers. Amid the pile of rubble sat a gaping, black hole in the cliff.

Faith shook her head. She didn't know much about archaeology, but she knew a dynamite hole when she saw one. She stepped back along the boulders toward the section of the cliff where she'd entered the little valley. As she made her way across a hot patch of burning rock, she sensed a change in the cliff, a sort of gap that hadn't been caused by an explosion. Brushing the sticky strands of hair off her forehead, she stepped cautiously to her right. There was a dark hole. From it came a cool, musty breeze. It was a cave, a real cave leading right into the cliff. Jutting out above it was a shelf of stone that looked like a curved surfboard lying on its side.

Faith was excited. She ducked her head under the shelf of rock and peered into the darkness. The cave smelled moist and cool. She stepped in, ready for exploration, ready for adventure. On her own.

The cave opening was wide, but the roof was low, and Faith had to stoop low to get in. From somewhere deep inside she heard the drip, drip, drip of water. She eased herself along the narrow path leading into the darkness. She hesitated. It was pitch black ahead of her, where a narrow trail headed through gigantic black boulders. On impulse, she flipped her backpack off her shoulder and unzipped it quickly.

Reaching in, her fingers closed over her flashlight. That was lucky, she thought. This was meant to be. Exploring a cave. Being on her own. She smiled as she flicked on the comforting beam of white light.

The walls glistened with moisture, and beyond the small, narrow space where she was standing, Faith could see a path heading deeper into the mountain. Along the right side of the wall were strange sticklike figures etched into the rock.

She stopped. The silence inside the cave was thick, pressing in on her ears like a pillow. But suddenly, from somewhere behind her, she heard a clattering sound, and then a whirring noise. Tires. A car engine.

Her breath stopped. Her heart banged against her ribs. Muffled voices reached her, carried on the wind. She strained to catch the words.

She moved toward the entrance again. Was it KC's friend Grady? Maybe he'd finally escaped Lance's buddies and come back to check on the caves. She wrinkled her forehead. But hadn't the guy in Las Altas said they'd "roughed him up"? That they were keeping an eye on him so he *wouldn't* come back here? She took a few steps along the damp wall, then stood poised, her fingers nervously rubbing the ridges of her flashlight handle.

"Yeah, that first blast was a beauty," a voice said from beyond the entrance. "We'll be able to get the gold out faster, though, when we set up this charge."

Faith swallowed hard. She recognized the voice. From the parking lot at Pinky's. From the CB radio in Jeff's cab. It was Lance Putnam. And he was standing in front of the cave opening. She peered under the narrow overhang, squinting at the bright ribbon of light shining from the outside. She saw jeans and hiking boots. And a hand.

A hand holding a gun.

Someone spoke from farther away. Lance scuffed his feet.

Scrambling quickly, Faith retraced her steps into the cave. The last thing she wanted to do was get caught alone with that creep and his gang. Look what he'd almost done to Winnie. And they'd gone after KC and Courtney, too.

"Looks good," Lance's voice echoed into the dark cavern. "But let's make sure. I don't want anybody poking around here. I don't want them finding *anything*."

Faith slid her hand along the moist rocks that led deep into the hillside. She hurried on. The deeper she went, the darker and colder and wetter the cave became. Along the wall, dancing stick figures etched into the black stones kept her company

The police cruiser slid into the shade under a tall pine. Courtney realized she'd been holding her breath. "Well, Dr. Sanchez, what should we do now?" Courtney asked, turning toward Dr. Sanchez, Ted, and Winnie, who sat in the back. Her face felt tight. "I guess Grady knew what he was talking about. I mean—"

"Grady Kiesling is an excellent field-worker," Dr. Sanchez said, nodding slowly. "I have the utmost belief in his finds."

Joe sent a quick look into the rearview mirror. "Now who's this?" he asked as a dilapidated pickup truck bumped up the rutted road and pulled to a stop.

"It's KC!" Courtney yelled, wrenching her door handle open and charging out of the car into the blazing sun. She ran to her friend and threw her arms around her. "Oh, KC. I'm so glad you made it. We missed you in Las Altas," Courtney said in a rush.

KC returned her hug, then backed up to gesture toward the tall, rather rumpled bearded guy beside her. "Grady found me in Las Altas," she said, smiling.

Courtney stuck out her hand and quickly shook Grady's. "I'm really glad to meet you, Grady," she said. "Here." She turned to gesture toward Dr. Sanchez, who was slowly getting out of the backseat of the cruiser. "Here's Dr. Sanchez."

Grady stepped forward eagerly to help Dr. Sanchez. Then he shook the man's hand firmly. "You really need to see this. You're going to be impressed," Grady said simply.

Dr. Sanchez squinted up at Grady, nodded, and let a small smile soften his mouth. "I hope we're in time," the professor said.

"Me, too," Grady said. "We get into the canyon this way, through these shrubs. Watch your step. The ground's pretty loose."

Courtney fell into step beside KC, who was hanging back and gazing toward the police cruiser. Ted and Winnie had stepped behind Grady and were walking toward the canyon. "Ted?" KC asked quickly. "Where's Faith?"

"She's gone," he answered. "It's a long story." He turned back toward a big shrub covered with blue flowers, then stepped behind it to follow the party that was making its way into the canyon.

KC stared at Courtney, who just shrugged and headed for the canyon. "Don't ask me about it, KC. Winnie and Ted don't want to talk."

With KC right behind her, Courtney stepped around the shrub and across the loose, brown rocks, coming quickly up beside Joe, who was staring up at a huge cliff house just inside the narrow entrance to the canyon. KC crossed the loose rubble to stand beside Grady.

Dr. Sanchez and Grady stood close together. "I told you," Grady was saying. "1250, at least. Maybe even older." Dr. Sanchez nodded as he studied the tall dwelling.

"What's the next step?" Courtney asked. If Lance Putnam were here, or about to arrive, shouldn't they do something? Get ready? Dr. Sanchez had the experience and the expertise to advise them. She wished he and Grady would stop staring at that pile of rubble.

And what about Joe? She drew herself up beside him. He was still admiring the cliffs. "Incredible, aren't they?" he asked.

Courtney nodded, feeling a twinge of worry. Would he be able to act when the time came?

Dr. Sanchez let his gray eyes travel across the cliff. "I'm afraid that pile of adobe over there is not a natural occurrence. A blast, no doubt," he said.

Grady nodded. "The cavern I found lies deep in this end of the mountain. Filled with pots and ceremonial jugs. My guess is that the inner caves were some kind of ceremonial storehouse for sacred objects."

"Well," Dr. Sanchez announced, suddenly pulling back his stooped shoulders, "let's see what you've got." He stepped toward the cliff dwellings, with Grady beside him. The others fell in behind.

Courtney and Joe headed toward a tall room that reached almost halfway up the cliff, and Ted and

Winnie walked toward the pile of blasted rubble. Grady and Dr. Sanchez and KC headed for a dark hole in the cliff face.

Suddenly, Courtney heard KC gasp. KC seemed to be looking at the wall in front of her. When Courtney followed her gaze, she froze in horror.

Lance Putnam stood ten steps away. There was a gun in his hand and a smile on his face. The gun was pointing straight at Grady's chest. "Well, well, well. It looks like you never learn," Lance spat. Behind him, Jake and Carson closed in. "Get out of here," Lance commanded, waving his gun at Grady.

"No," Grady said. He crossed in front of Dr. Sanchez.

"Carson," Lance snapped to a redheaded guy dressed in baggy jeans and a grimy T-shirt. "The old man."

He flicked his head toward Dr. Sanchez just as Grady lunged for Carson.

"Stop!" KC screamed.

Carson lunged past Grady and grabbed Dr. Sanchez. Pulling a gun from his belt, he jabbed it into the professor's ribs. Jake reached Grady, pulled him in front of his broad chest, and wrenched Grady's arms behind him, twisting them with bone-crunching pressure. An anguished spasm of pain crossed Grady's face.

Courtney lunged forward.

"Courtney, no!" Joe shouted.

She clawed at Carson, grabbing at his hands. She

didn't care about anything except getting the old man free. His cheeks had gone white with pain and fear. She had to do something. Suddenly, from behind her, Lance grabbed her shoulder and wrenched her backward, sending her sprawling. She crashed against a boulder. A sudden, stabbing pain pierced one shoulder.

KC instantly leaped toward Jake. Courtney could see his terrible smile as he reached for her. He flung a fist at KC's chin, glancing a blow off her face and sending her flying.

"KC!" Grady yelled.

She fell heavily onto the stones, then dragged herself up. "I—I'm okay, Grady."

Courtney struggled up, crossing quickly to KC. As she helped her to her feet, Courtney sent a desperate look at Joe. He was staring at Lance, his face rigid, his jaw set. But he wasn't doing anything. It was obvious that they wouldn't be able to overpower the gang.

Courtney rubbed her shoulder slowly, thankful that it was just bruised. A clatter of stones from behind her made her flinch.

Winnie's voice echoed through the canyon. "What are we doing, guys? There doesn't seem—"

Lance spun, then a broad grin spread across his face. He was standing just beside the cave opening, and as Winnie came up from around Courtney and Joe, she stumbled and stopped. "Well, if it isn't Ms. Gottlieb. I've been looking for you. This is just perfect," he crooned. The smile vanished and his eyes grew cold. "My work always deserves an audience."

"You won't get away with this, Putnam," Grady barked. The guy who held him pulled up on his arms, and he groaned.

"Wanna bet? I just set enough explosives in that cave to send this mountain into orbit." Lance gestured quickly back toward the cliffside where a shelf-like rock hung over an opening. "All that historical junk will go with it. I'll pick up gold like driftwood off the beach." He focused his harsh gaze on Dr. Sanchez. The professor's face got even paler, and his mouth tightened into a thin line.

"That's right, Sanchez," Lance said. "You've got two choices here. You can keep your mouths shut." Putnam stared at the group, and let out a harsh laugh. "Or you can get shoved into your precious caves and get blown to bits."

Ted had come up from behind Winnie and was standing beside her. His arms were crossed over his chest. "You're totally wacko, Putnam. You think we're just going to let you blow this place up? What do you think we are?"

Lance's face set into hard lines. "No one in this entire valley will believe I had anything to do with this," he sneered. "No one."

A horrible laugh erupted from his throat, and Courtney looked at Joe. She couldn't believe there was nothing they could do. She couldn't believe that this greedy madman could do anything he wanted, and that they could only stand there and watch.

"You'll pay for this, Putnam," Grady spat again. His voice was tight, constricted with pain. Tears shone in his eyes. "Somebody will stop you. One of these days, you're gonna get caught. And when you do," Grady snapped, his eyes burning, "I hope they lock you away for a couple of centuries."

Lance laughed again. "Give me a break, Kiesling. I'm opening a mining operation here. Nobody will ever know there was anything on this hillside. Besides, mines create jobs. People *like* jobs. Somebody should pin a medal on me for improving the employment situation of Las Altas." He shook his head and chuckled.

"You're nuts," Grady mumbled.

Lance shrugged. "Now get out of here," he shouted. "Nobody squawks. I mean nobody!"

They stood still. They were all frozen, highlighted by the white-hot sun. Then, without warning, Lance drew back his hand and hit Dr. Sanchez hard.

"I said *move*!" Lance screamed at them.

As Dr. Sanchez recoiled from the blow, Lance stuck his foot out, shoving Dr. Sanchez across it. The professor crashed to the ground with a heavy thud.

Courtney ran to help him, but Joe's hand restrained her. She couldn't stand this! Why wasn't anybody doing anything? Sure, Lance Putnam had them outgunned. But surely they weren't going to just allow him to beat up an old man, to destroy an important historical monument.

She looked up into Joe's eyes. There was a

flicker, an intense flash of sheer determination deep in them. Courtney gasped, then held her breath.

Before she could say anything, Joe stepped forward. Slowly, in one fluid motion, he pulled the gun at his waist and pointed it at Lance Putnam's face. "Drop the gun, Putnam," he said. His voice wasn't loud, but there was a razorlike intensity to it that made the skin on Courtney's neck tingle.

"Oh, that's right," Lance taunted. He turned toward Jake, bobbing his head toward Joe. "We've got a big cop here. Big important policeman with his shiny badge and his brand-new gun."

Courtney could feel Joe's body clench beside her.

"You've gone too far," Joe said in a low voice. "You've given me enough evidence to put you away. And don't think I won't do it."

Lance started to smile but then caught sight of Joe's face. He hesitated for an instant, then his grin was back in place. "Ooooh. I'm scared. Let's see. I know your boss. A few words in his ear about your wimpozoid act at Pinky's the other night should do the trick. You'll be flipping burgers at the drive-in by the end of the week."

Lance laughed, and his buddies joined him.

Joe stood completely still, and Courtney could see the fury etched in his face. She knew he was scared. They were all scared. If he let Lance get away with this, Joe would never be able to live with himself. She knew helping others sometimes meant getting tough. But did Joe know it?

"*I SAID DROP THE GUN, PUTNAM!*" Joe's voice boomed through the canyon and echoed back from the cliff walls. Everyone flinched. Lance's face froze, the smile sticking to his lips awkwardly.

Joe lunged forward. Jake, who was holding Grady, sprang back, shoving Grady into Joe's path. Joe side-stepped him, then snapped his hand against Jake's wrist. His gun dropped like a stone into the dust. Jake moaned and held his arm.

"You wanna be next, Lance?" Joe barked. He steadied his gun again and thrust it at Lance's face. "I said drop it," he roared. This time, Lance didn't hesitate. He flipped his gun into the dirt.

"Looks like you're outta business, Putnam," Joe snapped.

Lance backed away toward the entrance to the canyon. "Maybe. But the charge is all set. See if you can stop it," he shouted. Jake and Carson nodded, exchanged a quick look, then bolted away from the cliff with Lance right behind them.

There was a moment of stunned silence. Courtney stared at the cliff, where the shelflike rock jutted out from the face, where the houses stacked one on top of the other. At least no one was in there.

Suddenly everyone started cheering and whooping. Winnie even hugged Dr. Sanchez. Courtney felt the rush of excited joy flood through her. They'd done it! They'd actually made Lance Putnam back down! Courtney flung her arms around Joe's waist, giving him a tight squeeze. "Oh, Joe!" she squealed.

"You were fantastic! You did it! I didn't know—"

KKKAAABBBOOOOOOMMMMMM!

Courtney staggered back as a blast exploded from the hillside. Rocks and bits of stone peppered her face. She was blinded by smoke and dust, and she coughed. Around her she heard others coughing loudly. Footsteps clattered around her. Someone grabbed her hand, and she was running. She felt herself shoved down behind a huge boulder, with Joe crouched beside her. Someone was screaming.

A thundering *CRASHHHH!* sounded from the cliff and the face collapsed into a pile of rubble twenty feet in front of her.

BBBOOOOOOMMMMMM.

Faith plunged into a damp, narrow chamber. She'd been heading back to the front of the mountain. Ignoring the occasional sounds of footsteps that echoed faintly beyond her, she'd been stepping carefully around pots and fragments of pottery.

In front of her, she heard a low, rumbling growl from the other end of the cave. The mountain seemed to shift and move. Thick black smoke poured into the chamber. She froze for a minute, then charged away from the booming, covering her face with her arm. She coughed. Her eyes burned. She turned, disoriented by the swirling, choking smoke. She had to get back. The way she had come. But which way was it? Suddenly, the narrow path through the rocks shuddered. Then it disappeared.

"Oh no!" she gasped. She stumbled through the thick smoke, tripping over a pile of rock that hadn't been there a minute ago.

Sticking her fingers out in front of her, Faith groped frantically. The flashlight beam was swallowed by the swirling black smoke. There hadn't been a wall here! She'd just come through this section.

She ran her fingers across boulders and dirt. The air seemed to close in around her ears. The path she'd just come through was completely sealed off! It blocked her way out. She was buried alive.

"Help!" she screamed. "Help!" She coughed, her throat clogged by smoke and dust. The air was so thick she couldn't breathe. She dropped to the floor. She frantically wheeled around her flashlight beam. There had to be something, some way out.

There had to be a crack, a fissure, some sign of a break in the impenetrable blackness. Smoke still swirled through the darkness, and her lungs felt as if they were going to explode. There was nothing. The air was thick with choking dust.

Then she saw it.

A tiny fleck of white. Light! It was sunlight!

Scrambling up the pile of dusty rocks that blocked her way, she tried to reach the opening. Her hand came forward. Just beyond her fingertips she could feel the flow of warm air from the outside. Desperately, she clawed at the rocks. If she could pull back a few, just a few rocks, she could make the opening large enough for her head. From above her, she heard a clatter and a scraping sound. Then a rush of air.

Crash! Something hit her head, and she saw a blinding flash of colored light. Then blackness.

Twenty-three

Ted stood staring in horrified silence at the blank face of the cliff where moments before elegant cliff dwellings reached toward the blue sky. A short time ago the hillside had been glorious remnant of the ancient past. Now it was a pile of adobe and dirt. Emptiness yawned inside him like a gigantic black pit.

The sun blazed down on all of them as they stared at the destruction Lance Putnam's blast had caused. They were unable to speak or move. Joe shook his head slowly. "Jeez. I can't believe that lowlife did this. I just can't believe it!"

Ted glanced over at him. Joe had his arm around Courtney's waist. Tears were streaming down

Courtney's dirty face, leaving tracks through the grime. Ted looked around. They were all covered with grit. Winnie had a small cut on her cheek from a flying rock. She dabbed at it with the back of her hand. KC and Grady had their arms around each other's waists, too. Their faces were gray.

Dr. Sanchez turned away from the sight, an expression of total defeat on his face. "I'll send out an excavation team from the university immediately. There may be something left. Perhaps the inner chambers weren't destroyed." His voice was flat and hopeless.

Joe nodded. "I'll file a report. You can bet on it. Lance Putnam's troubles are just beginning."

Ted headed for the patrol car. He was numb. The empty feeling intensified until he felt as if he could fall into it and never come out. It was more than the destruction of the mountain and Lance's arrogant selfishness. Seeing Putnam again triggered something in his brain, and he couldn't shove it aside or ignore it. He trudged toward the blue and white patrol car. The dust at his feet sank slightly under his hiking boots. He missed Faith. The collapse of the cliff had made a gaping hole in the side of the mountain, a hole that matched the one inside him.

He stepped over a pile of rocks and veered around the side of the cruiser toward a stand of chaparral. Leaning against the car, he crossed his arms tightly against his chest and stared at the shrubs. He saw Faith's face in his mind. Smiling as she gave him a sweet kiss. Laughing as they put up the tent. Playing Frisbee with him on campus, studying with him. He needed to get back to Springfield. He had to find her. He had to find out if he could make up for his stupidity.

He stared at the chaparral. Thick, spreading limbs made it look like some kind of deformed sculpture. He blinked. Through the twisted branches he saw something red. With a canvas top, and a tarpaulin in the back.

The Jeep! *His* Jeep?

What the hell was it doing here?

He shook his head. The person who stole it in Las Altas drove it out here? But why? Maybe the thief was one of Lance Putnam's goons. He ran to it and made a quick check of the inside. All the equipment was there. The raft, the cooking supplies, everything. It didn't make sense.

He dashed back for the others. Joe needed to know about this. Ted stumbled around the very edge of the crumpled cliff where a pile of rock lay scattered up against the base.

Then he stopped. There was nothing but rubble and dust and stones and adobe—but there was also a sound. It was a weak sound, a faint sort of moan. The hair on his neck tingled. It was eerie.

Ted listened some more, tilting his head toward the face of the cliff. There it was again. He turned toward the rocks. The heat was intense, reflecting off the rocks like a blast furnace. Sweat trickled down his neck.

"Pleeeaaassse!" the faint sound shaped itself into a word.

Ted flinched. It was a voice! And it was coming from inside the cliff.

He launched himself over the strewn debris. "Hey! Help!" he yelled. "Joe! Courtney! KC! Winnniiieee!" he shrieked. "There's somebody in there!"

The group, which had begun straggling back to the cars, looked up. "What? What did you say, Ted?" Joe barked.

"There's a voice. Inside the cliff!" Ted sputtered.

"Where?" Joe hurried over. He hesitated at the base of the cliff where the pile of rubble lay.

Ted ran up behind him. "There." He pointed to the place where, at shoulder height, a large, curved outcrop jutted from the side of the mountain. It was the only solid-looking rock in a hillside of rubble. Joe stood still, the others rushing up behind him.

Silence.

The wind whistled through the pine trees and the locusts buzzed. A hawk soaring above their heads flicked a shadow across the face of the cliff.

Joe gave Ted a skeptical look. "It must have been the wind. I don't—"

"Help," a faint whimper came from the rocks.

Winnie gasped. "It *is* a voice! I heard it."

KC, Courtney, and Grady exchanged worried looks. Joe leaned down in the rubble. "Maybe Lance left one of his buddies behind."

"Pleeaasse!" the voice cried. It was faint, ragged. "I—I'm trapped. Help!"

Joe stood up. "I'll radio for assistance. Ted, see if there's an opening somewhere. But don't move any rocks!" Joe dashed to the patrol car.

"Ted," the voice cried weakly. "Ted, help me."

A cold stab of pure terror went right through his chest and he froze.

God, oh God, he thought. *It can't be.*

"KC," the voice murmured. It seemed to be getting fainter.

KC fell on her knees in the pile of sharp stones. "Faith? Is that you?" she screamed. Her face was a mask of white. "FAITH!"

Ted felt as if his bones had turned to solid lead. He couldn't move.

Winnie flung herself down beside KC in front of the small opening. "Faith," Winnie called. "Are you in there? Can you hear us?" She peered under the rough overhang of splintered rock. "I think— I think there's a cave there."

Grady joined them. He peered under the rock. "Yeah. Doc, what do you think?"

Dr. Sanchez examined the ledge. "Definitely. You see the slight curve in the rock. I'd say there's a cave there. No telling how big it is. Or if it's intact after that blast." Grady helped him to his feet. "An excavation team will have to shore up this hillside, though," he added. "It's very unstable."

A shower of rock tumbled down from the cliff,

and the group scrambled out of the way. Ted staggered back slightly as rubble covered his shoes. KC and Winnie retreated fast as a hunk of rock crashed beside them.

Ted rushed back up the loose rock and grabbed the ledge of rock, hanging on to it as he leaned sideways to peer under the shelf. Winnie dove onto the rocks beside him. "FAITH!" she screamed. "*CAN YOU HEAR ME?*"

"Winnie? Is that you? Help me."

Ted flung his knees onto the stones and began digging with his hands. Rocks and stones went flying in every direction. "Ted!" KC screamed from behind him. "You'll make it worse! Stop!"

"She's hurt!" he screamed. "We've got to get her out of there."

He cleared a small space under the overhang and stuck his head into it. It was so small, the jagged rocky edges brushed his ears and stabbed his neck. A small, flat opening about twice the size of a football appeared in front of his face. He squeezed his head sideways and peered into the blackness. Cool, musty air hit his face.

"Faith," he called. "Can you hear me?"

A pale hand appeared, covered with dirt. The long fingers waved limply.

"Ted?" Faith whispered.

He grabbed her hand. It was ice cold. And her voice! She was close to him, but her voice sounded as if he was ten miles away.

"Are you hurt? Faith, can you move?" Ted called. He tried again to squeeze his head in some more, but his shoulders jammed against the opening. More rocks clattered around him.

"I—I can't. My head. It's so cold—" Her voice faded, and her hand went limp.

Desperation and panic welled up inside of him. He shoved himself forward, trying to claw a bigger opening. It widened a little, but then, just as he pulled away a large rock, a shower of stones rained down on his head, filling his mouth and burning his eyes. Somebody grabbed his feet and pulled.

"Ted!" KC shouted. "You're going to bring the whole mountain down."

He scrambled back, brushing the dirt from his mouth and eyes. "She's hurt, KC. She passed out. I can just see her inside the opening. If we could get in a little ways, we could pull her out. I have to try to get her out!" His heart felt ready to explode.

KC shook her head, grabbing his arms savagely. "But you don't know if her legs are trapped. You could hurt her even worse."

"I'm too big to get through. KC, you try," Ted said, his voice tight.

KC held his gaze for a moment. "All right." She scrambled under the ledge. Ted watched as her head and neck disappeared into the opening. Then she stopped.

"KC?" he called. *"KC?"*

KC's voice came from under the ledge. "I—I can't

fit. I can see her. She's unconscious. She looks . . ." Her voice faded, and her legs scrambled back quickly. She stood up, her eyes wide with fear. "She's so pale!"

"Let me try," Courtney said sharply from lower down on the loose rock. She bent down and edged her way toward the shelf of rock. Ted watched her head disappear, feeling a growing sense of panic.

As Courtney squeezed forward, Joe returned. "The rescue team is on its way. All we can do is wait."

"Like hell," Ted said fiercely.

Just then a huge boulder let go from above the remnants of the cliff dwellings and came tumbling toward Courtney's legs. "Look out!" Ted yelled. "Courtney, don't move." The rock bounced down the talus, then suddenly veered and bounced away toward the entrance to the canyon.

"Courtney," Joe called. "Get out. The whole mountain could collapse any second."

Courtney slid back, then clambered upright, coughing and rubbing her eyes. Ted could see she was crying. "Ted, I—I saw blood on Faith's head. I think she's really hurt." Sobs broke from her throat and Joe put his arm around her quickly.

"Listen, you guys," Winnie barked from beside Ted. "I can get in there. I can do this. I will do anything to help Faith." She looked at Ted, and he nodded.

"Do it, Winnie," he whispered. "If you can get a good hold on her, we'll pull you both out." Winnie nodded quickly, then dropped to her knees and slowly crawled forward. She could feel the sharp rocks digging into her knees and the dust sliding along her shins as she lay down flat to face the hole. "Okay," she said firmly. "Here I go."

Winnie had known, the moment they'd figured out the person trapped inside the mountain was Faith, that she had to help, even if it meant crawling through that mountain on her hands and knees. She was smaller than all of them. Compared to KC, Courtney, and Ted, she was a midget. But a midget who could crawl into a tight space. And she owed Faith.

Winnie pressed her body against the grinding stones of the hill and crept forward, inch by inch. She reached the opening, then pushed her head inside it, slowly, using her upper arm muscles to ease herself forward.

Her eyes adjusted slowly to the murky blackness in front of her, and she squinted slightly to try to spot Faith. Then, as she pulled herself over a hump of sharp stones, she saw her. A little to the left and down.

Faith's pale, limp hands were stretched in front of her. And her eyes were closed. Her face was white, pale, and covered with smudges of dirt. Her hair was matted on the back. Winnie gasped. It was matted with blood. "Oh, Faith," Winnie moaned. She reached forward to take her hand. It was ice cold. "Faith? Faith, can you hear me? It's Winnie," she said firmly, trying to make her voice steady. A sob rose up inside her, but she clamped it down. She would not cry. She would not fall apart!

Faith's hand stirred slightly. "Winnie?" she said weakly. "Wh-what are you doing?"

"I'm going to help you," Winnie said softly. She remembered at the Crisis Hotline in Springfield, when she didn't want to alarm or worry a caller, she'd use a steady, calm voice. Soothing. Confident. Reassuring. She swallowed. "I'm going to try to pull you a little, Faith. Now, can you grab my hands? Both of them?" Winnie stretched forward a little more.

From outside the cave opening, Ted's voice yelled, "Winnie! Look out!"

Just then, an echoing thud sounded from the cave, and a grayish-brown poof of dust jetted onto her head. She held her breath. For a minute, her air was gone as heavy dirt pressed her down into the rocks beneath her chin. Rocks thudded around her and loosened stones pelted her legs as they hung out of the opening.

"AArrgghhhh!" Winnie shouted. The rumbling stopped, and silence fell. "Faith? Faith?" she asked, terrified that the new collapse had injured her even more.

"Winnie? Can you hear me? Are you okay?" Ted shouted. He sounded frantic.

"Yeah, I'm okay. I'm going to try to grab Faith now, so get ready," Winnie called, twisting her head a little to shout back.

"Right!" Ted answered.

"Winnie? I lost your hand," Faith whispered, her voice growing weaker.

"Here . . . here it is, Faith. Now. Hang on." Winnie reached out both her hands and grabbed Faith's cold ones. She pulled a little. Faith was heavy. Winnie's elbows screamed in pain. She groaned. Then she pulled again, slowly, toward the opening. Every inch, the rocks and dust tore at her legs.

The loose rocks under her dug into her skin, and she bent her leg forward to get more leverage. She pulled again. "Faith," Winnie moaned. "Can you push a little with your legs?"

"I—I think so," Faith whispered.

Winnie felt the pressure on her arms ease a little as Faith's right leg came forward and she shoved slightly with her foot. Then Faith's head starting rolling. "Winnie, I—I feel sick. My—my head hurts."

"Come on, Faith! You've got to hang on. I know you can do it," Winnie spoke. Dust clogged her throat and tears stung her eyes. Faith's weight was getting heavier. *I can do this*, Winnie told herself. *I have to do this.*

Her shoe slipped on the rocks outside, and then, suddenly, she felt a hand grab her ankle. "Hang on, Winnie," Ted called. "Joe's going to get your other foot. Do you have her? Do you have Faith?"

"Yeah . . . yeah, I've got her." Winnie squeezed the words out of her throat. Her breath was coming in ragged gasps. "Hurry up. I can't hang on much longer." Sweat mingled with the dust on her face. She coughed, then tightened her handhold on Faith's hands. She could feel her grip slipping.

"Faith," Winnie shouted. "Hang on!"

Faith's head bobbed, and Winnie could see she was fighting unconsciousness. Winnie felt her knees sliding back. Faith's hands were at the opening.

"Just a couple more inches, Faith. Don't let go now."

"Winnie?" Faith's voice was so faint, Winnie could hardly hear it.

At last Winnie's waist was out, then her shoulders. Faith's arms were out of the opening. Behind Winnie, stones clattered, and she felt hands helping her.

Ted grabbed Faith's wrists. As he pulled her shoulders free of the cave, Faith sank back into unconsciousness. Ted put his hands under her and pulled her gently into his arms. He scrambled along the slope sideways, gripping Faith tightly.

Joe helped Winnie up.

"You okay?" he asked softly.

Winnie nodded. Her breath was choking her. The sun blazed into her eyes, and tears spilled across her cheeks as she looked down at Faith.

The group closed in around their injured friend. "Get back," Ted called. "Get back," he said more softly, holding Faith tightly in his arms. Faith's face was deathly white, and her lips were blue with cold.

Winnie staggered away, coughing loudly. KC jumped forward. Tears streamed down her face, and she hugged Winnie tightly. Winnie flung her arms around KC and began to sob.

Twenty-four

ourtney smiled with pure happiness as she gazed around the table set under the overhanging eaves of the outdoor patio restaurant.

Beside Courtney, Winnie sat eating a gigantic pile of huevos rancheros. Faith was next to Winnie, a square patch of gauze stuck in her hair. She'd joined them for breakfast at the Inn at Las Altas after spending the night in the hospital. On her other side was Ted, looking subdued. Then came Grady, and on Courtney's left, beside Grady, sat KC. Everyone was just about finished with the sumptuous breakfast. Except Winnie. "This place is absolutely incredible," Winnie whispered.

Courtney took a sip of her coffee and nodded. "Treating my friends to a night at the Inn at Las Altas is the least I can do. I'd say we deserve a little luxury, don't you?"

KC giggled softly. "Well, you *know* Winnie's impressed when she starts whispering."

Courtney, Grady, Ted, Winnie, and Faith laughed and settled back in the soft chairs. "How's your head, Faith?" Courtney asked.

Faith reached up to touch the gauze. "It's still attached." Her broad smile brought some color to her cheeks. "But it's sore. The doctor at the hospital said I should take everything easy for a while. Even though it's a slight concussion. Not to worry if I can't quite remember everything." She took a sip of tea. "And I had to promise not to do any cave exploring for a while."

Ted reached out and took her hand. "I hope not."

"Anybody have any quesadillas left?" Winnie asked.

"It's a buffet, Winnie," Grady said. "Go back and get another pile of food. We'll watch you eat it."

Winnie shook her head. "I better not. I don't want you guys to think I'm a pig or anything."

"Ohhhhhh nooooooo!" they all said together, then burst out laughing. Faith reached over and ruffled Winnie's spiky hair. Winnie gave her a huge smile.

Courtney felt serene again, secure. And relieved. They'd escaped Lance Putnam more than once. And they'd exposed his ruthless destruction of the ancient dwellings in the cliffs. Maybe they'd done some good. It was tragic that the beautiful cliff houses had been destroyed, but she hoped that Dr. Sanchez and Grady could gather enough evidence to stop Lance and his powerful family.

She was suddenly conscious of footsteps echoing across the bricks of the patio. Then she noticed that everyone was staring at her. Winnie wiggled her eyebrows. Courtney could feel herself blushing as she twisted slowly in her chair.

Joe was walking over to them. He smiled straight at her, and her heart flipped over in her chest. He wasn't wearing his uniform, but instead new jeans and a tailored burgundy shirt. He still looked intense, though, and calm. Seeing him out of uniform reminded her of the night she'd met him at Pinky's. The night she thought he was an artist or a poet. She gazed at him. Something was different, but she couldn't figure out what.

"Well, this group looks like trouble," Joe said, a slow grin spreading across his face. He let his gaze sweep around the table.

Courtney rose from her seat to stand beside him. The breeze ruffled his dark hair.

"Hey, Joe!" everybody said at the same time.

Winnie studied Joe for a moment. A wrinkle appeared between her eyebrows. "Did you get taller?" she asked him.

Joe nodded slowly, giving Courtney a warm look that washed through her. "Maybe."

Courtney noticed Joe pull his shoulders back a little further. He did look taller. The serious, intense, quiet look of the poet was still there, but added to it was an aura of self-confidence and assurance.

Joe let his gaze settle on Faith. "Are you all right? I checked at the hospital, and they said you'd been released."

Faith nodded. "Yeah. I've got a bump the size of Mount Vesuvius on my head, but I'm fine otherwise. I'm supposed to—"

"TAKE IT EASY!" everybody announced, laughing.

Joe nodded. "Yeah. Try to stay out of exploding caves."

Winnie bounced in her chair. "And Courtney and KC have promised to stay out of jail."

Joe's eyes crinkled into a warm smile. "That's a very good idea." He stood for a minute looking at everyone. Courtney could see an excited grin replace his cool smile. "I have some news for you," he said to the group.

Courtney glanced quickly at the faces of her friends. They all stopped moving. Even Winnie had stopped eating.

"The inner chambers are still intact at the Mesa Alta caves. The blast affected only the outer walls," Joe announced.

Everyone cheered. Grady jumped up and hugged KC. Ted and Faith and Winnie hooted and clapped.

"And . . ." Joe said, his eyes twinkling happily,

"Dr. Sanchez has agreed to testify against Lance. We've finally got enough evidence to really shake up the Putnam organization."

Courtney laughed as more whoops followed. Grady reached out and shook Joe's hand fiercely. "Great work, Joe," he said, his voice filled with happiness.

"Hey," Joe said. "It was a team effort. If you hadn't come down here on spring break, we would never have caught that guy."

Everyone started talking at once, and in the general confusion, Joe reached over and took Courtney's hand. He let his gaze settle again on her face. "Could I talk with you for a minute?"

She nodded and fell in step beside him as he walked toward the cool, deeply shadowed hallway leading from the patio to the main lobby of the inn.

Courtney squeezed his warm hand. She saw the slow flush ease up his cheeks. He looked down, and then back into her eyes. "I want to thank you, Courtney. For what you've done for me. You really helped me."

"I did?" Joe held her gaze for a long moment, searching deep in her eyes. She thought about how much had happened to them on this road trip, how many miles they'd been since they'd pulled onto the highway outside Springfield. She thought about how roads lead to other roads, how they touch and make connections and intersect. She was glad one of her roads had led her to Joe.

"Yeah." He ran his fingers along her cheek. "You

helped me find a part of myself I didn't know I had."

Courtney put her arms around his waist and drew him close. "It was always there, Joe. Maybe I helped a little. You're a very brave man."

"You helped find what I needed to find. I guess I've always been afraid of fear. I never thought I could get beyond it. I never thought I could get past it. To use it." He drew one hand from her waist and gently brushed her hair away from her face.

"If—if I hadn't figured that out, if you hadn't helped me, I don't think I'd have been able to go on and be any good at my job," he went on. "Thank you. I'll never forget you, Courtney." His words sailed into her heart and made her feel light-headed and free.

"I'll never forget you either, Joe," she murmured. He drew closer, and gently touched her lips with his. She leaned forward and gave him a long kiss. A kiss he'd remember for a long time.

"Red Jeep and vintage Bel Air convertible leaving driveway number 12 in fifteen minutes for Coyote Mountain, the Santa Maria Mission Church, and points north, ultimate destination—after twelve hundred hot, gruelling miles—Springfield, Oregon, and dormitory living."

Winnie made her voice sound like an airline announcer, and Faith laughed as she tucked in the edges of the tarpaulin then grabbed the rope that

Ted flung over to her from the other side of the Jeep. They were in the parking lot of the inn, packing for the long trip back.

"Ugh," Faith said. "Don't remind me. With this headache I don't even want to think about opening a textbook or memorizing Spanish verb tenses."

Winnie came up beside her and gave her a serious look. "Did you take another aspirin? Are you sure you'll be able to drive back? Maybe you should ride with us—I mean, we could put the top up so the sun won't shine on your head."

Faith patted Winnie's hand. "Thanks, Winnie. I'll be okay. I plan to sleep most of the way."

Winnie looked away, then let her eyes drift back to Faith's face. "Well, take plenty of water, and if you need to stop just pull over." She paused, then a small flicker of an apologetic smile appeared on her face. "And—I'm—I'm really, really sorry."

"I know, Winnie," Faith said softly. "Just give me time. Time to—"

"Forgive me?" Winnie said in a small voice.

"Yeah. And Winnie?" Faith paused. "Thanks for saving my life."

Winnie sniffed, her brown eyes moist. "Hey, Faith. I was glad to do it. I mean, after all, well, it was the absolute least I could do. I mean, I'm just glad you can stand to talk to me."

Faith smiled. "I still don't understand how you could have done what you did with Ted." She let her eyes drift over to Ted as he studied a map Courtney had laid out on the trunk of the convertible. "I know we'll never get back what we had, that some parts of our relationship are over. But I think we can still be friends."

"I'm just so sorry," Winnie said again. Tears shone in her eyes. Faith pulled Winnie into her arms for a big hug. "Thanks, Faith," Winnie whispered. Then Winnie backed up quickly and jogged to the convertible, climbing up over the trunk and falling into the backseat.

Ted looked over at Faith, folded the map, and returned to the Jeep. "Okay, KC is going to meet us at the Pueblo Grande Trading Post at the west side of town after she visits her grandmother. Then it's Coyote Mountain first, two hundred miles northwest. Then the mission, and then . . . straight, flat, endless highway to northern Nevada."

Faith nodded. Ted was trying to sound cheerful, but she could see the heavy sadness in his eyes, and she felt sorry, too, that his own impulses had broken them apart. She climbed into the passenger's side and settled into the seat. Ted came around to stand next to her. He gave her a steady gaze from regret-filled eyes. "It's over, isn't it?"

Faith felt the sadness, too. But she also felt she'd made the right decision. "Yeah, it's over."

"I thought so," Ted murmured. "I just want to say again how sorry I am."

Faith could sense his embarrassment, his confusion, his pain. But for once she wasn't going to try to make him feel better.

"I'm so grateful you're okay," Ted continued. "I would never have been able to forgive myself if—if anything had happened to you."

"I know," she said quietly.

"All you wanted on this trip was a few magical hours. And—I'm really sorry. I don't know why I did it. I'm a jerk." He looked down at his feet.

Faith nodded slowly. "Yeah, you're a jerk." His head came up and he stared at her. His cheeks were flushed. Even though part of her was sad at losing what she and Ted had shared, part of her was still tingling with that free sensation she'd gained with Jeff Warshasky. Even after her terrifying experience in the cave, even with a headache and with Winnie and Ted apologizing and regretting their actions, Faith felt light and strong.

She smiled and patted Ted's hand. "It's okay, Ted," she said in a soft voice. "Some parts of spring break weren't so bad."

Ted gave her a quizzical look. "What's that supposed to mean? Did something happen when you left in that truck?"

Faith watched a white cloud sail across the blue sky above her. "No, Ted. Nothing happened."

"Then why do you look so dreamy all of a sudden? Are you sure nothing happened? Where did you go, anyway?" Ted asked, frowning more heavily.

"Oh, just around. Here and there." Faith closed

her eyes. In her mind appeared a crimson sunset. A rainbow of rocks, glowing gently, lay scattered across the violet desert like the bones of a great giant. She could smell the heat of the stones, the dust, the sagebrush and juniper. At her feet bloomed the orange desert poppies that Jeff had pointed out. Around her shoulder, she felt the gentle pressure of Jeff's arm.

Ted's voice came faintly from beside her. "And you're sure nothing happened?" he asked again, all confused.

"No, Ted, nothing happened," she murmured. "Nothing you'd understand."

The little white house at 341 Hermosa Street shimmered like a pearl in the bright morning light. Grady had offered to drive KC over to her grandmother's house, while Courtney and the others finished packing. And now KC stood on the front porch, gazing around her, trying to memorize the garden, the light, the shadows on the grass, everything.

Especially her grandmother's face. The lines in Maria's tanned face deepened as she smiled. KC felt the love in that smile flow into her.

Grady was standing a little behind her. He'd been telling Maria about the caves at Mesa Alta. "And the inner chambers, deep in the mountain, have piles of pots."

Maria nodded slowly, her eyes growing thoughtful. "You are probably right to believe them to be ceremonial jars. The earlier pueblo dwellers stored sacred objects and healing herbs in the caves. Away from enemies."

Grady and KC exchanged smiles. KC could feel Grady's intense excitement. His eyes radiated enthusiasm. "I'm going up there tomorrow to see to the preliminary field mapping. Maybe, when we get everything started, you'd like to visit the site?"

KC felt a flood of gratitude for Grady's knowledge and generosity. When KC glanced at him again, she was amazed at the sweet smile on his face when he looked at Maria.

Maria nodded slowly. "Yes, I would like to see it, Grady," she said softly, smiling up at him with her dark eyes. "Now, I have some things for you, KC. I will get them," she said softly, slipping into the house and returning a few moments later with a bundle in her hands.

"Here are a few things to keep," she went on. Her soft hand patted the pile. "This is a native blanket to remind you of your heritage. Wrapped inside are two animals made of stone. One is a wolf, and the other is a bear. Wolf will help you find your power, perhaps alone. It teaches important lessons, new ways of being. Bear also guides you to inner-knowing. To personal truth. They are for protection."

KC stared at the small carved stone animals. She picked up the wolf. It felt cool and heavy. It reminded her of the cool, comforting cave above the

Cactus Cottage Motel, where she first felt the echoing voices of her ancestors, speaking to her. She'd gained so much on her trip. She wanted to show Maria what she felt, how grateful she was. But she felt tears closing her throat and an aching constriction in her chest.

Maria patted KC's hand. "And underneath, wrapped in the blanket, are the photographs you admired. Manuel. Beverly. Me."

"Oh, no. I can't take your pictures!"

Maria smiled. "They are yours, too. And I have many, many others. You must have your ancestors around you. Otherwise, you will not know who you are." She nodded slowly, giving the blanket one last pat.

KC felt a lump rise in her throat. "Thank you, Grandmother," she said softly. "I don't know what to say." KC felt as if she were suddenly full of history and life and hope. And the two people who helped her find these precious treasures were standing with her at this moment. She wanted the moment to last forever.

"I promise to stay in touch," KC said. "I'm so glad I found you."

Her grandmother studied KC's face for a long moment. "I am relieved you came to see me. I have thought of you often, Kahia. If you would send me a picture of yourself when you get home, I would be very grateful."

"Of course I will," KC said. "And thank you. I'll

write. I promise." She kissed her grandmother on her weathered cheek. "And I'd love to visit again."

Maria's eyes lit up. "I would like that very much, KC." She stepped back a little, holding KC's gaze with her own. "Good-bye, KC. Have a safe journey, no matter where you travel."

With a nod and smile, she turned. The front door creaked slightly as she closed it behind her.

Grady and KC returned to the truck and drove out of town toward the trading post where Courtney, Ted, Faith, and Winnie were going to meet them. The sun streaked across the sky in shimmering bands. The cacti stood tall like sentinels, always watchful, always alert, and the breeze was fresh with morning sweetness. Grady pulled off the road into a turnoff and stopped the engine. KC breathed in the rich smells of morning in the desert, the shrubs that smelled like dust and pine and tar, the sage, the grasses that clung to life in fierce surroundings. The desert was full of beauty and life. KC saw it all now.

Grady got out, came around to her side of the truck, and pulled open the door. "Come here," he whispered.

KC smiled and set her treasures down on the seat. She swung her long legs to the side and scrambled out of the truck. In front of them lay the valley, dotted with purple and rose. Along the eastern horizon lay the rippling mountains, shining as the sun caught them, and to the west stretched miles and miles of road. Cars zoomed past. KC smiled slowly.

She hoped the people in those cars got to experience the Southwest as she had. Its mysterious, ancient magic.

KC looked up into Grady's eyes. He took in every inch of her face. KC felt his breathing matching hers.

"I want to tell you something," Grady said. His rugged face looked calmer, relaxed, happy. "I will never, ever forget what you did for me. For us." He took her hands, and peered deeply into her eyes. "For the ancient ones. They'll remember, too. I didn't tell your grandmother—Maria—but the caves are one of the biggest Altaverdi finds of the decade." His eyes shone, and he reached forward and slid his hands around her waist. KC stepped into his arms smoothly. "Because you and Courtney talked Joe into letting you go, letting you find Dr. Sanchez. Without you," he went on, "everything would have vanished, like so much of our heritage has. Gone in a puff of smoke."

"It was more than just me," KC whispered. "Without you, I would still be running from people, afraid to trust, afraid to be who I am." She leaned in and put her head on Grady's shoulder. She felt him draw her tightly against him. "I couldn't trust anyone. I didn't know who I was or what I wanted to be. I just know I'd been hurt. And being distrustful was safer than risking getting hurt again."

She pulled back and twined her hands up around his neck. "And now," she whispered, "now I can go home renewed, hopeful, and happy. I can go on with my life, knowing how I'm connected. Thank you, Grady."

He smiled a wide grin. "I'm just glad you drove twelve hundred miles and ended up in my cave. I mean, when you think about all those miles, all those long, dusty roads that led you here. To me. To your grandmother. To your ancestors. It feels as if it was—"

"Destiny?" KC finished quickly. "Like it was my journey? I do feel that. Part of me will always be here, under this huge sky, gazing at the rocks and sage and canyons. I'll never forget."

Grady nodded. "And the desert will always hold you in its heart," he said, drawing closer, "and so will I." He leaned in, and when his lips touched hers, KC felt as though her ancestors were watching, and smiling.